# SAMANTHA MARTIN
# LATIUM

# LATIUM

For permission requests, write to the publisher, addressed "Attention: Permissions Coordinator," at the address below.

50/50 Press, LLC
PO Box 197
1590 Route 146
Rexford, NY 12148

http://www.5050press.com

ISBN-13: 9781947048348

Edited by: Megan Cassidy-Hall

Printed in the U.S.A.    First Edition September, 2018

# Dedication

For Sandra, Liyan, Diana, and Abigail

# CHAPTER ONE

"You're still doing it wrong." Danny rubbed the smooth stone between his fingers. "It's not so much a throwing motion as much as it is a *snap.*"

"Well, maybe it would help if you'd stop taking all the good stones." I rolled my eyes, letting the chunk of granite fall from my hand into the warm sand at my feet.

"Here. Try this one."

"And steal the glory from you?" I winked. "No, go on. It must be hard to be second best all the time."

Danny scoffed. His warm brown eyes lit with a smile. He held the stone up, examining every inch of the surface. After a moment of consideration, he tossed it into the smooth water, snapping his arm over his body. The glass-like surface rippled as the stone skipped over it, bouncing three times before sinking into the water.

"You're right. I do like this too much to let you win." Danny crossed his arms as he watched the last of the shimmering ripples fade away. A smirk rested on his face. His messy brown hair fell into his eyes as the breeze washed over us, filling the air with the scent of saltwater.

"Look, it's not my fault that Dad's always liked me best," I teased.

"Hey, low blow." Danny bumped my shoulder, and we started to walk. The sand washed over my bare feet as I took slow, careful steps along the water line. "When the Drillers come, who's going to be able to fire a gun and stop them? Me, or you?"

"That depends on who can run away fast enough to get to the guns," I quipped, shooting my brother a look over my shoulder. "It's not my fault I'm not sixteen yet, but I think I can understand the concept of 'point and shoot' as well as you."

"I'd stick to the typing for now, if I were you." Danny looked down and stopped in place, letting the water wash over his feet. I mimicked him, cringing as the cold brushed over my toes. Shivers ran up my spine as I gazed out at the horizon. The clear blue sky was dotted here and there with fluffy white clouds.

"Yeah, like typing is what's actually going to win this war," I muttered, more to myself than to my brother. "If it ever ends at all."

"Hey." Danny put his arm around me. "We'll get there, okay? And for now, we're safe. The world hasn't gone *completely* to shit yet. This is more like a preliminary war to decide who'll be in charge when it does."

I shook my head, pulling away. "I don't want things to be safe. I want them to be different."

"Different how?"

"Oh, I don't know." I bit my lip, staring out at the waves. "Like…"

"Lydia Melrose, if you say *like they are in the movies,* I swear to God I'm going to kill you."

"Forget it." I turned away from the water. The corners of my eyes started to burn. I blinked rapidly into the sunlight, trying to get the sting to go away.

"Wait." Danny fell into step beside me. "I didn't mean it, okay? How do you want things to be different?"

I stayed quiet, pressing my lips together. The pain in my eyes spread to my chest and I gasped, trying to force air back into my lungs.

"Lydia."

"Just forget it, okay? It doesn't matter, and it's nothing I haven't said before." I scuffed my toes into the ground. Sand gathered on my feet like a swarm of ants that latched on and wouldn't let go. My skin crawled. "We should get back."

Danny looked at the ground, his brown eyes focused on the tiny shells that dotted the shore. "Things will get better."

I scoffed. "Yeah, Danny. Sure, they will."

"I mean it," he insisted. "They won't be like they are in the movies, but someone will make a breakthrough soon. Discover that you can actually make electricity from dirt or something."

Some of the pressure in my chest loosened with my laugh. "Right. Sounds plausible."

"I'm serious. You know they're planning something. Let's say that what they're planning actually works. Let's say that the war is over by next Wednesday, and you can do anything you want. Where do you go first?"

"Danny, this is stupid."

"Where?"

I sighed. "Oh, I don't know." I cast my mind around, to every movie I'd ever seen, every book I'd ever read. Out here on the base, there weren't exactly hundreds of old movie reels lying around, but everything was still on the internet. Just tricky to access, given the weekly checks to my Rosett computer to make sure that I wasn't a Driller spy. With the amount of digital pirating I did, it was lucky I knew how to cover my tracks.

Someone had designed the small Rosett computers when they figured out how to make the keys themselves change between languages. The Rosetts replaced laptops and turned international communication into a breeze. I can imagine they were a lifesaver for my mom back when she was alive. She was born in America, like my dad, but still learned Korean to talk to her family back home. Then, the wars started, and it didn't matter how easily she could reach South Korea anymore. It didn't matter that she spoke Korean at all. It just mattered that she and my dad survived the violence and poverty sweeping most of the nation.

But in the end, even that didn't make a difference. She died the day I was born. By then, everything had changed. Now, there are no more movie theaters, milkshakes, or midnight diners. Gone are the pep rallies, sleepovers, and coffee dates I see in the old films. Everything I've ever wanted just isn't there anymore. All that's left is sand, sunshine, and the promise of disaster on the horizon.

"I can stand here all day," Danny said.

"Fine." I shrugged. "A football game. I'll go to a football game."

Danny released my arm, laughing. "A football game?"

The small smile on my face slipped away. "Let's just go home, okay?" The hot sun beat down on the back of my neck like a heat lamp.

"I'm not laughing at you." Danny's eyebrows furrowed together. "I just—"

"You just what, Danny? You thought that getting me to talk about how I wish things could be would help me accept the fact I can't have any of it? Yeah, I want to go to a football game. I want to be in the stands cheering for the team, *like they do in the movies.* I want to go to high school and date and go to prom, okay? I want life to be *normal.*"

"I didn't mean to—"

"I know you didn't, and I know you want all those things, too." I looked away from my brother and back towards the ocean, at the deep blue water and pale blue sky. The sunlight glimmered off of the gentle waves; white foam rose to the surface with each crest. "We have a big day tomorrow."

"Lyd, that's not the point."

"Then what is the point, Danny? Is it sitting at a computer every day, typing? Working towards a breakthrough that probably doesn't exist? Is the point that we can just pretend the war doesn't matter because we're perfectly safe from it as long as we're here?" I threw up my arms. "I would take a high school that gets shot up daily over one more quiet, peaceful evening playing scrabble with Dad. I don't care about this anymore!"

As the last word left my mouth, the world around me exploded into noise, smashing the silence like a glass window. I threw my hands over my ears, looking frantically from Danny to the trees just beyond the sand, but the sound was gone. Waves lapped onto the shore; silence drifted through the air. I slowly lowered my hands. My heartbeat pounded behind my eyes.

"Danny." Fear lurched in my abdomen. "What the hell was that?"

Danny's face was completely bloodless. "I don't know."

"Dan!"

Suddenly, Chris tore through the trees and raced towards us. He stumbled and almost fell flat before righting himself.

"Chris?" Danny's voice was sharp. "What's going on?"

Chris straightened up, dragging his sleeve across his forehead to clear the sweat away. His face was splotched; his eyes flickered from Danny to me as he panted, trying to catch his breath. "They're here."

"The Drillers?" I demanded. Every thought I'd ever had about what would happen if they found us ran through my mind, tangling around each other, making it impossible to think straight.

Chris nodded, running a hand through his sweat-soaked hair. "I can't imagine who else it could be, but at this point it doesn't matter. They're here, and they have guns. And Danny, they're killing people."

"Killing people?" I echoed, my voice high. Danny and Chris stayed focused on each other. I dug my nails into my arms hard enough to draw blood, forcing myself back into the here and now.

Chris scrambled for his pocket and pulled out a black handgun that he handed to Danny. "Get Lyd somewhere safe." Chris nodded to me. He pulled out a second gun. "See you over there."

With these words, Chris turned and ran back towards the gap in the trees. The second he was gone, Danny loaded the gun and held it out to me. "Take this."

I backed away. "I can't take that. You need to go! You need to make sure Dad's okay!"

"Dad knows how to take care of himself. You don't."

"I'm fourteen," I snapped. Heat gathered at the base of my neck. "If they find me, I'm dead no matter what, so please, just go." I crossed my arms, glaring at my brother. Fear bubbled in my stomach, but I swallowed it down. If the Drillers really were here, I had no chance against them, gun or not. But for Danny, a weapon could mean the difference between life and death.

Danny shook his head and yanked my hand, pressing the gun into my palm. I shied away at the contact as if burned. "Danny, I can't!"

"You have to," Danny snapped. "You're always going on about how you understand 'point and shoot.' Go hide in the lighthouse. If anyone except Dad, Chris, or I come to get you, shoot them first and ask questions later."

"The lighthouse? I can't be that far away! What if something happens?"

"If something happens, at least I know you'll be safe. Lyd, you're smarter than this. You know you can't take them on."

"Neither can you, without this. Just take the gun!"

A tear trailed down my face as another explosion rocked through the air. Danny grabbed my arm, meeting my eyes.

"Go to the lighthouse," he repeated. "Stay there, no matter what you might see or hear. Don't come looking for me."

My voice caught. "Be careful!"

Danny squeezed my arm and brushed a tear from my cheek with the ghost of a smile on his face. "Always."

He turned away from me, crossing the beach to follow Chris's path through the trees. I simply stood there for a moment, too numb to move, but as another gunshot rang through the air, I turned and ran.

The warm sand rose and fell under my feet as I flew across the beach. I stumbled more than once, but I held my stride. I kept the gun at arms' length, fingers ironclad around the handle. The beach blurred in front of my eyes. The sea air burned my lungs. Worry formed a huge, painful knot in my chest. Every step that I took was a betrayal to Danny; the further away I got, the more danger he was in.

Still, I kept going.

Faces flashed in front of my eyes. My brother. My father. Chris, my only friend in the world who didn't share my DNA. My stomach lurched. Bile rose in the back of my throat.

*What if I never get a chance to tell him I want to be more than friends?*

My bare feet caught on something, and I tumbled to my knees. I threw my hands out to stop my fall, but thankfully, the ground was soft, and I sank painlessly into it. The gun flew out of my hand and landed a few feet away. For a moment, I simply lay with my head pressed into my arms, pressure building behind my eyes. What if Danny and the rest couldn't hold off the Drillers? What if they killed him—all of them? What if the world had finally gone *completely* to shit, and that was why the Drillers were here?

A million more questions circled around my mind, crashing against each other until I couldn't string two thoughts together. I sat up, gasping. The sky, which a moment ago had been pale blue, was now scattered with dusty grey clouds. A clap of thunder echoed across the silent shore.

My stomach lurched.

*Thunder, gunfire, or something even worse?*

Scrambling to my feet, I grabbed the gun and continued on. The lighthouse rose on the horizon ahead of me, a tall, steady structure made of weathered gray bricks and broken glass. Holding my breath until spots danced in front of my eyes, I sprinted the remaining distance. I wrenched open the door. Jabs of pain stung my skin as the rusted handle dug into my palm. The door swung shut behind me. The metal scraped against the stone foundation beneath my feet.

I closed my eyes and pressed my back against the door, sinking to the ground and pulling my knees to my chest. The musty air burned my lungs. My chest heaved up and down. A beat of sweat trailed down my cheek, mingling with the tears on my face as I pressed my head back against the door, staring up at the spiral staircase that reached to the top of the lighthouse. Faint memories of summer nights and clear, starry skies teetered on the edge of my mind, but I forced them away. Thinking only of the Drillers, I cradled the gun in my lap, listening desperately for something—anything.

Danny's voice echoed in my mind. *Don't come looking for me.*

I pressed the heels of my hands into my eyes until spirals danced in front of my vision. A chill ran across the back of my neck, and I shuddered.

*Don't worry,* the memories whispered, drifting around me like ghosts. *There's nothing to be scared of.* There's just the endless summer sky, and the spark when Chris's hand brushes your shoulders.

I jumped as I heard a pattering sound across the lighthouse's broken glass. Tearing my hands away from my eyes, I realized it was only the rain, peppering the bricks and cracked roof. I wished more than anything that I was with my brother.

# CHAPTER TWO

*Three Years Later*

"Morning," I muttered as I entered the kitchen, pulling my hair into a messy knot at the back of my head. The smell of coffee hung thick in the air, and I headed straight for the pot on the counter. I poured myself a cup before turning to face my dad.

"Morning," he echoed, closing his Rosett and rubbing his tired eyes with the back of his hand.

I took a sip of the coffee and winced as the hot liquid scalded my tongue. "Long night?"

"The day didn't end for me." He offered me a wan smile and raised his own mug. "Thank God for this stuff, right?"

"Yeah. Can't have the head of security sleeping on the job now, can we?"

"No more than our best coder." My dad smiled, but sadness weighed down his gaze, teetering just on the edge of his eyes. "Speaking of which, are you ready for today?"

I scuffed my bare feet into the cold tile floor. "As ready as I can be."

My dad rose from his place at the table and crossed the room. He put his hands on my shoulders and peered down at me. "You can do this, Lyd. I wouldn't have chosen you if I didn't have complete faith."

I stared at my feet. "I know. I just wish…"

"Me too. I'm sorry it had to be today." He sighed. "Are you doing okay?"

"Yeah," I answered automatically. "Absolutely. Ready to go."

"Lyd, if you want to talk about it—"

"I don't want to talk about anything." I swallowed the rest of my coffee in one bitter mouthful. "The best thing that I can do for *him* is to do my best today. I should get going." I slipped on my shoes.

"Alright." Dad's voice was soft. "I'll meet you there soon."

I offered a half-smile as my dad ran a hand through his short salt-and-pepper hair. He retook his place at the table, and his eyes glazed over as he resumed his work. I hesitated, one hand on the doorknob. After a moment, I pulled open the door and stepped into the sunlight.

I took a deep breath, trying to relieve some of the pressure around my lungs. The air was light and clear, but the sunlight dazzled me as I followed the long, weaving path between the houses. My eyes roamed over the short brick buildings and lush green lawns. Hardly anything had changed since that day three years ago.

But everything had changed. One explosion and everything was different. Broken.

"Hey." Someone bumped my shoulder from behind.

I jumped. "Chris!"

Chris raised his arms in mock-apology, smirking at me. "You're a little jumpy there, aren't you? Nervous for later?"

"Not at all," I replied coolly, glancing up at his deep green eyes. "Are you?"

"Nope. We won't get caught." He tilted his head at me. "Speaking of which, you find that movie you were looking for?"

"How did you—"

"You forget how long I've known you."

"Too long." I bit the corner of my lip. "Please don't say anything."

"Have I ever?"

"Fair point." I sighed, staring straight ahead as we continued down the path. The sooner that we got to the lab, the sooner today would be over, and I could stop replaying my brother's funeral in my head.

The shiny black building rose on the horizon in front of us and some of the pressure pounding against my chest lifted. Chris held the door, letting me step through into the dim hallway before he closed the door behind us. I took a deep breath, waiting for my eyes to adjust to the light.

Chris brushed a hand across the small of my back, crossing behind me. He pressed his hand to the glowing scanner on the wall and I mirrored him, placing my hand on a scanner of my own. Red light pulsed beneath my fingers. After a moment, the door at the end of the hallway swung open.

"Here goes nothing," Chris murmured into my ear. I ignored him, holding my head high as I walked into the computer lab. The guard raised his eyes as we entered but returned to his work after only a glance. I pressed my lips together, staring straight ahead until I rounded a corner and reached my desk. I switched on my computer.

Chris followed me. He hopped onto the desk and swung his feet over the edge.

"Can I help you with something?"

He just shrugged.

"Chris, come on. We have work to do."

"I know." He reached over and picked up the photograph that rested on my desk.

I jumped to my feet. "Put that back."

"I'm just looking at it." Chris set the photograph of Danny and me back onto the desk. "I took this picture, remember? I miss him, too."

I picked up the photo. We'd taken it just a few weeks before Danny died. It was a beautiful afternoon, and we somehow managed to get permission from Dad to take our small sailboat onto the water.

"Just to the buoys," Dad warned, but I was ecstatic. The cool water, the sky, and being away from the latest news of a food shortage or tornado sounded like heaven. We packed a lunch and headed out, just the three of us— me, Danny, and Chris. Everyone else on the island was either older than forty, or younger than ten. We only had each other.

"What do you think we'd hit if we kept sailing?" Danny asked as we sunk the anchor a few yards away from the buoys. They bobbed with the waves, flashes of red against white and blue.

"First off, we'd probably die before we hit anything at all. You two didn't exactly pack enough snacks for an extended voyage." Chris threw a grape at me with a grin.

"Hey, I worked hard on that sandwich," I said. "You may take it for granted, but there's a perfect ratio of peanut butter to jam on that bread."

"Lydia Melrose. Brilliant coder, but much more importantly, sandwich aficionado," Chris said.

"Damn straight." I grinned back at him and took a bite of my own. We were lucky to live where we did. The soil was fertile, and the climate was perfect. Most of the world lacked access to food that didn't come out of a plastic bag, but not us. There were no bombs or fires threatening our fields or vineyard. It was a perfect little paradise, protected by the vast ocean and a state-of-the-art security system.

"You two. Photo." Chris reached in his bag. He pulled out a polaroid camera and held it up.

"Woah." I reached for it. "Where did you find this?"

"My dad's stuff. He was old-school, I guess."

"Polaroids did make a comeback around 2015, so maybe not *that* old-school," I pointed out. The camera certainly looked brand new, with a flawless black exterior and sharp, clear lens.

"Ever wonder what would happen if you spent half as much time studying chemistry as you do pop-culture history?" Danny asked.

"I'd know a lot more about chemistry and be a lot more miserable." I pushed his shoulder. "History's important, Danny. It's who we are."

"Knowing facts about the Constitution, the Civil War, or the Obama administration is important. Reciting the winners of the 1973 Oscars isn't," Danny said. "You know I'm kidding," he said as I fixed him with a glare. "Come on. Take the photo."

"I don't want a photo with you anymore," I pouted.

"Do it," Chris said. "Pretend you like each other."

I rolled my eyes, but I didn't protest as Danny wrapped his arms around me.

"Stop!" I shouted, shrieking with laughter as he tickled me. Chris snapped the photo at the perfect moment, just before I managed to push Danny off the side of the boat.

Chris and I jumped in after him, drifting dangerously close to the buoys as the cold water rushed over our clothes. Chris pulled a towel over my shoulders for the trip home. His arm lingered on the side of the boat, brushing my skin. Accidentally, I told myself. But I always wondered if, just maybe, it had been on purpose.

If he felt it, too.

I almost smiled, but the chime from my computer pulled me back into the present. I scowled.

"Just go get to work. I can't think about this today."

Chris frowned. "Lyd, it's been three years."

"And that's supposed to make it easier?" My voice echoed through the silent lab. The man across from me looked up from his work. I lowered my voice, glaring at Chris. "It shouldn't be me here today. It should be him."

Chris hopped down from the desk and stepped towards me. "You don't mean that," he murmured. I crossed my arms and stared at the ground, but Chris placed a hand under my chin and tilted my head up, forcing me to meet his eyes. "You're the smartest one here, and you know it."

"Danny was smarter."

Chris shrugged. "You know what? Maybe he was. But he's gone. And we still have you. Maybe all of this happened for a reason."

"There wasn't any reason for it," I muttered bitterly. Hazy memories lingered on the edge of my mind, but I shoved them away. "He never should have…"

"Never should have what?" Chris's eyes searched mine.

I shied away from him. I turned and pressed my hands onto my desk. Pressure built behind my eyes. After a moment, Chris put a hand on my shoulder. Every single muscle in my back tensed.

"Just go."

Chris grabbed my shoulder and pulled me around to face him. "No. No, I'm not going anywhere."

"Why not?"

"Because I haven't told you everything that happened that day."

I jerked my head up. "Haven't told me everything?" I stepped closer. "Chris, you never told me *anything* about that day."

"Exactly." His breath brushed over my lips. I tensed. But I didn't back away. "Alright, look. I know you blame yourself for what happened—"

"I don't just blame *me*."

"Okay, fine. You blame me, too. I can feel it every time you look at me. But mostly, you blame yourself, and you shouldn't."

I hit Chris's shoulder, pushing myself away from him. "Why not?" I hissed. "Why shouldn't I blame myself for my brother's death when he only died because he gave his gun to me?"

"That's what I'm trying to tell you. Danny might not be dead."

I backed away from Chris, shaking my head. My mind raced, trying to make sense of what I was hearing. Three years ago, Danny ran into a burning building and it came crashing down around him. Suddenly, there was a chance he wasn't dead?

"What the hell do you mean?" I hissed.

"We can't talk about this now."

"And when do you propose that we do that? What'll be the right moment for you to explain why my brother might not be dead? And why you haven't mentioned this in the *three* years since he's been gone?"

Chris raised his voice. "It's not that simple—"

Before Chris could finish his sentence, gunfire crashed through the air and shattered the silence. Screams erupted around me. I threw myself to the ground. Pain crashed through my arms as my elbows cracked against the cement. The lab was suddenly filled with voices and the smoky smell of gunpowder. I locked eyes with Chris. He slid a gun across the floor to me.

"What the hell are you doing?"

Chris shook his head. He pressed his palms to the floor and fixed his eyes on something or someone that I couldn't see. I scrambled to fit the gun into my hand and loaded it, clenching it in my fist so tightly that my knuckles ached. The voices around me faded out until they sounded like they were coming from an old-fashioned radio. For a heartbeat's space of time, there was silence.

*"Lydia!"*

I unfroze and scrambled to my feet. The edge of a shoulder appeared around my desk, and I yanked the gun up in front of my face. I tried to stop my hand from shaking as I took aim and fired, but my unsteady grip kicked the gun out of position and the bullet sailed harmlessly over the man's shoulder. The intruder had a gun of his own, one much larger than the one I held. He was dressed in black from head to toe. His weathered face was pulled into a glare.

I looked at the gun and then back at the man, who raised his own weapon with dull fire in his eyes. I reacted without thinking. Instead of shooting the gun, I threw it as hard as I could into his abdomen. The man dropped the gun he held with a grunt and doubled over. It went off with a sound like a cannon, but the bullet bounced harmlessly off of the concrete floor. I rushed forwards and kicked the man's gun away from him, towards Chris.

"Lyd!"

I snatched my own gun from the floor and aimed it at the man with an unsteady hand. "Who are you? Are you a Driller?"

The man leered at me, his eyebrows drawn low over his dark eyes.

"What do you want?" I shouted.

The man made no reply. He darted around the corner before I could stop him.

I lowered the gun, heart pounding. "Chris?" I called, tossing a glance over my shoulder. "Chris!"

The gun clattered to the floor as I whirled around and rushed to Chris's side. I pulled his head into my hands. He was bleeding, a bright splash of ruby red spreading over his chest like ink in water. Every other sound in the air, every other scream was drowned out by this moment. Air left my lungs as I brushed my hands over Chris's pale face.

"Chris?" I whispered, my eyes searching his. I knew that this wasn't the time to stop and ask why, why Chris was shot instead of me. I knew I needed to pick up my gun again if I wanted any chance of getting out of here alive, but all I could do was look at him. All I could do was kneel, frozen, as my only friend died right in front of me.

"Lyd." A trickle of blood ran out of Chris's mouth. I wiped it away with my sleeve. The corners of my eyes burned, threatening tears, but they wouldn't come. "I need to tell you—"

"Shh," I murmured, brushing Chris's dark, messy hair off of his forehead. "You're going to be fine."

More gunshots echoed from somewhere far, far away.

Chris coughed. Blood spattered onto my shirt. "You can't trust them."

"Trust who?"

Chris's eyes fluttered closed. I seized his shoulders, shaking him. "Chris!"

He made no reply. As the rise and fall of his chest slowed, I whispered his name again, but Chris's head lolled to the side.

The rest of the world zoomed into focus again. My ears were suddenly filled with the sound of footsteps. Black shoes surrounded me. I lunged at the gun, but someone kicked it away from my grasp. I tried to scramble to my feet to do something—anything—to hold them off, but it was useless. Men twice my size surrounded me on all sides. There was no way out.

My hands trembled as I backed into my desk, looking desperately for an escape that I knew wasn't there. My eyes landed on Chris's still figure. As I looked at my oldest friend, silent and still, something inside of me broke. A tear trailed down my face. Faint memories and what-ifs and should-have-beens played in my mind, but they all vanished as something drilled into the center of my back and my world exploded into a sea of sharp, burning pain.

I doubled over and crashed to the ground. My head bashed into the floor and I rolled to my side, in too much pain to move—to think.

Tears flowed freely down my face as my wavering gaze focused onto Chris's body. The world around me was filled with noises, but they were filtered as though through water.

The last thing that I saw before my world faded was Chris's blood spreading across the concrete floor underneath a pair of shiny black shoes.

# CHAPTER THREE

The first thing that I noticed as the world faded back in around me was the pain. It was dull at first, like a punch to the small of my back. Then it spread, branching out like poison trickling through my veins, splintering them until I thought they were going to rip apart. I strained against the pain, aching to cry out, but I couldn't move. Couldn't scream. Couldn't *think*. I was swimming through a thick fog that stung my every nerve.

Pain hit my back like fire. I gasped, shooting bolt upright. I whipped my head around, trying to make sense of my surroundings. At first, I couldn't see anything except for a bright, white light.

Then a voice reached my ears through the haze. "Calm down, hon. Calm down."

I became aware of a hand on my shoulder as the pain in my back gave a particularly nasty stab. An old woman stood in front of me. Her face was lined, her deep-set blue eyes peered at me, anxiously. I clenched my hands into fists around the clean white sheets I rested on and tried to keep from shaking.

"Where am I?" I whispered. I coughed as pain prickled down my dry throat. The woman placed a hand on the side of my neck, checked for a pulse, and clicked her tongue.

"You should lie back and rest. You have some nasty injuries."

"Injuries?" Pain jabbed into the crook of my left arm. An IV was drilled deep into it, buried so far that seeing it made me nauseous. A monitor to my right kept track of my heartbeat, beeping shrilly. Light reflected off of the clean white walls, brighter than the summer sun. I closed my eyes and took shaky breaths.

I was alive, and that was all that mattered. Right? The room was bright and spinning and painful. I blinked, and the spinning slowly eased into a gentle rocking, like a boat on the waves.

I seemed to be in a standard hospital room, all white walls and sharp, shiny medical tools. As the pain in my back intensified, everything came rushing back. The attack. The men in black from head to toe. Chris.

"What happened?" I demanded.

The woman moved away from me, her bottom lip caught between her teeth. She pulled out a clipboard and made notes on it as she surveyed me. "My name is Donna. Can you raise your right hand for me?"

Pain shot through my arm as I lifted it. I grimaced at Donna. Something about her chin-length grey hair and weathered skin looked familiar, like I'd once seen her in passing. But that was impossible. I took my eyes off of her and focused instead on the hand I'd raised. It was trembling. I curled it into a fist.

"Your blood sugar is still off balance." Donna frowned. "I'll let the doctor know that he should increase your dosage of—"

"I don't want my dosage increased. I want to know what's going on." I forced myself into a sitting position. Pain trickled up my spine. "Where's my dad?"

Donna dropped her eyes to the floor and flipped a page of her clipboard. "You've been recovering quite well, considering the circumstances. If this continues, you should be off of the IV in a few hours."

I glared at Donna. The worry in my chest swelled. "I want to know what happened."

Donna sighed. She placed the clipboard onto the nightstand and made a big show of aligning it to the edge. "How much do you remember?" She asked finally.

"Everything. I think."

"Do you remember getting shot?"

"Getting *shot?*"

"Yes. Do you know how much blood a person can lose before they die?" Donna asked.

I swallowed. "No."

"Forty percent. Do you know how much you had lost when we found you?"

I said nothing.

"Thirty-four percent. It's a miracle you're alive. I'm surprised you remember anything at all after something like that."

"How did you find me?"

"It's a long story." Donna adjusted something on the machine counting my heartbeats. "I'm not sure that I'm the one to tell it."

"Then get the one who is," I snapped. Pain jabbed into my back as I pushed myself up, but I didn't care.

"You need rest, Lydia." Donna placed a hand on my shoulder and pushed me back into the pillows.

"Donna, please—"

"That's enough," said a new voice, this one low and cold.

I peered over Donna's shoulder as the door across from me opened and a tall man stepped into the room. He wore a black suit that hugged his thin frame. His jet-black hair was slicked back, exposing his lined forehead and the veins that snaked beneath his pale skin. "Donna, thank you. Please leave us."

Donna nodded, ducking her eyes to the floor. The door slid back into place behind her, concealing the exit. There was no doorknob.

The man turned towards me and offered a cold smile with white, even teeth. "Hello, Lydia." His heels clicked sharply on the tile floor. "My name is Dominic Reed. For all intents and purposes, I'm in charge here. I'm sure you have many questions."

"That's an understatement," I muttered bitterly.

"Well." Reed spread his hands. "What would you like to know?"

"Where am I?"

"You're in the hospital. Quite an ordeal you went through."

"I've heard," I said through gritted teeth. "Quit talking in circles. I want to know what's going on, and I want to know now. Who were those men? How did I make it out alive? Where's my dad?" Every question that had been tormenting me since the second my eyes opened came pouring out of my mouth, and each syllable was like a knife to my sore throat. "Where the hell am I? When can I go home?" My voice broke. "Please. I just want to know what's happening."

"That's quite a list of queries." Reed's voice was smooth and even. "To answer your first few, your home was the victim of a targeted attack by the Drillers."

A thrill of nausea punched through my stomach. *I knew it. But how had they managed to find us again? They said that'd be imposs—*

"Reinforcements were called immediately, but by the time they arrived, it appeared as though you were dead. This is likely why the Drillers moved on after shooting you only once. You're very lucky, Ms. Melrose.

"This place is called Yucca Mountain School. I said I was in charge. Think of me like a principal. Our school is located deep within the bedrock of a mountain range in what used to be south Nevada. You'll be safe here."

"Why was I brought here?" I frowned. Our island was in the middle of the Pacific Ocean. It didn't make any sense that they would bring me to Nevada.

"You are here, Ms. Melrose, because this government recognizes your unique potential to aid us in the current conflict," Reed said. "And you are here because, as I said, Yucca Mountain is, above all else, a school."

"A school? I don't need to go to school."

Reed raised his eyebrows. "What you need to do will be determined by this government, Ms. Melrose. Not you."

"Where's my father?" I interrupted. "He could clear all of this up. I live on a military base, it's safe."

"It may have been safe, but it isn't any longer. And you still need an education."

"My father teaches me, and I take courses online," I tried to explain. His words blurred in my mind, fighting against the pain in my body. *Why wasn't the island safe anymore?*

"Even if I thought that these courses were an appropriate replacement for learning inside the classroom, returning home isn't going to be an option."

"Why not?" I whispered.

"The base has been compromised."

"Compromised?" I stuttered. "Where's my dad?"

Reed fixed me with an icy gaze. Chills of fear ran up my spine. "I'm very sorry to be the one to tell you this," he hesitated, "but your father is dead. He was shot by the same group that tried to kill you."

I heard Reed's words, but somehow, they didn't seem to reach my ears. I opened my mouth, but my lips couldn't form words. "I..."

"I'm sorry," Reed repeated, but his words snapped together like pieces in a jigsaw puzzle. Tense and unemotional. "I know that this may be hard to accept. But your father wanted, above all, for this war to end. Don't you want to honor that?"

I swallowed. Fire ran down my throat. "Did you know him?"

"We had a mutual acquaintance." Reed pulled a piece of paper out of his back pocket. A numb tear trailed down my cheek. "Now, as I was saying, Yucca Mountain is a school for gifted students such as yourself."

"You don't know anything about me."

"I do, actually. You took the entrance exams for the state education program just like all of the other students here, even though you were never enrolled. As a licensed educator, I have access to all of these records. And you are quite gifted."

"Thank you," I bit my lip, trying to form my next argument. "But as I was saying, I don't need to go to school. My dad taught me everything he could about computers and coding. The rest I need to learn for myself. In a real lab. Who else survived the attack? Did Holbrook?"

Reed stared at me.

"Mathews?"

Silence.

"Did... Did anyone?"

"Very few," Reed snapped. "They have all been placed where we feel they can best assist the cause. And your place, Ms. Melrose, is here." Reed pulled a crisp piece of white paper out of his pocket. "It has been decided that you will attend school here until you finish your senior year, at which time your status will be reevaluated. Is this clear?"

"Yes, sir," I said, teeth gritted. I had always wanted to go to school, to be a normal teenager. But not like this. Not without my dad by my side. But it seemed that, whatever my feelings, I wasn't going to have a choice.

"This is the schedule of classes that you will attend. When you're well, you will be relocated to the student housing. Do you have any further questions?"

I shook my head, accepting the page that Reed offered me without looking at it. Reed turned on his heel and moved back towards the door. He pressed his palm to the wall and hit a series of what seemed to be invisible buttons. The door slid open, and Donna's anxious face appeared over his shoulder. The pair exchanged a few hushed words and then Reed left, the slight heel on his shoes clicking away until he was out of sight.

"How are you feeling?" Donna stepped into the room and the door slid shut behind her.

I placed the sheet of paper onto my knees and shrugged. I knew that if I tried to speak, nothing intelligible would leave my mouth. Donna sighed and bustled over to one of the cabinets that lined the left side of the room. She pulled out a needle, a tube, and a few glass vials that she arranged on the nightstand.

"What is that?" My voice came out hoarse.

"I just need a blood sample." Donna tilted my right arm so that the crook of my elbow was exposed and ran her finger down the length of my arm. "Standard procedure."

Her skin was cold, and I shied away from her touch. The last person who touched me was Chris. Now, he was dead. Skin colder than the hands touching me now. Skin covered in blood.

"Couldn't you have gotten some when I was bleeding out from a bullet wound?"

Donna laughed, a tinkling, eerie sound that bounced off of the white walls and echoed ever so slightly. "You want to keep up your health now, don't you?"

I reluctantly returned my arm to its original position and looked away as the sharp needle broke my skin. Compared to the amount of pain in my back, a little blood should have been nothing, but the needle felt like fire in my veins. It took everything I had not to cry out.

"There," Donna said after a moment, twisting the cap onto the last vial of my ruby-red blood. "That wasn't so hard, was it?"

I shook my head.

Donna offered a smile and pulled another syringe out of her pocket. "This is medicine," she clarified as she injected the liquid into my IV. "It'll aid the healing process. You should be able to begin school in a few days' time."

I nodded as I watched a drop of completely transparent liquid travel down the IV and into my left arm. Suddenly, my eyelids felt incredibly heavy and I blinked once, twice, three times, trying to force them back open.

"There are some side effects." Donna's voice reached me from far away. "Dizziness, shortness of breath…"

"Fatigue?" My eyes slid shut. Donna's laugh was the last thing that I heard before the world faded away.

\*\*\*

The next few days and nights passed in a drug-induced haze. I barely knew where I was, could barely find the strength to open my mouth when Donna tipped glasses of clear water into it several times a day. When my eyes were open, everything was blurry, like I was looking at the world through murky ocean water. But I fought to keep them open. Because when they closed, all I could see was Chris's face.

I lost count of the amount of times I'd replayed those last few moments in my head.

Chris's body on the floor.

*Danny might not be dead.*

*You can't trust them.*

Trust *who*? Someone on the island? Someone far away? Someone here? I spent forever staring into the memory of those haunted green eyes, wishing I could read his mind.

Of course, I couldn't. So instead, I focused on those last moments when his skin had skimmed against mine. Pretended for a while that everything was okay. That all of this was just a nightmare. Chris was still alive.

And so was my father.

My dad, who'd kept me sane after Danny's disappearance, who played with me on the beach when I was little, who taught me everything he knew, who kept me safe no matter what… was dead. I was never going to see him again. Somehow, I was supposed to navigate the rest of my life without him. Without him, or Danny, or Chris, or anyone else I'd ever known and loved.

If I could have found the strength to lift my arms, I would have dug my nails into my skin hard enough to draw blood. Anything to chase the pain away. As it was, all I could do was lie there.

I hadn't felt this helpless since the week after Danny's death. The Drillers had attacked our armory and killed anyone they ran into along the way. They'd set a bomb underneath it with four people trapped inside. Danny ran in to help, and then the place was blown to pieces.

There was no casket at his funeral, just a jar of white sand with his dog tags buried inside. They were charred black in places, but we could still read the name. Someone had found them inside wreckage, because of the way the sun glinted against them like a beacon. Since I was technically a member of the military, I had my own somewhere, but I'd lost them ages ago. When I saw the dog tags, all I saw was Danny.

I wore a black dress at the funeral. I think it used to be my mother's, because the only clothes I owned were standard-issue jeans, shorts, t-shirts, and sweatshirts. The dress was hanging over my bedroom door when I woke up that morning, which was smart of my dad, because I had been planning to lie in bed all day until I died, too, instead of attending the funeral. Looking at the dress, I knew Danny would want me to get out of bed and honor him. I wore it the again the next year, on the anniversary of his death, and the year after.

I never found out where that dress came from. Dad never told me. There was so much I wish he'd told me.

Chris wore a suit to the funeral. The bags under his eyes were almost as black as the fabric of my dress. We didn't say anything that day. He just put his arms around me and kept them there for a long time. When we finally broke apart and sat side by side in the tiny church, it was with our hands laced together.

I laced my own hands as I lay in the hospital bed and closed my eyes.

Chris's last words echoed in my head. *You can't trust them.*

# CHAPTER FOUR

"You're going to have to wake up eventually, you know."

Something tapped my face and I wrinkled my nose, raising my hand to brush away whatever it was.

A laugh. "Hey, you're alive."

I cracked open my eyes and the world swam into focus. I sat bolt upright, kicking the thin blankets off of my legs. I wasn't in the hospital anymore.

The girl sitting across the room laughed and tossed a Cheerio into the air. She caught it in her mouth and grinned.

"I knew we'd get there eventually." She stood up and held out a hand. "I'm Kat."

I wrapped my arms around my legs. "Where am I?"

Kat dropped her hand and gestured around the small space. "You're in our room." She rolled her eyes. "God, how many drugs did they shoot you up with last night?"

I stepped off of the bed and raked a hand through my messy hair. "I have no idea." A few Cheerios fell from my shirt and bounced on the tile floor.

"Well, that figures." Kat grabbed a bag from beside the desk she leaned against. "You remember your name after all of that?"

"Lydia. Lydia Melrose."

"Melrose," Kat echoed. "Melrose, like Battle of Montara, Melrose? Like Sebastian Melrose?"

I nodded. "Yes. Sebastian is—" The words burned my throat like acid. "Sebastian *was* my father. He's gone now."

The smile slipped off of Kat's face. "I'm sorry," she stuttered. She slung her bag over her shoulder. "They told me…" she trailed off.

"What did they tell you?" I snapped.

Kat shrugged. "Just that you're new here. Not about your father or anything like that."

A sharp sound rang through the room, loud and clear as a bell.

My stomach jolted, and I jumped, looking to Kat. "What was that?"

"The five-minute bell."

"Five minutes until what?"

Kat raised an eyebrow. "Class?"

I sank back down onto the bed. "Oh God." My stomach was suddenly a bundle of knotted nerves. Even though it had probably been days since I'd eaten, I felt like I was going to throw up.

Kat crossed the room and laid a hand on my arm. "Hey. Are you alright?" She peered into my eyes, her face scrunched with worry.

"I'll be okay." I took a deep breath. A piece of my wavy black hair fell into my face. "God, I'm such a mess." The corners of my eyes burned. My first day here, and I was expected to meet all of my classmates looking like this? Without so much as a warning that I was being released from the hospital?

Kat bit her lip, bouncing on her heels. She crossed to the closet that stood open a few feet from my bed and tugged a dress from the hanger. She tossed it at me and I caught it one-handed. The fabric was soft in my hand.

"School uniform," she explained. Kat held out a hand that I grasped, and she pulled me to my feet. She put her hands on my shoulders and spun me so that I was facing another door that I hadn't noticed. It was cracked open; I could see that it was a small bathroom. "You have about six minutes to clean yourself up, but then we have to go."

I took a deep breath. "Thank you."

Kat patted my shoulder. "Don't thank me yet. I wouldn't put it past Jamison to kick your ass for being late, even if it is your first day."

"Jamison?"

Kat pushed my shoulder again. "Get cleaned up. We'll have time for questions later."

I wanted nothing more than to whirl around and demand more answers from Kat, but I knew she wouldn't have the ones I wanted. And Reed had made it pretty clear that disobedience wasn't going to fly at Yucca Mountain.

I pulled the bathroom door shut behind me and peeled off my clothes, moving into the shower as quickly as my injured body would let me. The soap and hot water from the shower stung my wound like poison, but I gritted my teeth and scrubbed my body with the soap, avoiding only the bullet wound. It was square in the center of my back; I couldn't even see it.

I could only hope that the doctors here knew what they were doing when it came to treating wounds.

I toweled off as quickly as I could and stared at myself in the mirror as I pulled on the dress. A pale girl with scared brown eyes stared back at me, her lips shaking. A bruise scrawled across her forehead; blood webbed beneath her skin, purple and blue.

I turned away from the mirror and tossed my hair over my shoulder. It was so hot inside this room that it was already starting to dry.

"Lydia?" Kat pounded on the door. "We have to go!"

"Coming!" I took one last look at myself in the mirror and gave my head a small shake. I was about to go to *class*. To *school*. I'd only ever seen schools in old television shows and movies; the only people I'd ever known that were my age were Danny and Chris.

My breath caught. I couldn't think about them right now. I just couldn't.

"Here." Kat dropped a bag into my hand the second I opened the door and beckoned me forwards. "They left a bunch of stuff for you. I shoved most of it into here. Door in to here opens with a passcode—3-3-7-9."

I fumbled with the bag as Kat wrenched open another door. "Come on," she called. "We're already late."

I barely had time to catch my breath before Kat took off at a run, navigating the narrow halls like she'd been doing it all her life, which, for all I knew, she had. I stumbled as I caught up with her, knocking into the walls as I went. How the hell was she so agile?

"Class isn't far," Kat shouted over her shoulder as we took another left. "Everything is pretty central since there aren't that many of us."

My heart leapt. "How many students are there?"

Kat didn't reply. She skidded to a stop in front of a blank door and wrapped a hand around the doorknob. "Okay," she huffed, her chest heaving, and her olive skin tinged with red. "Just act natural. Take any open seat. And try not to die."

"Try not to—"

Kat pulled open the door and ducked inside. I had no choice but to follow, but I froze at the scene in front of me.

A classroom.

Filled with teenagers.

Every single gaze was locked onto me. My mouth dropped open. I gaped into the small classroom until Kat grabbed my arm and wrenched me forwards. She marched me down a row of desks and shoved me into one. I stumbled, gripping the edges of the desk while locking eyes with the boy who sat next to me. He looked me up and down with warm brown eyes, a smirk painted on his face.

My heart jumped as our eyes locked, but I barely had time to say a word before a voice rang from the front of the room, loud and clear.

"I've given you more than a few warnings about punctuality, haven't I, Ms. Romero?"

I snapped my eyes to the front of the room, where a middle-aged man with jet black hair and a sharp chin gazed at us with eyebrows raised. He leaned back against a shiny silver desk, his posture pin-straight. A pocket scarf stuck out of his suit, an impeccable triangle of red against the black.

"Yes, sir." I recognized Kat's voice from behind me as I dropped my bag to the floor. "It's just that I…"

"Have a blatant disregard for established polices?" The teacher offered, his expression stoic.

Kat laughed lightly. "Professor Jamison, I—"

"You know what, Ms. Romero? I'll make you a deal. If you can tell me the exact date of the Battle of Incitement, and the name of the location where it took place, we'll wipe your attendance slate clean." He raised an eyebrow. "Does that sound fair?"

My heart pounded in my chest. Easy. December 13th, 2026. I knew those dates like the back of my hand, but did Kat?

"Well, Professor Jamison…" Kat's voice tapered off.

"No, that's enough." Jamison held up a hand. "I'll see you after class to arrange repercussion for your tardiness. Now—"

"It's not her fault," I blurted before I could stop myself. Eyes swiveled to me again. Dull murmurs rose up here and there throughout the small classroom, and one boy craned his neck to get a good look at me. I faltered, "Sir, it's my fault. It's my first day, and Kat was just helping me."

Jamison's eyes locked onto me. His gaze was stone cold. "They told me I'd be getting a new student." He tapped his chin. "While I sympathize with your situation, Ms. Melrose, I'm afraid I can't bend policies for your more troublesome classmates." Jamison looked to Kat again. "After class, Ms. Romero."

"What if I can answer the question?"

The boy next to me coughed into his hand. I looked over, and he shook his head, flicking his hand across his neck in the universal sign for *stop talking*.

I grimaced in his general direction. It was already too late.

"Excuse me?" Jamison raised an eyebrow.

"The Battle of Incitement. December 13th, 2026. It was an underwater battle on the US base, The Washington," I recited. "It was the first sign of aggression from either side, and even though the Drillers were on the offensive, they weren't able to take the base. It is still standing today."

I looked to my left, at the boy who'd warned me not to say anything. He scoffed as his lips spread into a smirk. He flashed me a thumbs-up underneath the desk. Warmth spread to my cheeks, and my lips fell into a smile.

It quickly vanished.

"That's correct." Jamison's forehead wrinkled. "But that doesn't excuse Ms. Romero's lateness."

"But it wasn't her fault," I repeated. "It's my first day."

"And?"

"Kat was only late because she was trying to help me. If anyone's going to be punished, shouldn't it be me?"

Jamison threw up his hands. "Well, if you're so insistent, then *you* can meet me here for in-school detention tonight at seven o'clock."

"Fine," I said. At least Kat was out of trouble.

Jamison hit a switch on his desk. The lights dimmed as a projector lit the wall behind him, detailing a map of the United States. He cleared his throat. "Now, before we start on our new material, let's review the tensions that lead to the war. I'm sure you all did the reading, so we'll begin with the dissolution of the United Nations. You," he pointed at a girl in the front with curly black hair.

"Uh, it happened in 2024."

"And?"

"It was all Russia's fault?"

A chuckle rolled through the class.

"In simple terms, yes." I was surprised to see Jamison crack a smile. I frowned. Nothing was *all Russia's fault*. My dad was *at* those talks. The United States, Iran, China, and Great Britain were as much to blame for the dissolution as Russia.

"Can someone walk us through the conflict? Taylor?"

The guy next to me cleared his throat. "The air pollution from cars and stuff made it impossible to use solar power, so everyone started redoubling efforts to get to the oil under the ocean. When things didn't go too well, there were divides."

"And these divides were? Melrose?" I jumped when Jamison said my name.

I stuttered. "One side wanted to keep drilling, and the other wanted to focus all efforts on finding renewable solutions to the problem. Everyone was pretty surprised when the U.S. sided with renewables, given our history." I laughed lightly, but no one joined me. "Because of our history with oil," I said.

Jamison cleared his throat. "Let's move on."

I opened my mouth to reply but thought better of it. Maybe I was the only one here who found historical irony funny.

Jamison started to ramble on about recent territory acquisitions and I slumped in my seat, sighing. He was skimming over the most important parts, like what we were even fighting for. Danny always said the war was about who would be in control of the world when it went completely to crap. When there wasn't a single barrel of oil or battery left to fight over, this war would decide who got to pick up the pieces.

"And that brings me to your next assignment," Jamison interrupted my thoughts. "I want you to break into groups of three. Using the articles I've loaded onto your Rosetts, pick a battle and prepare a report for the class. Specific requirements will appear in your inbox by this evening. Questions?" When no one raised any, Jamison nodded. "Class dismissed."

Almost in unison with his words, a bell rang through the room. I winced at the sound. The students around me gathered their things, shoving notebooks into bags and laughing. A few eyes turned my way, but most of my classmates seemed keener on exiting the room than gawking at me.

Someone tugged on my arm. "Let's go." Kat pulled me to my feet. I grabbed my bag and slung it over my shoulder. Jamison looked my way as we passed him but said nothing. I ducked my head until we were in the hallway and the twenty-some students dispersed, going this way and that down the maze-like hallways.

Kat dropped my arm and leaned one shoulder against the wall, facing me. Her face twisted into a glare. "What the hell were you thinking?"

My mouth dropped open. "What?"

"Lydia, you... you don't talk back to Jamison. He'll murder you."

I paled. "Really?"

Kat laughed, shattering her hard expression. She hit my arm. "No, not really." She sighed, shaking her head. "What you did in there..." A pause. "Thanks."

I offered a small smile. "Anytime." I glanced around. "Now what?"

Kat beckoned me. "This way."

I turned to follow her.

"Hey, new girl!"

I stopped and glanced over my shoulder. The boy from class waved and pulled his bag higher on his shoulder as he walked over to us.

Kat threw her hair over her shoulder and raised her eyebrows as he approached.

"So," he paused, looking me up and down. "I've come to the conclusion that you have a death wish."

I just stared at him.

"But also, that you're crazy badass." He held out a hand. "I'm Aaron."

I grasped his hand, warmth tingling in the pit of my stomach. Aaron was tall, with warm brown eyes, light brown skin, and a kind smile.

"Lydia." I drew my hand back and hooked it around my neck. "I'm… new."

"Yeah. I can see that."

I offered a wan smile. "That obvious, huh?"

Aaron laughed. "Don't sweat it. You'll learn. Hey, you guys want to work on the project together?"

"Uh, sure," Kat shrugged.

"We'd love to," I said, doing my best to smile.

"Great. Meet later to figure things out?" he asked.

"I've got detention tonight."

"At dinner, then. See you at five."

"Okay," I said as he tossed a grin over his shoulder. "Goodbye!"

Kat tugged my arm again. "First rule of the schedule here? Five minutes between classes means not much time for conversation."

"Okay." I glanced over my shoulder to see if I could see Aaron, but he was gone. "Where to next?"

"Well, we have five classes a day, with lunch in between the third and fourth," Kat explained as she led me down another hallway. "Most of them are hell, but we'll be finished and out of here soon enough, right?"

"Right," I echoed, matching her pace. "What did they tell you?"

Kat tossed a glance over her shoulder. "About?"

"Where you'll go after," I gestured around us, "whatever this is?"

"Oh." Kat shrugged. "Not much. I just know that this is a lot better than where I was before."

"Where was that?"

Kat's face darkened. "Let's just say that this school is underground for a reason."

# CHAPTER FIVE

"Never enter the laboratory without your scrubs and goggles on. We work with a lot of dangerous chemicals here, and one slip could mean an acid burn that takes half of your skin off." The woman in front of me pushed a bundle of gray clothes into my hands. "Have you ever worked in a lab before?"

I shook my head. "Only a computer lab."

The woman, Ms. Khan, clicked her tongue. "Well, you'll have a lot to learn. I see here that your roommate is Katerina Romero, is that correct?"

I nodded.

"You can join her for now." She tilted her head towards the entrance of a large laboratory. Students wearing scrubs and goggles milled about, mixing chemicals, and creating miniscule flames. A knot grew in the pit of my chest as I pulled on the scrubs and goggles. I pulled my hair back with the rubber band she'd put in with the clothes. *What the hell had I gotten myself into?*

I stepped tentatively into the lab, dodging a boy carrying a test tube filled to the brim with bright blue liquid as I made my way over to Kat.

"Hey," I mumbled as I joined her.

Kat looked up from the beaker that she was swirling. "You look hot."

"Very funny. What can I do?"

"Um…" Kat flipped through her notebook. "Grab me ten milliliters of acetic acid." She pushed a beaker into my hand.

"I… okay."

"Over there." Kat pointed to a fume hood surrounded by students. I nodded, trying to ignore the tightness in my chest as I crossed the room and stood behind two tall girls with their hair pulled back into messy buns.

"...going to get into so much trouble."

"Who the hell cares?" asked the blonde. "What can they do?"

The brunette frowned. "Throw us back out on the street, for one."

"They won't do that." The blonde dismissed her with a wave of her hand. "It'll be fun."

The brunette sighed as another student moved away from the hood and they moved closer. "When is it again?"

"Next month. Plenty of time for you to get a date."

"Yeah because that's my biggest priority..."

Their conversation trickled into laughter. I frowned, watching them. *What the hell are they talking about?*

I shook the questions away as I measured out the acid, trying to keep my hands from trembling. Giving myself a chemical burn would just get me a trip to the hospital, returning me to square negative one. I had no wish to see Donna again. Ignoring the laughter, I took a label from beside the test tubes and marked mine. I carried it back to Kat with slow, painstaking steps.

"Thanks." She took it from me and made a small note in her book. "So, you just record the exact volume of the liquid, see? Easy." Kat poured the contents into a beaker and hit a few buttons on the computer that hung above the station.

"What are you doing?" I peered over her shoulder.

"Titration," she answered. "We're finding the concentration of the acid, so we can know how much to dilute it by before using it for other purposes." She stirred the liquid with a glass rod. "It's pretty nasty stuff all on its own."

"Interesting," I mused, staring at her careful handwriting. "Why don't they know the concentration already?"

"They do, silly. This is just to train us." Kat pulled the beaker from the stand and handed it to me. "Can you pour this into the red waste barrel over there?"

"I think I can handle that." I weaved through the students to the fume hood and poured the contents into the barrel. It hissed faintly as it made contact with whatever substances lay at the bottom. I replaced the lid, barely paying attention to what I was doing until I crashed headfirst into someone just in front of me.

I gasped as cold liquid spilled over my exposed wrist. Someone's beaker had tipped.

"Shit, I'm sorry." The boy I'd crashed into backed up immediately and set his test tube inside the fume hood. "Are you okay?"

I wiped the liquid from my arm with my rubber gloves. "I think so." I raised my eyes and locked my gaze onto the boy in front of me. Green eyes peered at me from pale skin; a mess of dirty blond hair tumbled over his forehead. Freckles danced across his nose.

"Carver!" Ms. Khan's shrill voice echoed through the room. Every station went silent.

The boy rolled his eyes and turned to our teacher. "What?"

Ms. Khan rushed to me and took my arm, examining the clear droplets on my skin. "Are you alright? You should rinse this with water immediately."

"That's just it," Carver cut in. "It was just water." He shrugged and held up the test tube.

Ms. Khan, far from looking relieved, only glared at Carver. "Why aren't your test tubes marked?"

"I tend to make remembering which test tubes contain things that can kill me a priority. This one is filled with water. Test it if you don't believe me."

Anger flashed across Ms. Khan's face as she picked up the test tube and poured the contents down the drain. "Detention." She pointed at Carver. "Safety is the top priority here. See me after class."

I looked down at my scrubs instead of at Carver. Between calling Jamison out this morning and running headfirst into Carver, my plan to fly under the radar was backfiring tremendously. I stared at the ground as I walked back to the lab station. By the time I reached Kat, chatter had refilled the lab.

"You sure you're okay?" Kat asked, frowning.

I stared at my dry, pale skin. "Yeah." I couldn't get Carver's face out of my head. "Yeah, I'm fine."

\*\*\*

After history and chemistry, I had calculus. The concepts were ones I'd learned years ago, but I kept my head down. Everyone's eyes were already on me. My skin prickled like there were hundreds of tiny bugs crawling all over me, inside and out.

By the time I walked into the cafeteria for lunch, my whole body was shaking. Everyone was looking at me. The walls were closing in. Every table was filled. Where was I supposed to go? I froze in the doorway as idle chitchat hummed in my ears like radio static.

"Woah. Deep breaths." Kat appeared at my shoulder. Concern settled on her face. "Come with me."

Relief flooded my body; my shoulders sagged forward. I nodded shakily and followed as she led me over to the food and explained that each counter had a different option. There was anything I could want here, from salad to roast chicken to mac and cheese. I gaped at the seemingly unending mounds of food.

I found my voice again as Kat and I found an empty table right in the middle of the room. "How is there so much food here?"

"It's a combination of waste reduction and state-of-the art greenhouses. Or so I've heard. For all you know, that was grown in a test tube," she said, jabbing her fork at the chicken breast on my plate.

I set my fork down. "You know what? I'm not hungry."

"Lydia, I'm kidding. Eat," she said, and shoved a huge bite of spinach into her mouth. "None of this'll get any easier on an empty stomach."

"I guess you're right." I took small bites, trying to settle my stomach. It sort of worked, even if I was having trouble swallowing. "Can I see your schedule?" I asked. Even though I'd only known Kat for a few hours, I was terrified of going through another class without her.

"Give me yours. I'll look it over." She studied it. "Hm. No dice on gym class—that's your next period, but I'll see you in computer science later."

"Oh. Okay." I think my voice was trembling, but I was having trouble hearing it.

"Listen." Kat reached for my hand and gave it a squeeze. "You seem pretty freaked out. I was the same way when I first got here. It'll get easier. I promise."

"Not if I fall and kill myself in gym class."

"Well," Kat laughed, "don't do that."

I shot her a smile. "I'll try."

We spent the rest of the meal in relative silence. Slowly, my appetite returned. Looking at the variety of food, I couldn't help myself, and I went back for seconds.

Before the bell rang, Kat walked me to the gym, a huge room with high ceilings and a jumble of exercise equipment. She introduced me to the trainer, Mr. Amari, a muscular and kind-faced man. He gave me some clothes to change into, and I spent the class with a group of girls around my size, lifting weights and doing squats.

It wasn't bad. It even helped me rid myself of the nervous energy radiating off my skin. By the time I walked into computer science, hair damp from a quick shower, I felt remarkably better. Even computer science wasn't bad. The assignment was easy, but it was a good chance to brush up on my coding. Everyone was too focused on their own screens to pay me any attention. They even gave me my own Rosett, for school use. When my hands hit the keys, it was like I was breathing for the first time in weeks. A computer was power. It was life.

I figured out pretty quickly that the Rosett was connected to an internal network. There were websites, but only those that were relevant to our classes. Apart from the few, select websites, my assigned textbooks, and a school email account, there didn't seem to be much else loaded onto the computer. No books, no movies. Nothing from the outside world.

But there had to be a way to get to the real Internet, and I was determined to find it. When I walked into the cafeteria at five o'clock with Kat for dinner, I wasn't shaking anymore. And when Aaron waved us over to his table, my stomach only gave a small twinge.

"Hey, New Girl. How was your first day?" Aaron asked with a grin. He bit into an apple.

"It was fine." I shrugged. "And also, terrible."

"Well, it's about to get better, because we're just about to dive into the wonders of the Battle of Montara," Aaron said.

"Woah." Kat sat next to me and set her tray down. "Maybe we look at another battle."

"Why?" Aaron asked. "It's the most interesting one on the list."

"I just think…" Kat started.

"It's okay," I said quickly. "Battle of Montara. Sounds great." Even though the pit of my stomach felt like it was full of poison, I knew it was a good idea. I knew more about that battle than anyone. I'd heard firsthand accounts from my father.

"What's wrong?" Aaron looked between us.

"Nothing," I said quickly. "In fact, that's one of my favorite battles." I gave a strained smile. Judging by the confused look Aaron was giving me, my discomfort was showing. "Really. Let's do that."

"Okay," he said slowly. Together, we drafted an email to Jamison with our group and project choice. Kat started an outline for our report, and after an hour of work, we agreed on another time to meet and parted ways. It was weird, hearing my dad's name thrown around like he was a fictional character, but the way that the articles talked about him filled me with pride. When the Drillers went after the Montara Oil Field, my dad was the one who lead the charge against them, but not with weapons—with code. He hacked into their ships and planes, and that was it. We crushed them without a single casualty on our side. The victory was incredible, and it made my dad famous.

For a moment, I stared at the black-and-white photograph that topped the article I'd been reading. He looked younger. Still weathered, but hopeful. We had the same laugh lines around the eyes. I brushed my finger over them, lost in thought.

"Lydia?" Kat touched my shoulder gently. "You probably want to get changed before you go to Jamison."

I nodded and switched off the Rosett. Once back in our room, I changed into a gray t-shirt and black sweatpants. Kat was right. I *was* more comfortable.

I glanced at the digital clock on the wall—six thirty. I sank onto my bed, getting a good look at the room for the first time. There wasn't much here: two beds, two desks, and a bathroom door. The carpeting was a soft, dull gray. While there was nothing on my desk, Kat's was jumbled with papers covered in code and math problems. In the margins, I could see doodles of flowers, faces, and clouds.

Tacked to the wall above the desk was a blurry polaroid photo. I stood and gazed at it. A much-younger Kat peered at me through the shiny paper. Her hair was tied back into two messy, carefree braids, and three teeth were missing from her mouth. On her left side was a boy of around the same age. Their arms were wrapped around one another, eyes shining. Uneven, cracked brick stood behind them, covered with artful graffiti.

"Who is he?" I asked curiously, pointing to the photograph.

Kat joined me beside her desk, gazing at her younger self. "He was my brother," she said finally. "My twin brother Ivan."

The word *was* punched me in the gut. "I'm sorry."

"It's alright," Kat said quietly. "It happened a long time ago."

I hesitated. "Was it bad out there? Where you came from?"

"No worse than anywhere else," she said, sighing. "We had enough to eat, usually, so we were luckier than most of the world."

I bit my lip. An insatiable curiosity flowed through me. What had happened to Kat's brother? How old was she when he died? Was it because of the war? But I saw the sadness shining from Kat's eyes like rays of dusky sun and decided to drop it.

"We've all lost so much," I said softy. "I've lost everything." First, my brother. Then my dad. Then my best friend.

"Hey. You're here now. It's going to be okay."

"Thanks, Kat." I shied away and rummaged through my closet. "What's detention like?" I asked. I'd seen my share of teen romance movies, of course, but something told me that true love and a gang of plucky new friends was the last thing I would find when I walked into Jamison's classroom.

"It won't be that bad. Just keep a low profile and you won't have to do it again."

"I'll do my best." I sighed, flopping down onto my bed. "How did I let everything go so wrong?" I muttered, more to myself than to Kat.

"What do you mean?" Kat asked as she pulled a red hoodie on over her tank top. "It's just detention. Not a big deal."

"No, not that... forget it," I mumbled as Chris's face appeared in my mind, pleading for me to listen. Telling me not to trust them. I closed my eyes. What would have happened if the attack had never come? Would we have succeeded? Would my father still be alive?

"I should get going," I said loudly. "Can you show me the way again?" Kat pointed the way to the classroom, but I still managed to get turned around on the way. By the time I made it to the right room, I was out of breath, and late.

"I see that punctuality is going to be a continual struggle for you, Ms. Melrose." Jamison raised an eyebrow as I stepped into the room. "Have a seat."

My heart leaped as I saw the boy from chemistry, Carver, sitting in one of the seats with his feet kicked up on the desk. He looked me up and down, frowning, but didn't say anything as I dropped into the desk next to his.

"You two will be doing some grading for me today," Jamison said shortly, dropping a stack of paper the height of four large textbooks onto my desk with a thump. "There's an answer key on top of each of your piles," he added as he set a similar pile on Carver's desk. "Enjoy yourselves." With this, he turned on his heel and left the room, sliding the door shut behind him with a snap.

I sighed and turned my attention to the stack of paper in front of me, pulling the answer key off of the top. Luckily, the tests were multiple choice. I cleared my throat and got to work, trying my best to ignore Carver, who ruffled his hair and yawned as he flipped through the pages. For a few moments, we worked in silence.

"So, what are you in for?"

I jumped as Carver spoke. I turned to face him. He leaned back in his chair, offering me an easy half-smile.

"Nothing all that interesting," I said finally, turning back to the papers. The back of my neck burned. My pen ripped through the page as I crossed out an incorrect answer.

"You're new here, aren't you?"

I looked back at Carver. He hadn't returned to his papers and was now gazing at me with a half-frown on his handsome face.

"Yeah, I am. I'm Lydia." I tried to smile, but my features felt stiff, frozen.

"Jared Carver," he grinned and reached a lazy hand over his desk. I grasped it, apprehensive. Nervous tingles ran up my spine as we shook hands. Unsure what to do next, I ducked my head and returned to my work. But something had changed; the air was charged with electricity, a nervous energy that hadn't been there a moment ago.

White-hot pain shot suddenly through my back and I gasped, jumping out of my chair.

"Hey, you alright?" Jared stood and brushed a hand across my shoulder. He peered at me in concern.

"Yeah, I'm fine," I managed through gritted teeth. Hot tendrils of pain snaked across my back, up my arms.

"You don't look fine." Jared put one of his hands over mine and my heart spiked. "You're bleeding."

"What?" I pulled my hands away from my back and my fingers came away red. I gasped, pulling air in through my teeth.

"Stay still a second," Jared said, circling around to my back. Slowly, he pushed my shirt up above the wound. I stood stone-still and silent. My nerves thrummed as his fingers skimmed my skin.

"How the hell did you manage this?"

"I…" I sighed, trying to think of a plausible lie. But nothing came. "I kind of got shot."

"Got shot?" Jared repeated sharply.

I turned to face him and bit back a gasp as I found our faces inches apart. One of his hands still rested gently below my wound. "It's a long story," I whispered.

"You can't have," Jared said. A frown pulled at the corners of his mouth.

I looked down at my shoes. "I didn't believe it at first either."

"No, you don't understand." Jared shook his head and circled back around me. His breath skimmed my neck as he slowly pulled the bandage away from my skin. "This isn't a gunshot wound."

"What?" I whirled around, craning my neck to try and see it.

"It's not a gunshot," Jared repeated. He reached behind me and pressed the bandage back into place. He pulled my shirt back down. "Who told you that you got shot?"

"Principal Reed." My mind was racing. How the holy hell did Jared know what a gunshot was supposed to look like?

Something like fear flashed through his eyes. "You said your name was Lydia?"

"Lydia Melrose," I affirmed.

"Melrose?" Jared repeated, his voice sharp.

"Yeah. I'm guessing you've heard of my dad." Sadness pulled at my heartstrings.

"Yeah." Jared hooked a hand around the back of his neck. "Yeah, I have." He sank back into his chair and pulled the tests back towards him, marking the grades at double time.

I mirrored him, my mind swimming with confusion. What had just happened? Was it just my imagination, or was Jared's response about more than my famous father? What had triggered the flash behind his bright green eyes when he'd heard my name? Questions danced on the tip of my tongue, but I couldn't bring myself to ask them. Muscles stood out in Jared's arms while he stabbed at the tests with a new vigor, like he was desperate to get away from here as fast as possible. I returned to my own tests and tried to ignore the pain and tingling at the back of my neck.

After a moment, Jared stood up, arranging his jumble of tests into a neat stack.

I just stared at him. My pile was still half as thick as it'd been when I started. Jared turned and met my eyes. He held out a hand. "Here."

I raised my eyebrows. "What?"

"Here," Jared repeated. "We'll get out of here faster if I help you."

"I can do it," I said quickly, speeding up the strokes from my red pen. "I don't want you to do extra work."

"I just want to get out of here," Jared said, snatching half of my stack away from me. I jumped, startled at the ice in his voice.

I fumbled with a test of my own, slicing a flash of red ink across it as my pen slipped. "You can go," I said quickly. "You don't have to wait for me."

"I know I don't. Jamison has cameras in here, and that door won't unlock until all of those tests are marked."

The back of my neck prickled as my eyes darted around the room, scanning for any sign of a camera. "Are you kidding?"

"I wish."

I gaped at him. Was this the same boy who'd been checking my wound with a gentle touch just a moment before?

As the pile of tests in front of me dwindled, I bit the side of my cheek, hard. Jared was silent as he rushed through his own exams. Even though our stacks were roughly the same size, he finished much more quickly than I did. But maybe he had done this before.

"Done." I threw my pen down onto the last page and gathered up the papers, tapping them into a neat pile. Immediately, a click sounded from the doorway and the door swung open.

Jared leapt to his feet and dropped the tests onto Jamison's desk. He glanced back at me.

"You coming?"

I scrambled to my feet and dropped my tests on top of Jared's pile. Jared turned on his heel and stalked out of the classroom. He set off down the hall without so much as a backwards glance. The cool air of the hallway was like a slap in the face as I watched him go.

"Jared!" I shouted before I could stop myself, hurrying to catch up with him.

He turned, a glare on his face. "What, Melrose?"

I stepped back, stung. "What just happened?"

"What do you mean?"

"I *mean*, one second you're making small talk, and the next you're acting like I shot your puppy or something. What happened?"

"What happened was that we're not friends, Melrose. And we're going to keep it that way." He gave me a small salute. "Have a nice life."

"Jared," I protested, frowning. "Why did you freak out when I mentioned Principal Reed?"

"I don't have any idea what you're talking about." A cold smirk curled over his lips. "Are you feeling okay?"

"I...yeah..." I took a step back as a wave of dark intensity rolled over me. One of the lights overhead flickered, casting Jared's face with shadows. I swallowed. "Never mind."

"See you around, then." Jared turned away. I watched him until he was out of sight, my feet rooted to the spot like they were full of lead. I shivered as a wave of cool air brushed over my skin from a vent overhead and set off back towards my room, unnerved. The wound on my back throbbed with every step, and with every stab of pain, Jared's voice echoed in my mind.

*It's not a gunshot wound.*

Why would Reed lie about how I was hurt? What did it matter as long as I was alive now? I wrapped my arms around myself as I wandered down the hallway, wishing that I had brought a jacket. I wanted nothing more than to burrow under my blankets and let the world fade away. I sighed as I turned down the final hallway, staring at the wall. My eyes fell onto a row of photographs that I hadn't noticed earlier.

I slowed to a stop and gazed at the frozen smiles behind the glass. Just over a hundred students were lined up in rows, all dressed in shades of red, black and white. My gut tingled as I looked at the rows of previous Yucca Mountain students.

A girl in the front row had her arm thrown around a friend; their white smiles were frozen on their faces and their unblinking eyes seemed to stare into mine. They looked like the girls that I used to watch in the movies back at home, their faces porcelain beauty and their golden hair thrown over their shoulders. I sighed and curled my fingers over the glass, moving on to the other teens in the photo.

A girl with dark skin and a strained smile.

A boy with thick glasses set on his pale nose.

And in the top row, almost hidden, a boy with brown eyes and hair. With a sad smile on his lips. A boy who looked like me.

*My brother Danny.*

# CHAPTER SIX

I only have one photograph of my mother. She died the same day that I was born, so all I know of her is frozen in that single plastic frame, the one dotted with tiny polka-dots around the edges. Tall and slender, she's wearing glasses and holding a clipboard. A white lab coat hugs her frame; her dark, almond-shaped eyes seem to stare into mine through the glass.

*Just like Danny's stare at me now.*

I stumbled backwards, hand over my heart. I closed my eyes, hard, then opened them again. My brother's face was still there, almost hidden in a sea of others. The standard red polo reached up to his neck, buttoned just below his chin. I traced my finger over the glass, gaping. What the hell was going on? Is this where Danny had been since he disappeared three years ago?

And if Danny was here when we thought he was dead, could they have done the same thing to me? What if everyone I knew was still alive, and I was the one that was gone?

*Could Chris be alive?*

*Could Danny?*

I gasped audibly and clawed at the plaque set into the bottom of the photograph.

*Yucca Mountain School Students, 2046.*

2046. The year that he disappeared. The year that he...died. I dragged a hand down the length of my face, breathing hard. I'd spent the last three years believing...*knowing* my brother was dead. But here, staring me in the face, was irrefutable proof that he wasn't. Not in 2046, anyways. Anything could have happened since then.

I reached frantically for the next photograph, whose plaque read *Yucca Mountain School Students, 2047.* I scanned every inch of the photograph. The four girls laughing in the front. The sullen-looking, dark haired boy in the middle. I ran my fingers over every single face, searching for my brother.

But he was nowhere to be found. I raked a hand back through my tangled hair. What did this mean? Had he been taken somewhere else? Had he...

*"Danny might not be dead."* Chris's words crashed into me.

Chris. He'd tried to tell me more than just that before those men burst into the lab, but he hadn't gotten the chance. He'd known something. Was that why they'd killed him?

I pressed my hands into my eyes and slid to the floor, trying to recall every detail from that day. The walk to the lab. Chris's hand on the small of my back. Watching him sink to the ground and whispering not to trust them as his eyes slid shut.

My eyes flew open as the pieces came together. The wound on my back wasn't a gunshot. My brother's picture was on the wall in front of me. I wasn't allowed to contact anyone outside of this school. Was anything that Reed had told me so far, the truth?

Was my dad alive, too?

Shaking, I stumbled to my feet. There wasn't anything I could do right now, not when the halls were dark and there was no way for me to figure out a plan. For now, there was nothing I could do. For now, I was trapped.

\*\*\*

"We really have to stop meeting like this."

I shot bolt upright as something bounced off my nose and fell to the floor.

Kat laughed and threw another handful of cereal at me. "Rise and shine."

"Oh God." I kicked the tangled blankets off of my legs. "Are we late again?"

"Nah." Kat shook her head and skipped to her feet, shoving various supplies into her bag. "You've only got twenty minutes, though. Better hurry."

"Sure thing," I grumbled, rising, and stretching my arms over my head. Sleep burned into my eyes. I'd spent what seemed like endless hours suspended in darkness before finally slipping into a restless doze.

"What kept you so long last night?" Kat called as I washed my face and pulled my hair back, peering at the dark circles under my eyes.

"Just detention," I called back, trying to force the image of the photograph out of my mind.

"What did he make you do?"

"Grade papers."

"Rough."

"You have no idea," I muttered under my breath. I grabbed my Rosett from my desk and shoved it into my bag, brow pulled together in thought.

"Hey, is there a registrar here?" I asked, trying my best to sound casual. "You know, like, a list of all the students?"

Kat frowned. "Not that I know of. Why?"

"But would the teachers have one? Would Principal Reed?"

"Probably?" Kat said the word like a question.

As I tried to decide how much to tell her, I must have been staring off, because she snapped her fingers in front of my face. "Hello! Earth to Lydia. Are you okay?"

"How hard would it be to break into Reed's office?" I blurted before I could stop myself.

"Break in?" Kat demanded. "Lydia, what's going on?"

"I saw something yesterday," I muttered. "Something that shouldn't be possible."

"You're not making any sense."

"Why were you brought here, Kat?"

Kat tilted her head. "What?"

"Why were you brought here?" I repeated. "What did they tell you? Did you sign up for this school? Did your parents register you? Do you ever talk to them?"

"Lydia, we have to get to class—"

"Please," I whispered, "I need to understand."

"Lydia, honestly, right now, I don't understand *you*." Kat took my hand and squeezed it. "I want to. I really do. But we cannot be late. As much as I want to help you figure this out, getting another detention isn't going to do either of us any favors."

As the words left her mouth, the warning bell sounded overhead. I yanked my bag higher on my shoulder, huffing out a breath. "You're right," I muttered. "Let's go."

\*\*\*

"Morning, new girl." Aaron grinned at me as I slid into my seat. He spun a pencil between his fingers. "Looks like you had a rough night."

I sighed and leaned my head on my arms. "Something like that."

"Damn, how late did Jamison keep you?" Aaron asked, peering at me sideways.

I didn't reply.

Aaron leaned back, running a hand through his messy hair. "I guess I should know the answer to that," he mused. "I had my fair share of detentions freshman year. I swear that guy never grades anything we give him. Whenever there's a test, someone ends up in detention, and you can guess what they end up doing."

Something Aaron said registered with me. I sat up and faced him fully. "Freshman year? You're a senior now?"

Aaron offered a confused smile. "Yeah, this is a senior class."

"So, you've been here for four years."

"Of course. You feeling okay, Lydia?"

"Yeah," I muttered, leaning back in my chair. If Aaron was telling the truth—and as far as I knew, there was no reason for him to lie—then he'd been here when Danny was. But what were the chances he'd come across Danny in a sea of a hundred students? Even if Aaron saw Danny at some point, what were the chances he remembered him?

"My first year, I did most of his work— literally me and one other guy every week. What was his name? Damon? Daniel..." Aaron scratched his head, brow scrunched.

"Danny?" I blurted.

"Danny! That was it," Aaron smiled to himself. "Hey, you okay?"

I gripped the edge of the desk, heart pounding. "Danny?" I whispered.

"Yeah. Danny Morris, I think it was. We always had detention together."

"Morris—?" My words were drowned out by the bell and Jamison's voice as he drew attention to the front of the room.

"Today, we're going to continue our discussion of post-UN politics." I fell silent as Jamison launched into another lecture. I chewed my lip, glancing between him and Aaron. Talking in class was sure to get me into trouble, but my mind was racing a mile a minute.

Something was going on at this school. In order to figure out what, I was going to need help from someone who knew the ropes—several someones, ideally. I'd said all of two words to Aaron. Could I really trust that he would help me? Or did I think I could trust him just because he had pretty eyes?

*He has more than his pretty eyes. He knows about Danny,* a voice whispered in the back of my head.

Sitting through class was torture, like someone was jabbing my skin with hundreds of tiny needles. When the bell finally rang do dismiss us, I grabbed Aaron's arm.

"Would you recognize him if you saw him again?" I asked.

"Who? That Danny kid?" he asked, confused.

"Yeah."

Aaron shrugged, twirling a pencil between his fingers. "Yeah. I mean, I guess so. Why?"

Kat caught my eye and motioned for me to join her. "No reason," I lied, taking my hand from his arm. "See you tonight. Library?"

"Yeah, see you," Aaron called as I joined Kat.

"What was that about?" she asked.

"Nothing," I said quickly. "Everything's fine."

\*\*\*

Everything wasn't fine, and my head was still elsewhere when Kat and I met Aaron in the library that night to continue working on our project. I couldn't help but wonder why they called the room a library when there wasn't a single book in sight. Instead, there were tall gray walls, black armchairs, and a few metal tables. We grabbed one near the wall and got to work.

"What do we have so far?" Aaron asked, frowning at his Rosett.

"Just our outline. We should start with each side's motivations," Kat said. "The US wanted to protect the oil fields, so the atmosphere could heal, right?"

"And the Drillers wanted the oil to further their own agenda," Aaron said.

"That's just it, though. What *is* their agenda?" Kat asked frowning. "These articles are all about facts and figures, but there isn't much about what they actually want. Why waste resources fighting over something there's no guarantee you'll even get your hands on?"

"It was about power," I said. "The outside world is bad, right? Like, Great Depression era bad?"

"Worse, I think," Kat said, biting her lip. "All I know about the Great Depression is that a lot of people lost money and had to sell apples and stuff."

I tried not to roll my eyes. Didn't this school teach any real history? "It's like this," I explained. "A lot of people out there are suffering, but it's not apocalyptic. I mean, it's not the end of the world. Not yet. But sooner or later, the world's going to break completely. This war? It's not even about oil. It's about who'll be in charge when all hope seems lost. That's why they want the oil. So, they can power their warships and take control when everything falls apart."

For a moment, they both just stared at me.

"Did you get all that?" Aaron asked, grinning at Kat.

"Most of it," she replied. "That's interesting, Lydia. I've never thought about it like that."

"Most people haven't. They just know we're fighting, and they know people are dying. People who deserved a future."

People like Danny. People like Chris. People like my dad.

I couldn't say any more. Suddenly, I felt like I was going to throw up. My stomach churned with acid. I jumped to my feet. "Where's the nearest bathroom?"

"It's down the hall, to the left. Are you okay?" Kat asked, her eyes wide and concerned.

I didn't answer. I just jumped to my feet and left, hand pressed over my mouth. Heads turned as I ran through the library. Somehow, I managed to make it to the bathroom before I threw up everything in my stomach. Nauseous and dizzy, I slumped to the floor and leaned my head back against the bathroom stall. Danny had taught me all that stuff about the war. He was so much smarter than me. So much smarter than all of us. But he was gone, frozen in a photo fixed to the wall. Trapped there.

I stayed there, head buried against my knees, for a long while.

"Lydia?" Kat's voice rang through the bathroom. "Are you alright? You've been gone a long time."

I took a deep breath and got to my feet, shivering. "I'm fine." I grimaced as I washed my hands and rinsed my mouth out with water. Kat watched me cautiously, bouncing on her heels.

"We can still switch the project, you know. We have plenty of time."

"No, Kat. It's okay. Really." I wiped my mouth with the back of my hand. "My dad's famous. It's not like I'm going to go my whole life without hearing about him." I walked past her and pushed open the door. Aaron stood on the other side, holding my bag.

"Hey," he said softly. "You forgot this."

Had he heard me? I cleared my throat. "Uh, thanks." I slung the bag over my shoulder.

"You might want to see the nurse," Kat suggested gently. "You don't look so good."

I hesitated. I didn't trust anyone at this school, least of all the woman who had treated me for my injuries, but Kat was right. I looked awful, and a dull pain was thudding behind my eyes. At the very least, I could get some pain medication.

"Come on." Aaron took my arm, keeping me steady. "We'll take you."

Somewhere, beneath the aches and worries, warmth spread through my chest. "Thank you."

"'Course. We'd never finish this project without you," Aaron joked.

I laughed, and together, the three of us set off down the hallway.

"So, what do you think of Yucca so far?" Aaron asked.

"I don't really know what to think."

"Fair," Aaron squeezed my arm as the three of us took a left down a hallway that seemed slightly darker than the one we were in. Suddenly, the lights overhead flashed twice.

"What was that?" I asked.

"Curfew. We're not supposed to be out of our rooms after ten," Kat explained. "Don't worry. They don't enforce it much."

"I can make it on my own," I said. "I don't want you two to get into trouble."

"We can handle it. Right, Romero?" Aaron said.

"Uh, yeah," Kat said, but she bit her lip. "It's not far, now."

I nodded, grimacing as the pain gave a nasty jab.

"Woah, hold on a second," Aaron said suddenly. The three of us stopped, silent. I strained my ears. Voices drifted from around the corner.

"It was reckless, Dominic. You know we can't keep doing this. The Helifax trials aren't safe."

"I'll do whatever I want. It's your job to fix it." Principal Reed's voice sounded.

Donna huffed loudly. Their footsteps grew closer, along with a shrill squeaking, like the wheels on a cart. Aaron pulled Kat and me into a doorway, hiding us from view. I peered around the edge of the wall just in time to see Donna and Reed walk by. They weren't alone. Donna was pushing a gurney, and a pale body lay atop it.

My heart leapt with fear. I stumbled back into the doorway, hands pressed over my mouth. I'd only gotten a glance, but a glance was enough. The girl on the gurney had been deathly pale. Her arm hung limply, dangling towards the floor. Blood trickled from her mouth.

I met eyes with Kat and saw my own shock mirrored in her face.

For a long while, we just stood there, frozen. Too scared to move.

"Who was that girl?" Aaron whispered, breaking the silence. "Was she dead?"

"She can't have been," I said shakily. "She can't have."

"She looked pretty bad," Kat said, her eyes wide with fright. "Maybe we should get back."

"Yeah. We should." Aaron hiked his bag higher on his shoulder and set off down the hall.

"Wait!" I said.

Kat turned. "What?"

"Nothing," I decided. It was already after curfew. Even if we probably wouldn't get caught, there was no reason to pull her into this. Either of them. So, we made the walk back in silence. Every one of my nerves was on edge as we navigated the halls. If we were caught, would it be us on those gurneys? If I had anything left in my stomach, I was sure I would have been sick again. Every time I blinked, all I could see was the girl's face, pale and bloody.

I blinked again, and it was Danny's body on that gurney instead of hers. I could barely manage a shaky goodbye to Aaron when he set off down a different hallway to his room.

"Here," Kat said after we reached our own room. She held out a pill bottle. "Pain meds. They're not as strong as whatever the nurse would have given you, but they should help a little."

"Thank you," I sighed. I closed my fingers around the bottle with some difficulty; my hands were trembling.

"You're welcome," Kat said softly. She watched me carefully as I took two of the pills. "Hey. I don't think we should say anything about what we saw earlier."

"Say anything to who?" I asked cautiously.

"Anyone. Whatever we saw, it looked dangerous. I don't think we want anyone to know we saw it." Kat bit her lip.

"What are you saying?"

"I don't know. Just that it's best to keep a low profile here. The last thing we want is to be thrown out."

"Right." I nodded, even though I wanted nothing more than to get out of here and back to the island.

"Okay. Night, Lydia."

"Night," I replied. I climbed into bed, eyes wide open. I knew that if I closed them, I'd see my brother's face, pale and bloody, pushed down a dark hallway to God knew where.

I didn't sleep a wink that night, but it was like nightmares had found a way to hover in front of my eyes even when I was awake. Chris, bleeding out in the lab. Danny being blown to pieces. My dad, bullet holes through his skin. The pale girl on the gurney. And then there was that photograph of Danny. He'd been here, for however brief a time, and Aaron had seen him. I needed to know what he remembered, if he'd seen what happened to him.

\*\*\*

By the time history was over and I had a proper chance to talk to Aaron, my lip was bleeding in three separate places from how hard I'd been biting it. "Aaron?" I asked, stopping him with a hand to his chest. "Can I talk to you?"

"Yeah, sure," he said, leaning back against his desk. "What's up?"

"Not here," I said. I gave Kat a small wave and pulled Aaron into a crowded hallway. "Can I trust you?" I asked.

Aaron frowned, confusion scrawled all over his handsome face. "Yeah, of course. What's wrong?"

"You said you'd recognize Danny if you saw him again," I said. "The guy you had detention with a few years ago."

"Yeah, I think so. Why?"

I took a deep breath. "Because I think the person you're remembering is my brother." I explained everything, as quickly as I could. Almost everything. I didn't know if I could trust Aaron—every nerve in my body was screaming that it was incredibly stupid to be trusting so much to someone I'd just met. But I needed to tell someone. I needed *someone* to help.

"Run this by me again?" Aaron hissed as I pulled him away from the crowd. "Your brother, who lived with you on a deserted island for the first fourteen years of your life and then died following a mass killing on said desert island, is somehow in a yearbook photo that's up on a wall here? Thousands of miles from your home? And he's the same kid who did detention with me all those nights?"

"In a nutshell." I ducked around a pair of brunettes walking arm-in-arm.

"Damn."

"Yeah, that about sums it up." I glanced back at Aaron, dropping his hand abruptly. "The photo isn't that far, I promise."

"No worries. I'm not in a hurry to get to Russian Lit anyways. We're reading *War and Peace*. I guess it's supposed to be ironic or something." Aaron grinned and stuck his hands into his pockets as we rounded the final corner, to a passage occupied only by a small girl heading in the opposite direction.

"It's right up here," I called, taking the last few steps at a run. "Class of 2046." I came to a stop in front of the photograph. I ran my hand over the smooth glass, over the red uniforms that shone at me through the years like a glistening pool of blood. "He's in the back."

Aaron stood at my shoulder, leaning down to my level to peer at the photograph with me. "Where?"

I scanned the last few rows, searching for my brother's face.

He was nowhere to be found.

"This can't be. He was here!" I ran my thumb over each and every face in the back few rows, but Danny's neat brown hair and crooked smile had completely disappeared. I turned back towards Aaron. Desperation shone in my eyes. "He was here. I promise."

"Okay...." Aaron trailed off.

"I don't understand." I pressed my hands into my eyes. "I'm sure it was him. It's like he's been erased or something."

"Hey." Aaron put a hand on my shoulder. "After what we saw last night, I believe you. And we're going to figure this out."

"How? He's gone from the photo. There's no proof."

"There are other ways to get proof." Aaron offered me a mischievous smile. "Like I said, I was in detention plenty of times. I've learned a thing or two in my four years here."

"You ever break into Reed's office?"

Aaron barked out a laugh. "You're joking."

"I wish."

The smile slid off of Aaron's face. "You don't have a chance."

"I have to try. I need to know."

Aaron sighed. "We can't do it alone."

"We?"

"Of course." Aaron's tone was suddenly businesslike. "You don't think I'd let you tackle this by yourself, do you?"

A smile tugged at the corner of my mouth. "I guess I'm not really sure what to expect."

"It's okay, New Girl." Aaron slung an arm around my shoulders and guided me back towards the classrooms. "You'll learn."

\*\*\*

"Hey." Kat glanced at me as I set my lunch tray down next to her. Her eyes swiveled to Aaron as he sat on her other side. "Um, hi."

"Hi." Aaron bit into an apple and offered a smile. "Fancy meeting you here."

Kat didn't smile. "What's going on?"

"Remember when I asked you about Reed's office the other day?" I asked.

"Unfortunately." Kat looked between Aaron and me. "Because of last night? You're not…"

"Not because of last night, but I need to get in there, Kat. I think that my brother might have been here a few years ago."

Kat frowned. "I didn't know you had a brother. Why didn't you tell me when I told you about Ivan?"

"I didn't know how to tell you," I said. I lowered my voice and explained my suspicions under my breath. I left out the part about the fake gunshot, though. That was something I'd have to muddle through on my own.

"So, let me get this straight. You think that Reed attacked your island, kidnapped your brother, and brought him here? Just because he's gone from the photograph you think you saw him in two days ago?"

"That about sums it up," I muttered into my cup of milk. "I know what I saw."

"I," Kat scratched her head with the handle of her spoon. "I believe you, Lydia. It's just…" she trailed off.

"You won't help me."

"Look, it took a lot for me to get here. I don't think I can risk getting thrown out of here. Or worse."

"I get it," I blurted. "We both saw that girl last night. You're obviously scared. It's fine."

Kat sighed. "Lydia, I want to help. I just don't think I can."

"It's okay," I repeated. "Just don't tell anyone what I'm planning."

"I won't."

I pushed my tray away. My mouth was suddenly too dry to eat. "Thanks." I stood and turned away, heart pattering against my ribs. Kat wasn't going to help me. I had no right to expect her to. So why did I feel sick to my stomach?

"Lyd, wait up!" Aaron called after me, but I ignored him. I strode through the bustling cafeteria and didn't stop until I'd reached the hallway. I leaned my head against the wall, trying to breathe normally. Should I have told them? About the wound, about the lies? Pain stabbed into the small of my back.

"Lydia, hey." Aaron pressed a hand to my shoulder, bringing me back to reality. "We're going to figure this out, okay?"

"No. You're not going to do anything. Kat's right. I can't make you risk that."

"Kat's just paranoid. They won't throw any of us out of here."

"But we might end up on Donna's lab table."

"She's a nurse, not a mad scientist," Aaron laughed. "Come on. Let me help."

"It's too dangerous."

"It's not." Aaron shook his head, like breaking into Reed's office was going to be the simplest thing in the world. "So, we ready to plan this thing or what?"

# CHAPTER SEVEN

"Are you sure this'll work?"

Aaron nodded. "I know what I'm doing. Trust me."

I huffed out a breath, chewing my nails as Aaron peered around the corner. Classes were done for the day; it was well after dinner, so there weren't many people milling around.

"Coast is almost clear."

"Aaron, wait…"

"Hey. We agreed on this." Aaron offered me a half-smile and tilted his head. "I can get you ten minutes. Make sure you don't move anything."

"I know." My heart pounded underneath my bright red hoodie. Why hadn't I thought to wear something less conspicuous?

"Wish me luck." Aaron quirked his eyebrows and rounded the corner. His knock on Reed's tall, mahogany door echoed through the empty hallway.

Aaron's muffled voice sounded, followed by Reed's sharp reply. For a moment, there was silence. And then, footsteps.

Three sharp knocks echoed down the hall, the signal that Aaron's ploy had worked. I held my breath, counted to ten, and then followed Aaron's path down the hallway. Reed's door stood open a crack, spilling yellow light onto the tile floor beneath my feet. With one more glance over my shoulder to make sure I was alone, I crept through the door and pulled it closed behind me.

I sucked in a breath and leaned my back against the door. My heart pounded against my ribs; my breath came in shudders. I gave myself ten seconds to calm down, taking in the office. A large desk rested against the wall in front of me, topped with three computer monitors over which neon screensavers were scrawling, bursts of bright color against darkest black. A tall chair sat in front, cocked at an angle. But what drew my gaze was the shiny silver filing cabinet that rested against the wall.

My shoes clacked against the concrete floors as I crossed the room and ran my hand over the cabinet. I tugged on one of the drawers experimentally but found it locked.

"Damn it," I muttered under my breath. My eyes drifted to the desk. Would the key be inside? One of the drawers was unlocked and open just a crack. I tugged on the handle, revealing a neat jumble of office supplies inside. Pens, tape, staples. And tucked into a corner, a tiny set of keys.

"Yes," I muttered under my breath, grabbing them. I closed the drawer as quietly as I could.

"What the hell are you doing in here?"

The door slammed shut.

I whirled around, eyes wide. "Jared?" I sputtered.

Jared grabbed my arm, fury swirling in his eyes. "Have you completely lost your mind?"

The key fell from my hand and clattered to the ground. I scrambled to pick it up, spluttering.

"Get out. Now!" Jared tightened his grip on my arm. "You're going to get caught."

"No, I'm not." I yanked my arm away from him. "What the hell is going on? What are *you* doing in here?"

"At the moment? Saving you." Jared pushed my shoulder with one hand. I stumbled. "Get out of here before he gets back."

"I'm not going anywhere." I backed away from him. "Judging from how eager you are to get rid of me, Reed doesn't know that you're in here, either. I think we can both do whatever we need to do without stepping on each other's toes."

"Not happening."

"What are you going to do, drag me away?" I glared at Jared. "Who the hell do you think you are?"

"God, Melrose, are you actually this stupid? I told you before that your injury wasn't from a bullet. You know Reed lied to you about how you got hurt. Did it ever occur to you that *he's* the one who hurt you? That he won't hesitate to do it again?"

My grip on the key slipped. "What are you talking about?"

"Forget I said that. Forget I said any of that."

"No, I'm not going to forget anything. Did you see something?" *Did you see me being pushed down the hallway on a gurney, covered in blood?*

"You want to have this argument *now*, Melrose? Standing in the middle of his office?"

"I have a feeling it's going to be hard to get you to answer any questions otherwise."

"Damn it." Jared tore a hand through his hair. "Fine. You win. Come with me, right now, and I'll tell you everything you want to know."

I narrowed my eyes. "Everything I want to know is in this office."

"I know it too." Jared dropped his voice. "I know about Danny." He looked me up and down. "Put that back."

And with that, Jared turned and walked out the door.

I watched him go, jaw hanging open. What the hell was going on? Did Jared really expect me to drop everything and follow him? How could I, when information about Danny was just inches from my hand?

Then again, at least six of the minutes Aaron had bought me were gone, thanks to Jared. Would I have enough time to search through the files, get the one I wanted, and get out before Reed came back?

My odds weren't good.

And then there was Jared. He claimed he had information about Danny. I didn't believe him—I *couldn't* believe him. But how would he know about Danny unless he was telling the truth?

I'd lost another one of my precious minutes. I couldn't afford to lose any more. Heart sinking to the floor, I replaced Reed's keys in his desk and eased the drawer shut. My heart jumped as I stepped back into the empty hallway, but it was completely deserted. I pulled the door almost closed and took the last few steps around the corner at a run.

Jared was waiting for me, leaning one shoulder against the wall. "Good choice."

I grabbed his arm and pulled him further away from Reed's door. I dropped it as soon as we were out of earshot. "What do you know?"

Jared cocked his head at me. "You're going to have to be more specific."

"About Reed. About Danny. About all of this."

"Still not specific enough." A smile played over his lips. Was he enjoying this?

I gritted my teeth. "What do you know about Daniel Emerson Melrose?"

"Not a lot." Jared crossed his arms and leaned back against the wall.

My hands curled into fists. "How did you know I was looking for information about him?"

"I didn't. I do now, though. Thanks."

"Enough with this!" I shouted, startling a couple who were walking past Jared and me. "Anything you know about my brother, I need to know. Please, Jared."

"Look, I saw him around a few times when he was a student here. That's about it. He was here for a few months, and then he was gone."

My stomach swooped to my shoes. "Where did he go?"

"I'm guessing nowhere good. And if you keep doing things like breaking into Reed's office, then the same thing will happen to you."

"*You* were in Reed's office too."

"Yeah, well, I know what I'm doing. You," Jared paused, looking me up and down, "clearly don't. So, do yourself a favor and stay out of there because I won't be there to save you next time."

"Save me?" A derisive laugh tumbled from my mouth. "That's what I'm supposed to think happened here? You think I should be thanking you?"

"I think you should know better than to do something like that without backup."

"Who says I didn't have backup?"

Jared considered me for a moment. He shook his head. "This conversation is over, Melrose."

Jared turned away. I opened my mouth, determined to call after him, but fury stifled my words. I couldn't believe that I'd blown my chance and put Aaron in jeopardy in the process. Now, I was alone in a long hallway, with nothing more to show for our trouble than a vague warning and frustration crashing over me in waves.

*You have more than that,* a voice in the back of my head pointed out. *Aaron's not the only one who knows about Danny. Jared saw him too.*

I hit the wall and curled my fingers into a fist against it. How could I have been so stupid?

Voices brought me back to myself and I jumped, whirling around. I recognized the tall blonde and the shorter, golden-skinned brunette from my chemistry lab. They barely acknowledged me as they chattered, and my eyes followed them down the hall. How did they manage to make the high-collared, knee-length dresses look like they belonged on a runway instead of in a prep school buried deep underground?

I sighed and yanked my bag higher on my shoulders. It would be curfew soon, and there wasn't much more that I could do from my dorm room. Tomorrow, I'd have to think of a new way to break into Reed's office. I couldn't make Aaron take any more risks for me.

\*\*\*

"Hey," I muttered, throwing my bag to the ground as I snapped the door shut behind me.

Kat looked up from her Rosett, her eyes wide. "What happened?"

"Nothing happened," I muttered bitterly.

"No file?"

"I don't know." I hesitated. "There was a filing cabinet in his office, but I couldn't find a key."

"Bummer." Kat chewed her lip. "Lydia, listen. I'm sorry that I didn't help you today."

"It's fine." I flopped down onto my bed, pressing my hands over my eyes. "I'll think of something."

"You know," Kat said thoughtfully. "If the offices have hard copies of files, they should have electronic ones too."

I sat bolt upright. My body suddenly thrummed with energy. "Electronic," I whispered. How could I have been so stupid? I clambered off of my bed and fell to the ground. I scrambled to my feet and pulled my Rosett out of my bag.

"What are you doing?" Kat asked, alarmed.

"You're a genius."

"Thanks."

"No problem." I flipped open the top and began typing furiously. Would I be able to access the network remotely?

"Woah, woah, woah. Are you trying to hack into Reed's computer?"

"Little bit."

"You can't *do* that," Kat protested.

I stopped typing. "Are you going to report me?"

Kat shook her head. "Of course not, but Lydia, they're bound to know. As soon as you get in, they'll detect you." She bit her lip in clear disapproval.

"Kat, please try to understand. I need to do this to find out what happened to Danny." I paused for a beat. "If you found out that Ivan might have been alive this whole time, what would you do?"

Pain flashed across Kat's face. "Ivan's not coming back."

"What happened to him?" I asked quietly.

"Life was hard. He died," she said shortly. "It could have easily been me."

"I know how you feel," I said. I took a deep breath. "It was my fault that Danny disappeared."

"Lydia, that's ridiculous. You were what, fourteen?"

"We were skipping rocks on the beach. It was the only thing he could ever beat me at. We heard the shots, and then," I swallowed hard. "Our friend Chris came to tell us what was going on. He handed Danny a gun to protect himself with, but Danny gave it to me instead."

"He was just trying to protect you," Kat said.

"It doesn't matter. I didn't need it. I was far away from the fighting, hiding in an old lighthouse we used to use. By the time my dad came to find me, all of the fighting was done. And Danny was gone. So, I have to do whatever I can to figure out what happened. For all I know, Donna and Reed killed him like they killed that girl."

"Don't say that. You don't know that she's dead," Kat said shakily.

"I don't know that she's alive," I argued. "We can't leave this place, Kat. We're trapped. And we need to stick together."

Kat didn't say anything right away. She pressed her hands over her mouth, memories shining in her eyes. "Wall ball," she said suddenly.

"What?"

"You ever play?" Kat asked.

"No."

"Oh, it's the best," Kat said. A sad smile settled on her face. "You throw a tennis ball against a wall, and your opponent has to catch it before it bounces twice. That was the only thing I could ever beat him at. Ivan. It's the little things I miss, you know?"

"I do," I said softly. "I would give anything to have him back. To figure out what happened. If you know anything that could help me, please tell me."

Kat leaned forwards, resting her chin on her fists, and chewing her lip. For a moment, she was silent. "I have a network key."

My eyes widened. "You do?"

Kat nodded, pulling her Rosett into her lap. "You didn't get this from me."

A smile crawled across my face. "Of course, I didn't." I copied the text into an open file on my Rosett. "Thank you."

Kat offered a soft smile. "I hope you find what you're looking for."

I placed my hands on the keys, and I felt the familiar energy flowing into my fingers. It reminded me of one of my old coding assignments. I'd stayed in the attic for hours, head buried in my work, completely fascinated.

*"How's it going, there, Champ?"*

*I jumped as Danny grabbed my shoulders. "Quit doing that!"*

*"Hey, if you want to fight in this war, you've have to be ready for anything."* Danny grinned and hopped onto my desk. *"Seriously. How are you doing?"*

*"Fine,"* I muttered. *"I can't get the algorithm right."*

*"How long you been working on it?"*

*"Four hours now."*

*"Took me sixteen. Trust me, you'll get there."*

*"How long did it take Chris?"*

Danny smirked. *"Why?"*

I blushed. *"No reason."*

*"Ask me in three years. Then maybe I won't feel so gross about setting my little sister up with my best friend."*

*"I'm almost thirteen!"*

*"Exactly."* Danny hopped down from his perch on the desk and rubbed my shoulders. *"Get back to it. I'll bring you some cocoa."*

*"How about some coffee?"* I asked hopefully.

Danny chuckled. *"I'll see what I can do. And Lydia?"*

*"Yeah?"*

*"Don't give up."*

I smiled. *"Thanks, Danny."*

\*\*\*

I sat bolt upright, as wide awake as if someone had thrown a bucket of icy water over my head. My Rosett fell from my lap and clattered to the floor. I groaned and pressed my hands to my eyes as the last of the dream faded away. I'd been up well past three o'clock in the morning trying to break through the school's firewall—with no success—so it wasn't surprising that the memory of my last day of training had come back to me. My heart ached. The dream—seeing Danny's face—had felt so real.

In all, it'd taken me seventeen hours to finish the program. I was crushed until Danny told me it'd taken Chris twenty. I had completed the training, but now, when it really mattered, I was stuck. How? Literally *how* was it less difficult to hack into the largest terrorist group on the planet than into the database of a high school? I pushed air out of my cheeks and snatched my Rosett from the ground. The home screen stared back at me, and the clock in the bottom corner indicated that it was five o'clock in the morning.

I sighed and lay back down, pressing my face into the pillow. It was Friday, which meant that I didn't need to be awake for a few more hours. But now that I *was* awake, the nagging questions left over from last night wouldn't leave me alone.

How had Jared known the precise words to say that would make me back out of that office? None of this added up, especially not if he knew as little about Danny as he said he did. I chewed my lip as I stared into the darkness, trying to remember the night that we'd had detention together. The way Jared had reacted when he'd heard my name. At first, it'd seemed like his reaction was about Reed. But looking back, his strange behavior had started when he'd heard my name.

Was it possible that he'd known Danny? *Really* known him, as more than a face he passed in the halls? Any other explanation seemed impossible. And if he knew Danny when he was here... was it possible that he knew what'd happened to him as well?

"Lydia?" Kat's groggy voice drifted across the room and I jumped.

"Yeah?" I whispered.

"Why are you awake? You find anything?"

"No," I mumbled bitterly. I closed my laptop and cut off the stream of light it'd provided. "Nothing."

# CHAPTER EIGHT

"Hey." Aaron leaned across his desk as I sat down in history the next morning. "What the hell happened yesterday?"

"I'm sorry. I got…" I trailed off as Jared entered the room and slid into his own seat. "Sidetracked."

"Sidetracked? Lydia, what the *hell*—"

"I'm sorry," I hissed. My eyes burned from lack of sleep. "I'll explain everything, I promise."

Aaron opened his mouth to argue more, but he was cut off as the bell rang overhead.

"Exam day," Jamison said sharply.

I paled. Exams?

I looked to my left and right. All around me, my classmates pulled out pencils and stuck their bags under their desk. My stomach lurched.

"Ms. Melrose, up front." Jamison beckoned with one finger.

I jumped. "Is he talking to me?"

"Unless someone else has recently changed their name," Aaron grumbled, clearly still annoyed.

"Aaron, I'm sorry—"

"Go." Aaron tilted his head. "I'll catch up with you later."

With a sick feeling in my stomach, I descended the stairs. I locked eyes with Jared as I passed him. The back of my neck burned.

"Sir?" I asked weakly.

Jamison jerked his head towards the door. "The nurse wants to see you."

"What about the exam?"

"Melrose, weren't you the one who insisted that you didn't need this class on your very first day here?"

I sputtered.

"No more. Down the hall, turn right. Third door on your left. Donna will be waiting for you."

"Should I get my things?"

"Yes. Quickly!"

I turned on my heel and jogged back to my desk, eyes cast to the ground.

"Lydia, what's going on?" Aaron hissed as I slung my bag over my shoulder.

"I'm going to the nurse's office."

"Are you okay?"

"If I'm still alive at lunch, I'll let you know."

"What's that supposed to—"

I ignored Aaron's question as Jamison strode up the steps, distributing exams. My heart pounded as I left the room. Why did Donna need to see me? To check up on my fake gunshot wound? To punish me for breaking into Reed's office? To throw me on a gurney and wheel me away into the darkness?

*Don't be ridiculous. They don't know about Reed's office. They can't know.*

I wiped my palms on my dress, breathing hard as I turned the corner. I counted the doors as I passed them and came to a stop in front of the third metallic door. I swallowed.

*It's going to be fine. She's going to give you a checkup. That's all.*

The door swung open before I had a chance to knock or back out.

"Lydia. It's nice to see you." Donna's wide smile appeared in the doorway. "Come in."

I didn't move. "What's this about?"

"Just a routine physical to see how you're adjusting. Being deep underground can be hard on your body." Donna stepped into the hallway and placed a hand on my shoulder, pushing me into the room with surprising strength. "Sit." She pointed to the medical table in the middle of the room. Unlike my other hospital room, this one seemed equipped for quick check-ups rather than long stays.

The paper crinkled underneath me as I sat. I clasped my hands in my lap.

Donna hummed under her breath as she snapped the door shut. I sat up straighter.

"I'm just going to start by taking your temperature."

I relaxed a bit as Donna went through a few routine medical tests. Temperature, blood pressure, heart rate.

"And how is your schoolwork going?" Donna peered into my ears with a light.

"It's, ah, fine."

"Are you sure? Many students experience a certain degree of anxiety when transitioning to a new school, and if you ever feel the need to speak to someone, our counselors are available."

"I'm fine. Really." I dug my nails into my arms. "Is this it?"

"Almost." Donna crossed the room to a white cabinet and pulled out a needle.

I bristled. "What's that for?"

"Just some routine bloodwork." She hooked the needle up to a narrow tube and handed me a small ball. "Squeeze this."

I took the ball and placed it in my other palm. "Why do you need my blood?"

"I've just told you. Routine tests." Donna's eyes sharpened. "Hold out your arm, please." She grabbed my wrist before I could comply and jammed the needle into the crook of my arm.

Pain sparked up my arm. I gasped. This was more than the pain of a needle digging into skin; something like electricity crackled from my elbow to my shoulder, stinging as it went. I yanked my arm away. The vial slipped though Donna's fingers and smashed to the ground. Blood, ruby-red and shiny, spread over the pristine white floor, mingling with flecks of broken glass. A bubble of red grew at the crook of my arm and burst, running down to my wrist.

Donna huffed, slapping gloves onto her hand and bending down to clean up the mess. "What happened?"

"Sorry. It really hurt." I set the ball on the table next to me and hopped down. "Can we do this another time?"

"No, we can't."

I tried to protest, but Donna pushed me back into the chair. She'd jabbed another needle into my arm before I had the chance to cry out. More pain, sharp and white-hot shot up my arm. I gasped, but managed to keep my arm in place.

I jumped to my feet the second the needle was out of my arm. My heart pounded furiously, my body flooded with adrenaline and pain.

"Ms. Melrose, you need a bandage!"

I ignored her. The bell rang overhead as I hitched my bag onto my shoulder and strode to the door. I slammed it behind me, hand clamped over the crook of my arm. Now that the needle was gone, so was the pain, but sparks still coursed through my arm. Every one of my nerves teetered on high alert. I leaned against the wall and squeezed my eyes shut, breathing hard.

Chemistry was next. I could handle that. Voices swirled around me, none of them in focus. Somehow, I managed to stumble through the halls to class and clamber into my lab scrubs.

Someone knocked into me from behind as I stepped inside. I turned to see Jared's green eyes and mess of blond hair. He pursed his lips and made to move around me, but then his eyes locked onto mine.

I just stared at him, lips parted. A trickle of blood ran down my wrist and onto my palm. Jared's gaze followed. He grasped my hand.

"What's going on?"

I tugged it away. "Nothing."

"Lydia." Jared dropped his voice. "Are you hurt?"

I shoved him away. "Like you care."

"What happened?"

"What happened is you lied," I hissed. "You don't know anything about Danny. And you might have gotten me caught." I pushed past him.

He caught my arm and pushed the sleeve of my scrubs, exposing the crook of my arm. His thumb hovered over the bubble of blood still trickling from the wound.

My breath caught in my throat as I looked at him. The rest of the class seemed to zoom out of focus as he looked at me, his skin hovering centimeters from mine and our eyes locked.

When his voice brushed my ears, it was all I could hear. "Who did this to you?"

"N—no one." I whispered. "Just the nurse. Donna."

"Doesn't look like she was very gentle."

"It's fine."

"It doesn't look fine."

"Jared…"

"Carver. Melrose. Care to take a seat?" Ms. Khan snapped.

Jared and I jumped apart. I ducked my head and stepped towards Kat.

"Everyone else is paired up. You two take the table in the back." Ms. Khan nodded to a lab station set well away from the others.

I looked at Jared.

He looked at me. "Do I have to be with her?"

"You prefer not to? Then most assuredly, yes." Ms. Khan clicked her tongue impatiently.

I shot a glare at Jared. If he didn't want to talk to me, why did he keep seeking me out? He avoided my gaze as we strode to the lab station and faced the front.

"Now that Carver and Melrose are all settled in," Ms. Khan glared at us. "Today, you will be solving a murder."

My breath hitched in my throat.

"DNA from different persons will contain different percentages of nucleotides. In front of you, you have six different vials—a control group, the DNA of four suspects, and that from a bloody knife."

I cast a sideways glance at Jared—Khan wasn't serious, was she?

"The liquid will change colors based on the composition. When you've caught the culprit, you may go." She clapped her hands together. "Get to work!"

I dropped my gaze to the vials. The knot in my chest loosened when I saw that the liquid that filled them was clear rather than red.

"You look like you just watched someone get shot." Jared snatched the vials from the lab station and peered into them.

"Sorry, I guess I'm a little on edge given your reaction of seeing me in Reed's office," I hissed. "You made it seem like if I'd gotten caught, it'd be my blood being used in this experiment."

"Don't be stupid, this isn't real blood."

"Well yeah, I can tell that much." I raised my eyebrows as Jared counted out droplets of clear liquid that he splashed into the vials. Different colors burst from where they fell; earthy green, pure blue and blood red. "Wow," I said softly.

"Wow what?" Jared's eyes flicked to me for a fraction of a second.

"Nothing, it's just…they're beautiful." I picked up one of the vials and watched the tangled webs of color spread through the clear glass.

Jared took the other end of the vial I was holding and looked at it thoughtfully. Our eyes met over the clear surface. "I guess they kind of are."

My breath hitched in my throat as he looked at me, and suddenly I wasn't looking at the vial anymore. I was looking at Jared. His eyes. His dimples. The centimeter separating our fingers. The freckles that darted across his left cheek. My heart jumped to my throat; sparks shot up my spine, warm and tingly. I swallowed, trying to clear my throat of the knot that settled there.

"We should keep working." Jared pulled his hand away and I started, nearly dropping the delicate vial.

"Yeah." Air rushed back into my lungs; a few of the sparks tingling through my fingers faded away. "Let's."

We moved through the rest of the experiment quickly, watching bright colors bloom and recording the results on a clipboard.

"So," I asked when all of the vials were colored, "who's the killer?"

"What?" Jared asked sharply.

"In the experiment. Who's the killer?"

"Oh. That." Jared scratched at the back of his neck. "Juan."

"Alright." I poured the liquid from the vials into a large beaker one by one. Together, Jared and I cleared the station. Chatter echoed around us; most of the other groups had finished as well.

"Can I ask you something?" I muttered as I dried the countertop.

"You can. Doesn't mean I'll answer."

"Why do you hate me so much?"

Jared studied the clipboard. "I don't hate you. I just think you're an idiot."

"I'm smarter than ninety percent of the people in this school."

"Okay, I'll tell you something." Jared set the clipboard down with a snap. "I'll tell you the same thing I told you yesterday. Keep your head down and stop making stupid decisions, okay?"

"My head has been down," I hissed. "And you know what I think? I think that the real reason you wanted me out of Reed's office was because you were doing the same exact thing I was."

"And what would that be?"

"Looking for answers."

Jared didn't answer right away. He pulled the lab report off of the clipboard and held it out to me. "Here. You'll need this for the homework." He leaned close to me. His breath brushed my ear and his hand skimmed my shoulder, sending nervous tingles up my spine. "There are ways of finding answers that don't involve reckless behavior."

"I'll keep that in mind," I muttered to Jared's back as he walked away.

\*\*\*

"So, you ready to tell me what happened yesterday?" Aaron asked brightly. He set his cafeteria tray down across from me with a snap.

"Aaron, I am *so* sorry."

Aaron bit into an apple, watching me expectantly.

"I couldn't find the keys to the file cabinet," I lied. "I took a wrong turn when I left the office and got lost."

Aaron frowned. "Got lost where?"

"Well, I don't know, Aaron. I was *lost.*"

"And you didn't think to find me after you found your way back?"

I stabbed at a piece of lettuce with my fork. "I'm really sorry, Aaron. Are you okay? How did things go with Reed?"

"Well, I probably shouldn't get into any shenanigans for several years after the wild goose chase I took him on. But I'm fine." He leaned forward. "What about you? You still think you saw your brother in that photograph?"

"I *know* I saw my brother in that photograph. He was here."

"Well, then, what now?" Aaron asked.

"I'm not sure."

"I am." Kat sat next to me, looking intently between Aaron and me.

"What?" I asked softly.

"Listen, Lydia. I'm sorry I didn't help yesterday. I thought about what you said. We need to look out for each other. I want to help." Kat smiled. "I think I have an idea."

"Let's hear it, Romero," said Aaron.

Kat glanced at him. "The electronic files."

"I tried that, remember?" I asked bitterly.

Kat shook her head, grinning. "You tried that virtually."

"What are you saying? That there's a way to physically connect to the database?"

"That's exactly what I'm saying." Kat grinned, a mischievous look in her eyes. "Ever been down to the basement?"

# CHAPTER NINE

After classes ended that day, Kat, Aaron, and I met in a back corner of the library. Given the lack of books, I was surprised when Kat pulled several large maps out of her backpack and laid them across the table.

"Where'd you get these?"

"Trade secret," she said offhandedly. "There are books here. You just need to know where to look."

"Damn, Romero. Is there anything you don't know about this place?" Aaron asked.

"Plenty." Kat flipped the maps open, revealing detailed blueprints of the school. I recognized some of the structures, but some of the maps were of places I'd never seen before—different floors, even.

"This is the basement?" I asked, pointing at what seemed to be a maze of hallways.

"Yup." Kat jabbed a finger at a small closet not far from Reed's office. "See this? This is the server room. If you want into Reed's private files, this is your way in. The problem is that this door is locked with a manual lock, not a number one. If it was a keypad, we could swipe a pair of glasses, no problem."

"Glasses?" I asked.

"All of the keypads are painted with a solution that can only be seen with ultraviolet filters. The faculty have glasses that let them see the passcode. That way, they don't have to memorize a bunch of passwords," Aaron explained.

"Handy."

"Yeah, well, it makes trying to break in anywhere a little easier—as long as you can get your hands on a pair of glasses," Kat said.

"But we need keys," I muttered bitterly, remembering the last time that I'd needed to swipe a set of keys.

"We do. There are only seventeen doors in the whole school that use traditional keys. There are two sets of each. One of them is kept by Reed. Judging by what happened the last time you broke into his office...we're better off going after the other set." Kat pointed at a room in the basement. "This is the main maintenance closet. Though most of the cleaning throughout the school is done by electronic vacuums and stuff, there are still a few things that have to be done manually. Those supplies are in the maintenance closet— along with a set of those keys."

"Romero, how do you know all of this?" Aaron asked.

"Because I actually pay attention to things instead of staring at Lacey Taylor every second that I get," Kat replied, her voice dripping with sickly sweet sarcasm.

"I don't stare at Lacey Taylor," Aaron muttered.

"Sure, you don't." Kat looked Aaron up and down. "There are some advantages to being an outcast, you know. Like when the janitor takes pity on you and tells you all his secrets."

"Either way, it's impressive. How do I get to the basement?" I asked.

"Through here." Kat pointed at a stairwell. "This is your best bet. It's in an older section of the school. No cameras."

"Cameras?" I asked sharply. "There are cameras?"

Kat frowned. "Are you seriously telling me you're surprised by the fact that every inch of this place is under surveillance?"

My heart sped up. I sputtered. "You didn't think to tell me this before I *broke into Reed's office?*"

"They don't check the tapes unless something goes wrong. Nothing did, so you should be okay." Kat shrugged.

I tapped my fingers on the table. If Kat said it was fine, it probably was. But all the same, knowing that my face was on some surveillance tape somewhere made me nervous. What if they decided to check it?

"Is the stairwell alarmed?" Aaron asked.

"Not that I know of," Kat said. "But keep the curfew in mind—even if they don't see you going in and out of the stairwell, being out of bed after hours will send up major red flags."

I pushed air out of my mouth. "So basically, in order to get this thing done, I need to find a time when no one else is around after classes and before curfew."

"Basically."

"And I'll also need to return the keys after I get into the computer, so they don't notice and check the tapes." I bit the inside of my cheek. "It's not possible, is it?"

"That's the spirit," Aaron muttered.

"It's going to be hard. But it'll be easier if you know where you're going. You should do a practice run as soon as possible," Kat said.

"What are you suggesting? That I break in there tonight?"

"I'm saying that getting acquainted with what you're trying to break into wouldn't hurt." Kat tilted her head. "How badly do you want answers? How quickly do you think you need them?"

I pulled the basement map closer to me. "Tonight, it is."

\*\*\*

A half hour before curfew, I stole along the hallway as quietly as I could, praying that it would stay deserted long enough for me to get to the stairwell. Plain white tiles spread endlessly under my feet; a light flickered overhead. I glanced behind me. I'd been walking down this straight path for almost ten minutes now, and the stairwell was nowhere in sight. *What if the blueprints Kat gave me were outdated? Or wrong altogether?*

Finally, I came to a tall steel door. Its rusty hinges and stained surface were stark in comparison to the pristine doors I'd become accustomed to seeing around the school. I wondered how long it'd been since someone had set foot in the basement. Was it really a basement if we were already so deep underground?

I pulled open the door. Bits of rust rained from the frame as the metal scraped against it. I held my breath, staring into the dim stairwell. I couldn't tell how far down the stairs went.

"Here goes nothing." I stepped inside and closed the door. Dust choked me immediately, coating the inside of my throat. I coughed, stumbling down the stairs as fast as I could. The last thing I needed was to suffocate in here. The bare lightbulbs above my head seemed to flicker in time with my footsteps.

I burst through the door at the bottom, panting. The light down here was a bit brighter, the hall lit by rows of LED lights above my head. Particles of dust drifted through the air around me as I rested, trying to remember which way to go. After a moment, I walked to my left, taking care to trail one hand against the stone wall. Each of the halls that I turned down was lined with doors, some with windows set into them and some without. I peered through one of the windows and frowned. The room was near-empty, and the few pieces of furniture inside were covered with white sheets.

*What were these rooms used for?*

I shook away my curiosity and continued on my way. Water dripped onto concrete somewhere nearby. I sped up. Right turn, left turn, another left. I prayed that I'd be able to find my way out of here.

Finally, after what felt like hours, I came to a stop in front of a rusty door that read JANITOR across it in faded black letters. "Gotcha," I muttered under my breath. I tugged at the doorknob.

It didn't budge.

Heart sinking, I looked down at the knob. Next to it was a small numerical keypad. Aaron's words drifted back to me.

*All of the keypads are painted with a solution that can only be seen with ultraviolet filters. The faculty have glasses that let them see the passcode.*

I dropped my hand to my side. Breaking into this closet was never going to be a cakewalk, but now that this keypad was in my way, it was going to be a whole lot harder. I stared at the keypad. How many numbers would the passcode have? Would an alarm sound if I got it wrong? I rattled the doorknob again, but it didn't budge.

"Come on," I murmured. I fixed my eyes to the keypad and frowned. Was it my imagination, or were some of the numbers…glowing?

I dropped to my knees and ran my hand over the keypad. Sure enough, two, four, nine and six were glowing, each a bit brighter than the last. Hand shaking, I punched in the numbers. The door clicked and swung open. I stood and peered inside, heart pounding. Had I just seen the passcode for the room without the glasses Kat and Aaron had mentioned?

Deciding not to question why I was somehow able to see the right passcode, I stepped inside the closet and pulled the door shut behind me. The space was small and crammed full of shelves, some covered with cleaning supplies and others with what seemed to be old-fashioned machine parts.

"Where are you?" I muttered under my breath, turning in a circle. Hanging near the door was a set of rusty keys, each a different size. I grabbed them, triumph spreading over my face. If only there weren't cameras on the floor above me...

I hung the keys on their hook and backed out of the closet. It'd taken me far longer than I'd expected to find this place, and I couldn't afford to get caught out here after hours.

*I'll be back.*

I ran from the door, following the path back towards the stairwell—or what I *thought* was the path. The brick walls blurred together as I ran, turning me around until I was definitively, hopelessly lost.

"Shit," I muttered under my breath as I turned away from a dead end. I should have brought something down here to mark my path. What if I couldn't get out of here? Would Kat and Aaron come looking for me? I bit back a frustrated scream as I met yet another dead end. I panted and leaned against the wall, staring at the brick wall in front of me. I frowned. One of the bricks was emitting a faint green glow.

Just like the one I'd seen on the keypad.

I stepped towards like the brick as if drawn towards it. If I was somehow able to see the ultraviolet paint...why was this brick covered with it? I skimmed my fingers across the surface, frowning. Immediately, the glow grew brighter. I stumbled backwards, shielding my eyes against the bright light. Through my fingers, I saw the glow fade away. The brick broke into four pieces that were pulled into the wall, leaving a hole where the brick had been. I frowned. *What the hell had just happened?*

Something clanged behind me and I whirled around. No one was there.

I backed away from the brick wall and took off at a run. Whatever the hell was going on down here...that was a mystery for another night. For now, I needed to find my way out of this maze and get to bed. Now I knew what I was dealing with. I was glad I'd listened to Kat about doing a "trial run."

I stumbled over the uneven floor, nearly crashing into a wall. I wagered that I had maybe five minutes until curfew, and if I ran into Reed after that, I was toast. A four-way fork loomed in front of me. I skidded to a stop in the middle of it and turned on the spot. Which way was the exit? No matter where I looked, the halls seemed endless. I took the left fork. The lights flickered overhead.

Curfew. Part of me hoped that Kat and Aaron had the good sense to stay in their rooms instead of come looking for me, but the other hoped that someone would come for me, rescue me like my dad had that day on the beach.

"Please," I mumbled as I turned down another corner. More walls, more doors. Dust tickled my throat and I pressed my hand over my mouth, trying desperately to stifle the sound of my cough. As my eyes watered and my chest heaved, I spotted the stairwell up ahead.

*Thank God.* I pulled the collar of my shirt above my nose to block the dust and took the stairs two at a time. When I reached the door at the top, I pressed my ear against it, panting. The last thing I needed was to run into a teacher right now. That would've been bad enough at a normal boarding school, let alone one where students turned up passed out and bloody.

After a moment of listening, I pulled open the door. The hall was deserted, the lights dimmer than usual. I set off down the hall and pulled my hoodie up for good measure.

I speed-walked down the hall as quickly as I could. Even though I'd only been here a short time, my feet knew where to go. I passed the cafeteria, and then the chemistry lab.

Out of nowhere, a door opened. I skidded to a stop, looking for somewhere, anywhere, to hide. I wasn't quick enough.

I locked eyes with the blonde girl from chemistry. Her hair was pulled into a ponytail, and she looked as shocked and scared as I did.

"I, uh," I said.

"Hi," she said, flashing a somewhat shaky smile. "You're Lydia, right?"

"Yeah," I said cautiously.

"Lacey," she said, snapping the door shut behind her. "I've seen you around."

I blinked. "You too."

"I was just working on some stuff and lost track of time," she said, gesturing behind her with a laugh. Was it a trick of the light, or were her eyes sparkling, like she was trying to hold back tears?

"Me, too," I lied quickly. "I mean, I just need to walk sometimes. When there's no one around."

"I get it," Lacey said, smiling. The shine in her eyes was gone—I must have imagined it. "Well, I guess I'll see you later."

My heart was still pounding like crazy, but I managed a shaky smile.

"Oh, wait!" she said suddenly. "I've been meaning to get the word out—some friends and I are organizing this thing down in the basement next month."

"Thing?" I asked doubtfully.

"A party, to celebrate the end of midterms," Lacey explained. "All you have to do is come down to the basement. We're going to mark the way with glow sticks, so you won't get lost."

"A party," I said.

Lacey nodded, a wide smile on her face. "Dancing, beer, and boys," she said, winking. "I'll see you there, right? I think you'd have fun," she said earnestly.

"I, yeah," I said, smiling in spite of myself. "Thanks."

"Don't worry, I'll remind you." Lacey smiled. "I've gotta run. See you around," she said, turning on her heel with a wave.

For a minute, I just stood there, blinking. What the hell had just happened? And why was my heart giving a nervous, excited flutter at the prospect of going to a party when there was so much going on?

I shook the flutters away and jogged the remaining distance to the room. I slammed the door shut behind me, breathing heavily.

"What happened?" Kat asked, leaping to her feet at once. "I thought you got caught!"

"I sort of did," I said, and explained what Lacey had said.

Kat snorted. "Lacey Taylor was out of her room after hours? Scandalous."

"What do you know about her?"

"Not much. Just that she always looks flawless and ends every sentence like she's asking a question. She's a walking cliché," Kat said.

I shrugged. "She seemed nice."

"Maybe I'm wrong. But a party after hours, in the basement? Sounds like a great way to end up in detention."

"I don't know," I said. "I've never been to a party before."

"Me neither," Kat said.

I bit my lip. I wanted her to say that we would go to the party together, like a pair of best friends in a trashy teen movie. We'd drink cheap beer, dance, and kiss boys. But as she yawned and flopped onto her bed, it was clear that Kat wasn't interested in going to a party. Was I crazy to be considering this when there was so much on the line?

"Anyways, did you find the keys?"

"Yeah," I said. I explained what had happened, leaving out only the magical glowing numbers. I pulled my Rosett out of my bag and typed idly. All I wanted to do was find a way to watch one of my favorite movies until I fell asleep. I opened a window to the school's web browser and got to work.

"Well, that's good. We can get into the server room."

I nodded, eyes fixed to the screen. "Probably."

"Look, Lydia, if you want to go to that party, why not ask Aaron?" she asked.

I looked up. Was it really that obvious that I was hung up on it? "Why would I invite Aaron to a party?"

"He likes you," Kat said.

"You think?"

"Obviously. You're gorgeous. And smart."

I didn't reply. Slowly, I closed my Rosett. Could she be right? He'd certainly risked a lot for me, considering we'd just met. "Maybe," I said.

Kat yawned again. "All I'm saying is, you've got options."

"Yeah. Options." I switched off the light and climbed into bed. I didn't feel very much like watching a movie anymore. I wanted to sleep, to dream that I was back on the island, with Chris's hand laced in mine and the warm summer sun on my face.

***

Kat woke me the next morning in classic fashion. I was still shaking Cheerios out of my hair when we walked into the labs later that afternoon. I stuck to Kat like glue; the last thing I wanted was to get paired with Jared again.

Today, the lab stations were littered with beakers full of different substances.

"Whoa." I picked up a shiny silver knife. "What's this for?"

"We need that in smaller pieces. Be careful," Kat replied. "It looks sharp."

"I've got it," I said, taking the knife to a block of some white mineral. The knife slipped and sliced across my hand, leaving a deep cut. "*Fuck.*"

"Told you." Kat clicked her tongue.

Blood trailed down my wrist despite my attempts to stem it. I muttered a string of swear words under my breath as droplets of my blood fell into the wide-mouthed beaker on the counter.

The effect was immediate. My blood sizzled against the black dust inside, forming a cloud of grey vapor.

"Whoa!" I jumped away from the counter, still cradling my bleeding hand.

"What's going on here?" Khan was beside us in a second, arms crossed and eyes furious.

"It's my fault. I spilled sulfuric acid into the vial of coal dust," Kat said immediately. "Sorry."

"Sulfuric acid wouldn't react like that with coal dust."

"It's a scientific mystery!" Kat declared. "Maybe you should write your next thesis on that."

"Be careful," Khan said testily.

"Sure thing." Kat saluted.

"What was that?" I muttered out of the corner of my mouth.

"What do you mean, what was that?"

"Why'd you lie to Khan?"

"See this?" Kat held up a vial identical to the one my blood had dripped into. It was half-full of black dust. "This is coal dust. It's basically just pure carbon."

"So?"

"So, blood doesn't react like that with carbon," Kat hissed.

I looked at the pool of blood in my palm. "What are you saying?"

"I'm saying that that's really freaking weird. We can't trust anyone but each other, and I especially don't think telling a chemistry teacher about something like *that* would be great for you." Kat wiped the bloody knife on a paper towel and turned her attention back to the experiment we were supposed to be doing.

"Wait. Why did my blood do that to the coal dust?"

"I have no idea."

"Well, what would make it disappear like this?" I held up the vial. Before, it'd been filled with black dust. Now, it was perfectly empty.

"Not many things," Kat sighed. She rubbed a hand over her chin. "Plutonium maybe."

"Are you saying—"

"I'm saying that this is weird," Kat repeated. "Lydia…" She shook her head. "Never mind. It's probably nothing. The sample must have been contaminated." Kat nodded to herself.

"Do you really believe that?"

"No. But I don't think this is the place to talk about it, either."

The back of my neck prickled, and I turned to see Jared staring at me, his mouth pulled into a frown. "Yeah," I murmured to Kat. "You're probably right."

I turned back to the experiment and the events of last night came back to me with a jolt. I'd seen the passcode on the keypad when it should have been impossible. And now, my blood had caused a reaction that shouldn't have been possible either.

*Just some routine tests.*

Donna's words echoed in my mind and I clenched my hands around the edge of the lab table, wondering what exactly those routine tests might be.

\*\*\*

We were due to present our project on the Battle of Montara the following week. The next day, I stood in front of Kat and Aaron in the nearly deserted library. My shaky hands curled around a stack of index cards. Dates and figures were scrawled over them in Kat's neat print.

"The Battle of Montana—sorry, Montara," I stuttered. I blinked, staring up at the ceiling.

"Hey." Aaron got to his feet and put his hands over mine. "You okay?"

I looked beyond him, at Kat. She looked back at me, lip caught between her teeth. I could see it in her gaze. She thought it was time to tell him, and I had to open up sometime, right?

"Not really," I sighed. I sank into an armchair and plopped the index cards on the arm rest. "This hits kind of close to home."

Kat stood and hovered at Aaron's shoulder, looking worried.

"Sebastian Melrose is my dad, okay?" I burst out. "He's the one who won this battle, he's the one we're talking about."

"You miss him?" Aaron asked, his voice full of knowing sympathy. "I mean, since you enrolled here?"

"I didn't enroll in this place." I threw up my hands. "He died. He died, and they stuck me here. I didn't have a choice. I didn't even get to go to his funeral. I... I never got a chance to say goodbye."

Aaron's eyes went wide. "Oh."

"It's fine." I wiped the tears from my eyes, suddenly feeling embarrassed at the outburst.

"We never should have done this battle. I should have known better, I—"

"Aaron, it's okay," Kat interrupted. "Lydia agreed to the project. In all honesty, we would've been hard pressed to come up with a battle that didn't mention her father at least once."

"Kat's right." I cleared my throat and jumped to my feet. "It's fine. I'm fine. I'm in school, and I have to do projects. Not a big deal."

"Lyd, you know it's okay to not be okay, right?" Aaron asked. "This is a lot."

"No, it's not," I said stubbornly. "I'm in school, I have friends. This is what I always said I wanted."

Kat and Aaron exchanged a glance I'd seen on screen hundreds of times. Small frowns, subtle head shakes.

"You think I'm crazy."

"We think you've been through a lot," Kat said softly. She moved close to me and placed her hands on my shoulders. Her hands were warm, her features soft and concerned. Tears prickled the corners of my eyes and I sagged forward into her arms.

"He's gone," I whispered into her shoulder. "My dad's gone. And I never got to say goodbye."

"I know," Kat murmured. "Come on. We're going to get you to bed. Aaron and I will figure it out, okay?"

"No, Kat, I can…" I pulled away and reached for the index cards, horrified at the speed at which my walls were crumbling. "I can do this."

"Come on."

My fingers skimmed the index cards one last time, and then I let her lead me away.

***

Once back in our room, I took a long, hot shower. I wasn't even crying anymore. Instead of tears, there was only a steady burn, fueled by the dry numbness behind my eyes. When I emerged, hair tangled and eyes puffy, there was a cup of hot chocolate next to my bed, waiting for me.

I avoided Kat's eye. Humiliation at my outburst tingled in my gut like poison. "Thanks."

"Thank Aaron," Kat said lightly, sipping from her own mug. She paused, "You want to talk about it?"

"Not really."

"Okay." Kat shifted, tucking her feet up under her. "He's right, you know. Aaron."

"About what?"

"It's okay to not be okay."

"No, it's not," I choked.

"Why not?"

"Because Danny is less okay. And I'm the only one who can figure out what happened to him. I can't do that if I burst into tears about a presentation."

"Yeah, you can." Kat shrugged. "So, you had a bad night. So what? You'll be better first thing tomorrow after you rest a bit. And we'll do a fantastic job on the presentation."

"But what if I don't?"

Kat just smiled. "You will. *We* will."

***

The next morning, I greeted Aaron with a sheepish smile. "Hey."

"You feeling better?"

"Yeah. I am." I took a deep breath. "I think I can do this."

"Well, if it turns out you can't, we're here for you, okay?"

"I know."

"But I mean, I really hope you can do it. Because God knows we aren't getting any help from Kat."

"Hey," Kat called from a few rows behind us. "I can hear you guys, you know."

Aaron winked, and I couldn't help but laugh. Maybe they were right. Maybe I *could* do this.

Jamison called for us to settle down, and I rested my chin on my arms as class began.

My dad was gone. I was never going to settle in next to him on the couch after a long day of coding again. Never drink mugs of coffee with him on the back porch and watch the sun rise on Saturday mornings. And it hurt worse than anything.

But I was strong. And it was going to take a hell of a lot more than a school project to break me.

# CHAPTER TEN

"Morning, sunshine." Aaron grinned as I sat next to him in history a few days later, dropping my bag to the ground with a *thump.*

"I haven't seen the sunshine in a month," I grumbled under my breath. The temporary high of acing our project had long since faded, as had the frenzy of midterm exams, but I wasn't sad anymore. I was pissed.

"Hey, don't exaggerate. It's only been two weeks," Aaron said.

"Two weeks since I..." I lowered my voice, "since I found the key, but three since I was first locked up here." Two weeks since Donna drew my blood.

Aaron rubbed my arm, frowning. "We'll get there, okay? Sooner or later, you'll get a chance to get that key. And you'll get the answers."

"Not if they kill me first."

"You don't know for sure that they *killed* him..."

"I don't know that they didn't. I don't know that they didn't kill that girl."

"There it is again. That bright, sunny disposition that we all love so much." Aaron winked. "Listen, don't worry. That girl might have hurt herself, for all we know. Kids get depressed sometimes, especially with everything going on in the world."

"Or she might have had an accident?" I tried to concede but couldn't quite get myself to believe it.

"Lydia, we don't know what happened. But the truth is, you can't control any of this. You can only control what you do. And right now, it seems like you're considering doing something stupid."

"Such as?"

"Cutting class to go get that key."

I looked away. "I…"

"Hey." Aaron grabbed my wrist. When I faced him again, his mouth was twisted into a frown. "If they *did* do something to Danny…what do you think will happen when *they* figure out that *you* figured that out? Be smart, okay?"

"Okay."

"Promise me."

"Aaron…"

"Promise."

I opened my mouth to reply, but the morning bell cut me off. Aaron frowned. Deep worry lines cut into his forehead.

"Settle down." Jamison waved a hand at the front of the class. "Today, as you should all know, is the post-midterm assembly to review school policies. Some of you could certainly use a refresher. If everyone will follow me to the cafeteria…" Jamison trailed off as the room burst into noise. I grabbed my bag and, together, Aaron and I followed the swelling crowd into the hallway.

"Lydia! Aaron!" Kat ran towards us, her face flushed. "Where are you going?"

"Assembly." I jerked my thumb towards the receding crowd as the last of our classmates trickled away.

"You're kidding, right?" Kat demanded, out of breath.

"Kat, what are you—"

"The assembly?" Kat burst out. "It'll go on for a few hours at least, and the whole school will be there—don't you get it?" She seized my hands.

"You can get the key," Aaron said, his eyes wide.

"Oh my God." My heart raced. After all this time, the perfect opportunity actually fallen into my lap.

"Go." Kat pushed me. "I'll cover for you if anyone asks questions."

"Are you sure we won't get caught?"

"Of course not."

"Then what—"

"For crying out loud, just *go!*" Kat shouted. She sprinted away from us, following the class, but Aaron turned to me.

"Where to?"

"I'm not putting you in danger again," I protested. "Go with Kat. I'll be fine."

"You won't be fine. You need a lookout." Aaron offered me a sideways grin.

I took a deep breath, considering. He was right—I *did* need a lookout, someone who knew the school and where the teachers would likely be.

"Fine," I said slowly. "Go to the server room and stay hidden. I'll meet you in ten with the key."

"Perfect." Aaron offered me a salute, and we took off running in opposite directions. My dress billowed around my knees as I ran; my shoes skidded across the slick floor. I slowed down before approaching each hallway, sure that someone was about to catch me at any second. *Why did the history classroom have to be so far away from the basement?*

Sweat dripped down the back of my neck and over my forehead. If I could just pass the next hallway, I'd have a straight shot to the basement. I was ten feet away. Five. Three…

"Melrose?"

I skidded to a halt, chest heaving.

Jared stepped around the corner, anger scrawled all over his face. "What are you doing here?"

"We need to stop meeting like this." I stepped back, raking a hand through my sweaty hair. *Go away. Please go away.*

"What are you doing here?" Jared repeated.

"I'm going to the assembly."

"The assembly's in the cafeteria."

"I know."

"The cafeteria's that way." Jared pointed behind me.

"This is a shortcut."

"Melrose, you can't keep doing this." Jared stepped closer to me and dropped his voice. "If you keep sneaking away like this, they're going to catch you."

"You say that like we're not already caught."

"Sweetheart, you have no idea what it's like to be *caught*." Jared's eyes flashed. Sparks tingled down my spine. "If you want to put yourself in the line of fire, fine. I'm done trying to protect you."

"I never asked you to," I breathed. "And it doesn't feel like you're doing much except standing in my way."

"Fine." Jared stepped away from me. Some of the electricity in the air fizzled away. "See you around, Melrose. Or not."

I stared after him, openmouthed. *What was that supposed to mean?*

*Get to the key,* a voice hissed in the back of my head. I started and broke into a sprint. Whatever Jared was up to, this was more important. Somehow, I managed to shove Jared to the back of my mind as I hurtled down the basement stairs and towards the maintenance closet. I'd given Aaron ten minutes, and I was already far behind that mark. Somehow, my feet knew where to go. Before I knew it, I'd skidded to a halt in front of the janitor's closet.

Hands on my knees, I peered down at the keypad. Sure enough, the numbers winked at me like a friendly stranger. I punched in the numbers and the door clicked open. I grabbed the keys from the hook by the door and used the last of my strength to sprint back to the stairwell and down the hall. I had no idea how long I'd been down there, but I knew that every second spent in the open doubled my chances of being caught.

"What the hell took you so long?" Aaron caught my arm as I slowed, looking me up and down.

"Got...lost," I panted. Sweat dripped down my flushed face. The keys clinked together as I held them up.

"Nice." Aaron took them from me. "Which one is it?"

"Hell if I know." I pressed my back against the wall. "Is the coast clear?"

"Yeah. But it won't stay that way, especially if we have to try all these keys." Aaron pulled me around the corner. "Come on."

Together, we stood in front of the door. "Okay." Aaron ran his hand over the lock. "It'll be silver."

"They're all silver."

"*Shit.* Try all of them."

I sighed and held the keys up to the light. If I had to try all of these, there was no way that I was going to have enough time in the server room. I flipped through them, looking for something, any kind of clue as to which key I was looking for. Finally, as the keys glinted in the light, something else caught my eye. One of the keys was glowing. I picked that one out of the bunch and examined it. Sure enough, a tiny, glowing circuit board shone from the shiny surface.

"It's this one."

"What?" Aaron followed me to the door. "How do you know?"

"Superpowers." The key clicked in the lock. The knob turned.

"Fair enough." Aaron and I peered inside the server room. There was barely enough space in here for one person between the huge servers inside. "How about I wait out here?" Aaron suggested, taking a step back.

"Great idea." I pulled my laptop out of my backpack and shoved the pack at him. "Knock three times if there's danger."

"Got it. Although, I probably won't have time if Reed catches us."

"That's the spirit." I snapped the door shut and turned to face the room. I raked a hand back through my hair. Green and blue lights flashed around me as the servers worked, presumably directing all of the network activity throughout the school. I gave myself ten seconds to drink things in, remembering the last time I was in a server room.

\*\*\*

*"Fancy meeting you here."*

*"Chris, hi." I jumped and hid the laptop in my hands behind my back. "What are you doing in here?"*

*Chris held up a hard drive. His green eyes glinted as he moved into the room and snapped the door shut. "Some of the drives need repair. But you knew that."*

*I stared at the flashing red lights around me instead of at Chris. My heart pounded. "Of course."*

*Chris grinned and moved closer to me. He slipped the hard drive into his pocket. "And what are you doing in here, Lydia?"*

*"Nothing."*

*"Keep it that way, okay?" Chris winked, and all of the air zoomed out of my lungs. "The last thing we need is for you to mess things up."*

*The nervous smile on my face slid away. "Whatever."*

*"Hey, wait. Lydia—that didn't come out right." Chris scratched at the back of his neck. "It was meant to be ironic—everyone knows you're the best one here."*

*"Do they?" My eyes sparkled with tears.*

*"God—yes, they do." Chris put a hand on my shoulder and tucked a piece of hair behind my ear with the other. "I'm sorry."*

*"I'm just gonna get out of your way." I jerked away from Chris.*

*"No, wait." Chris held up his hands in surrender. "If I give you ten more minutes alone in here, will you forgive me?"*

*"Ten minutes?"*

*"Fifteen?"*

*"Done." I frowned. "Why are you being so nice to me?"*

*"I'm always nice to you."*

*I raised an eyebrow. "Really?"*

*"Okay, most of the time." Chris gave me a half-smile. "I like you, Lydia. You know that."*

*"Do I?"*

*"I think you do." Chris grinned and ran a hand up my arm to my elbow. Sparks shuddered up my spine. "Fifteen minutes, okay?"*

*My mouth was incredibly dry. "Okay."*

\*\*\*

That was a week before the attack. It had only taken me seven minutes to get what I was looking for. What I was after now was a lot more important than a movie, and I'd probably have less time to do it. I took a deep breath and got to work.

First, I powered up my Rosett. The home screen shone back at me, and I blinked against the light as I scrambled to find a spare wire on the servers. I found one, plugged in the Rosett, and sat back against the wall, balancing the computer on my knees while I accessed the connection.

"Here goes nothing," I mumbled to myself. Heart still pounding from the run—or maybe the nerves—I broke through the first firewall. And the second. And the twentieth. My legs ached from my position against the servers. Letters and numbers scrolled past my eyes in neon green against the black screen. My fingers pounded the keys so hard, they could probably hear it all the way in the cafeteria.

After what felt like hours, the last of the firewalls fell away. My screen was now filled with hundreds of tiny file icons. A wide smile spread over my face, but it quickly vanished when I realized how many there were. How was I ever supposed to look through all of this in time? Desperately, I ran a search for any file that contained the words *Danny, Daniel,* or *Melrose.*

"Come on," I muttered as the search ran. A tiny spiral spun around and around as the computer searched the database. I held my breath for one, two, three seconds. Suddenly, the screen was full of documents and file folders. My eyes widened. *Why was there so much information in here on Danny?*

I scrolled through all of the files, mouth open. There was no way I was going to be able to look through all of these in time. After a few seconds of deliberation, I clicked on a file at random.

The file popped up. It was labeled *The Latium Project: Initial Clinical Trials.* I mouthed the word *Latium.* It fell oddly in my mouth. *Lat-ee-um.* I scrolled down. Pages and pages of text filled the screen. My eyes zoomed over them, trying to take in everything I could.

*Patient 347 A Daniel "Danny" Melrose was unresponsive following Day 6 Treatment—*

The screen fizzled. The pixels in the screen sparked—first to white. And then the whole thing died.

I jumped to my feet. "No. No!"

The door banged open and Aaron appeared, wide-eyed. "What's going on?"

I ripped the cord out of the Rosett. "We need to go. Now."

"What happened?"

"Something bad."

# CHAPTER ELEVEN

"So, it just died? Just like that?"

"Yeah, Kat. Just like that." I sighed and pressed my hands to my forehead. "God, what was I thinking?"

"Hey." Aaron nudged my head with his toe. "You were thinking that you're a good hacker—and you probably are. It's just that whoever designed the system was better."

I opened one eye and peeked at him. "Thanks."

Aaron grinned and flopped back onto my bed. I was lying on the ground, my hair spread in a halo around me. Kat peered down at me from her bed, frowning.

"So, did you find anything at all?" she asked timidly.

"Not really. Something about trials. And an experiment called Project Latium," I said.

"Latium?" Kat repeated. "What the hell is that?"

"No clue. Aaron?" I asked.

"Uh, no. Never heard of it." Aaron sighed. "It may not mean anything at all. It might be code or an anagram or something. Until we can get back in there, we won't know for sure."

"Yeah, I guess you're right."

"At least no one noticed you were missing from the assembly," Kat pointed out. "Things could be worse."

"How did that go?" Aaron asked.

"The assembly? Same as usual. A review of rules, a lecture about what will happen if we're caught out after curfew, even though they never really care. There's a shortage of corn on the outside world, which isn't surprising." Kat hesitated before continuing, "And, Lydia, they showed us a video about… about your dad."

I sat up. "Oh." We'd finished up our project on the Battle of Montara last week. Sometime after I'd told Aaron who I was, hearing Dad's name stopped hurting so much.

Aaron put his hands on my shoulders. "You okay?"

I leaned into his touch, eyes squeezed shut. "Yeah. I'll be fine. I wish now I had been there to see the movie. To see his face."

"I'm sorry. I shouldn't have brought that up," Kat said quickly.

"No, it's okay. It's good that people are…remembering him."

"What was he like?" Aaron asked.

"He, ah…" I wiped a tear away from my eye. "He was everything they tell you he is. And more. He loved me. And Danny. He always went out of his way to help people, like my…" I hesitated, taking a deep breath. "I had this friend, Chris. Chris's father died when he was pretty young, and my dad picked up all the slack. Had him over for dinner, helped him with his work. That kind of thing."

"He sounds like a good man," said Aaron.

"Yeah," I pushed myself to my feet and shrugged off Aaron's hands. Why had I mentioned Chris when it just made me want to start crying and never stop? "He was. Let's talk about something else."

"Like?" Kat asked.

"How do you think you did on midterms?" I grinned weakly.

Kat threw a wadded up piece of paper at me. "Ugh, shut up."

I laughed and flopped onto the bed next to Aaron. He put his arm around me and pulled my head onto his shoulder. His hand brushed my arm and I smiled in spite of myself. Aaron and Kat had risked a lot for me today. For the first time, there were people in my life that cared about me—really cared about me. People other than my dad, of course.

But he was gone now.

They were all I had.

But for now, as the three of us laughed and Aaron pulled me closer, they were enough.

***

The euphoria of the afternoon had long faded by the time I got ready for bed that night. It was easy to make light of the day's events when I was surrounded my friends, but with Aaron back in his room and Kat passed out in her bed, the full weight of what I'd discovered came crashing down on me.

There were so many files that had Danny's name in them—certainly that wasn't typical for a student record. And then there was that word—Latium. What did mean? What experiments were they carrying out here? There was no way to know without going into the database again, but I was lucky that my Rosett wasn't fried by my first attempt. Asking for a new computer would have raised some eyebrows.

I powered the Rosett up, ready to give the movie search another go. The air-tight security on the internal network was incredibly frustrating. Even more so was the complete lack of access to any information not explicitly relevant to our classes. It made me wonder if education was like this everywhere. Was every school kid being exposed only to what our government had approved? The thought sent icy chills down my back.

It's about power. Always about power.

After a few moments of frustration, I sighed and opened up my messages. There were a few there from teachers, detailing my assignments, but there was also one from Lacey.

*Hey, Lydia! Don't forget—the party's tonight!*

I sat bolt upright in my bed. The party. After everything that had happened, I'd completely forgotten about it. It was only midnight. There was still time for me to go. I couldn't pass up the opportunity to do what I'd been dreaming of for years.

I looked at Kat's bed. She was out cold. I thought about what she'd said, about asking Aaron to go with me. But I had no idea where his room was, and for all I knew, he was already asleep, too. If I was doing this, it would be alone.

Could I risk it? Risk everything for some music and beer? Something was tugging at my heart, begging me to get out of bed. I had to try. I had to know, just for one night, what it was like to be a normal teenager.

As quietly as I could, I took one of my dresses from the closet. I pulled it on and tugged my hair back into two French braids. In the movies, the girls always wore short skirts and dark makeup to parties, the nerd turned into the most gorgeous girl there. I couldn't do that. All I could do was stare at myself in the mirror, wishing I would magically become prettier.

Unfortunately, this would have to do.

I stole quietly down the hallway, following the path to the basement that I knew by heart now. Sure enough, there was a bright red glow stick hanging over the door to the stairwell. I couldn't help but smile. For the very first time, I was going to a party.

I held my breath in the stairwell and patted the dust off of my dress as soon as I was out of it. More glow sticks lined the hall down here, marking a clear path. My heart fluttered when I heard music echoing through the hall.

Suddenly, hands grabbed me from behind and slammed me against the wall. Jared's green eyes met mine as he held me in place, a deep scowl on his face.

"I don't even know what to say to you anymore," he hissed. "Do you have a death wish?"

I shoved Jared away from me, anger boiling in my cheeks. "Do you?"

"If I had a death wish, I'd be dead."

"I don't have a death wish. I just want to go to a party, so if you want to skip the lecture about how much danger I'm in and let me do that, that'd be fantastic." I glared at Jared. God, how was he *everywhere*?

"You're not going to that party. I'm walking you back upstairs."

"No, you're not."

"I am."

"God, Jared, I do *not* need your help! What happened to 'I'm done protecting you?' Let's get back to that. Stop stalking me and leave me alone."

Jared barked out a laugh. "You wouldn't last three days here without me."

"It's been three weeks and I'm doing just fine."

"I'm walking you back, and that's final," Jared growled, dark fury in his eyes. "You can come with me, or I can strong arm you and *make* you come. But I'd rather keep things civil."

My mouth went dry. *Was he threatening me?* "You won't hurt me."

"No. I won't. But if you don't let me help you, then *they* will hurt you." Jared gestured towards the way out. "Lydia, please."

"Lydia!" a new voice rang out before I could answer Jared. I turned, and Lacey trotted towards me, excitement shining in her eyes. "I'm so glad you made it! Is this your date?"

Before I knew what was happening, Jared slipped a hand around my waist and smiled at me. "Yeah, I am. Hey, Lacey."

Lacey smiled. "Lydia, come here. We have to get your dolled up." She reached into her bag and pulled out what I recognized as an eyeliner pencil.

"Where did you get that?" I asked. I didn't even know that makeup even still existed, let alone how she was able to get it here.

"Secret," she said. She pulled me away from Jared. "Eyes closed."

A smile tugged at the corners of my mouth as she ran the pencil over my eyes. There were butterflies in my stomach, their wings beating in time with the music echoing through the hall.

"Perfect," Lacey said, squeezing my shoulders. "Come on. We're just getting started." She trotted down the hall, her blonde curls bouncing as she walked.

Out of nowhere, Jared grabbed my hand, lacing his fingers through mine.

"What are you *doing*?"

"Making this look convincing. I need an alibi."

I tugged my hand away. "What are you talking about?"

"Don't worry about it. Just hold my hand, look pretty, and I won't tell Reed about your after-hours activities," Jared said with a wink.

"Are you threatening me?"

"Not necessarily." Jared took my hand again with a smirk.

"If I don't have to hold your hand any longer, answering to Reed might be worth it," I spat at him. But even though I was furious with him for pretending that we were together, some small part of me was thrilled at the thought. The same part that sent warm, nervous flutters through my gut as his hand tightened around mine.

I looked at the ground instead of at him.

"Almost there," Lacey called over her shoulder. She was now walking next to a tall, thin girl whose shiny black hair hung to her waist. Now that we were closer to the center of the party, the music pulsed louder. My heart sped up; my hand suddenly felt clammy even though it was linked with Jared's. I'd grown up watching movies from nearly every decade—from the early 1950s through the late 2010s. Back on the island, I spent hours watching boys toss girls up in the air and throw them into bed in crazy, acrobatic dances. I'd been entranced as the girl got the boy, the girl got the girl, and everything in between. Every school dance seemed to turn upside down. In later films, there were hidden parties, like this one, filled with red cups, short skirts, and couples making out in darkened hallways.

Now, for the first time in my life, that was going to be me.

As Lacey pushed aside a black curtain and music I'd only ever heard in old movies drenched my eardrums, a wide smile spread over my face. We were in a kind of indoor amphitheater; rows and rows of stone seats sank low, circling a stage in the center. Girls and guys crowded together on the stage, clinking glasses together, and dancing to the rhythm. Lacey and her friend trotted off to join some of their friends, but I stood stock-still, taking in the scene.

"Wow," I whispered, but my voice was lost in the music. I recognized the song—something recorded in the late 1990s.

"Okay, we made an appearance. We should go now," Jared hissed into my ear. He tugged on my arm.

I turned to look at him, eyes shining. "I can't."

"I'm sorry, did you say you *can't?*"

"Jared, I have to stay. At least for a little while." I slid my hand from his. "I have to know."

Jared's eyes flashed in the strobe lights. The corners of his mouth tightened, and I couldn't tell if he was still angry or just disappointed. For a moment, the scene whirled around us; bodies silhouetted against the dim light wandered past us and the smell of alcohol hung in the air.

And then he nodded. "Okay."

"Okay?"

"But I'm staying with you." Jared took my other hand. "As your date."

I jerked away from him. "Come on. You've got your alibi. Let me have fun."

"Lydia." Jared leaned close to me and put a hand to the side of my face. "This type of party is more dangerous than you realize. Can you take my advice for once? I promise, I'm only trying to keep you safe."

I bit my lip as Jared's thumb skimmed over my cheek. Here I was, finally living out one of the things I'd been watching on screens for years. And here was a boy, offering to keep me safe. A boy with eyes the color of evergreen trees and a smile that made me feel like I was about to melt. One who I hadn't known my whole life. One who made electricity course through the air whenever he was near.

"Let's dance," he offered.

I could barely breathe as I replied. "Okay."

# CHAPTER TWELVE

Hand in hand, Jared and I wandered through the darkness. Music pounded in my ears and heart as we settled a little away from the stage. I couldn't wipe the smile off my face for anything as Jared settled his hands on my waist. I looped my arms around his neck, and it was like none of our past arguments had ever happened.

"You look happy for someone who almost refused to hold my hand earlier," Jared murmured into my ear.

"You look happy for someone who was trying to drag me back upstairs," I shot back. But I was still smiling. There weren't any words for the way I was feeling right now. I'd been dreaming about a moment like this since I was ten years old, and now, finally, that dream was coming true for all the wrong reasons.

But I didn't care.

Jared's hands slid over my waist, and my eyes fluttered shut. I was drowning in him, in this crowd that had swallowed us. In this moment, I wasn't in the basement of a boarding school, trapped and fighting for answers about my brother. I wasn't an outcast. I wasn't the daughter of a fallen soldier. In this moment, I was the girl who went to her high school dance and found everything she wanted there. And more.

I drew closer to Jared, grinning as I tangled my hands in the base of his hair. His lips neared mine, but I couldn't tell which of us was leaning towards the other. Our lips were only inches away. Centimeters. Millimeters. The music dulled in my ears like it was traveling through water and getting stuck along the way.

Someone tapped my shoulder and I jumped back from Jared, heart pounding. "Drink?" asked a tall guy with dark hair, offering me a red cup.

I pulled my hands from Jared's neck and stepped away. "Um, sure. Thanks."

The guy smiled at me, flashing rows of white teeth. "I'm Mason. How about a dance?"

"She's with me." Jared put his arm around my waist again and tried to pull me away. "Lydia, come on."

"But I—"

"Don't drink anything you haven't pored yourself," Jared warned, leaning close to my ear.

A wave of nausea hit me. *What exactly did that mean?*

Before I could think, the guy grabbed my other arm and yanked me roughly against him. "He always speak for you?" he yelled in my face, spraying it with spit and booze. I tried to pull away, but his grip was like iron.

My stomach dropped to the floor. "L—let go of me."

The guy shook his head, drunken fire in his eyes. "I don't think so."

"I think so." Jared stepped past me and punched the guy square in the jaw. The guy released my arm immediately and crashed to the ground. I scrambled away from him. My cup tumbled to the ground and spilled, splashing over my shoes.

Jared grabbed my shoulders and pulled me backwards, away from the scene. The guy stumbled to his feet, rage scrawled all over his face. Jared laced his hand through mine again and pulled me away from the crowd. Luckily, the guy seemed too drunk to notice we were gone.

I leaned back against the wall, heart pounding. I'd seen that happen a hundred times on a screen, so why was I freaking out?

"You okay?" Jared leaned close to my ear.

I didn't answer. I just shook my head. Where a second ago, all I had seen were dreams and possibility, I now felt like I was going to throw up. The walls were closing in. Someone else stumbled into me, tipping their drink. Booze splashed onto my shoes. The music grew too loud. The glow sticks were too bright. And there were entirely, entirely too many people.

"Let's leave," I said.

Jared frowned, looking concerned.

"Now," I said, but I didn't move.

"Come on." Jared took my hand again, and together we climbed the stairs. Away from the crowd and sweat and stifling heat.

Once we were out of there and far enough that the music had faded to a dull thump, I pressed my back against the wall and my hands to my forehead.

Jared put a hand on my shoulder. "You okay?"

"No, not really," I said bitterly. "I never should have gone to that stupid…" I didn't even know what to call it. A party? A rave?

"I get it," Jared said.

"No, you don't," I laughed mirthlessly. "You think I'm an idiot."

"That's not true," Jared said unconvincingly.

"You're just saying that to make me feel better."

"Yeah, kinda." Jared shrugged.

"Well, that's new." I straightened up. "Jared, I can admit when I'm wrong. I thought it would be… different. But thank you. Thank you for staying with me."

Jared shook his head, looking down the dark hallway instead of at me. "Listen, I know you're scared and I know you want answers, but risking everything for a lame party like that is not the way to get them. What do you think would've happened if I hadn't been there just now?"

"I would've been fine."

"Maybe," he said. "But there are things people put in drinks, Lydia. Most of them are hard to come by nowadays, but… you could have been assaulted."

I felt my fingertips go numb and my legs felt like jelly. There was clearly a darker side to being a "normal" teenager—one I hadn't realized before.

"I might have been nothing, but that's not the point." Jared raked a hand back through his hair.

"What is the point, Jared?" My voice was softer now.

"The point is that this place is dangerous. And what they can do to you is a lot worse than the effects of an anxiety attack at some sad excuse for a high school dance. You need to stop taking risks. This was dangerous, and so was whatever you were up to this morning," he said knowingly.

"Jared, you keep saying that. I know you want to protect me. That was clear tonight, and in some ways, I *do* appreciate it. But you know I'm going to keep looking for answers as long as you don't explain who you're afraid of." I shook my head, corners of my eyes stinging. "Please. What happened to Danny?"

"It's not safe to talk here." He paused, seeing the frustration on my face. "It's okay. I know a place." Jared held out a hand. "It's not far."

"Okay." I whispered. I took his hand. And together, we set off down the hallway.

\*\*\*

"Where are we going?" We'd been walking for about ten minutes, deeper and deeper into the basement tunnels. I hoped that Jared knew where we were going, because I had no clue.

"Somewhere it's safe. At least I think it's safe." Jared pulled his hand from mine as we came to a stop in front of a stainless steel door. Rust sprinkled to the ground as Jared pulled it open. "Follow me."

I tentatively stepped into the space, which was no bigger than a closet. A shiny silver ladder sank into the ground in front of me and stretched higher than I could see. I turned back towards Jared. "Where does this lead?"

Jared gave me a mischievous smile and pressed a hand to the small of my back as he edged around me. He put both hands on the rungs. "Climb it and find out."

The rungs were cool to the touch as they slid under my fingers. Hand over hand, foot over foot, I climbed into the darkness for what felt like hours. I knew Jared was close above me not just from the sound of his breathing, but from the tension in the air between us.

Finally, my hand found a stretch of smooth stone instead of a rung. I pulled myself off of the ladder, arms sore from the effort. As I straightened up, I glanced around me.

What little breath I had left vanished. I was standing in what appeared to be a small nook in the mountain that Yucca was nestled under. Bathed in soft star and moonlight from above, the rock walls shone silver as they rose twenty feet above me in all directions. And when I cast my eyes to the sky, I found it shining with millions and millions of tiny stars that twinkled like a handful of sugar thrown onto a black table. The moon was nestled among them, a beacon of silvery light.

My eyes watered. I hadn't seen stars like this since my last night on the island. It felt like years ago.

Jared caught my eye and grinned. A million different words and things to say circled around my head, racing to the tip of my tongue and away again. Nothing seemed right. No words could come close to describing the way I was feeling right now.

"You like it?" Jared asked, stepping closer to me.

My voice was barely a whisper. "How did you find this place?"

"By doing all the things I've been telling you not to do. Sneaking around at night. Asking questions." Jared stuck his hands into his pockets. "This school isn't safe."

"So you keep telling me," I sighed. I sank to the ground, lying flat on my back and staring up at the stars. It was like staring into another world. A world of light and dark and dreams. One that I could reach and touch with my fingertips. "I feel safe right now, though."

Jared sat next to me, resting his elbows on his knees and looking skyward. "That's probably because I'm here."

I gave a soft laugh. "Probably."

I pushed myself into a sitting position, sighing. "I don't know anything about this," I whispered. "Jared, I don't know how to go to school. I don't know how to choose which table to sit at in the cafeteria, who to talk to, who to be. I grew up watching these movies and reading these books where the characters learn all that along the way by going to parties and football games and all of those things that don't exist anymore. I guess I thought that going to that party would help me figure that out."

Jared didn't say anything. He just looked at me, a crease between his eyebrows and lines around his mouth.

"You think I'm an idiot. As usual."

"God, no. I don't." Jared turned to face me fully. "But Lydia, you know those movies aren't real. They never were."

"Yeah, that's what my brother used to say."

"He was smart, your brother. And I bet if he was here right now, he'd say that you don't need things like parties to help you figure out who you are."

"Yeah, probably." I sniffled. "I really miss him."

"Me too," Jared said.

"You what?"

"I miss him too." Jared took a deep breath. "I lied when I said I didn't know Danny."

I wanted to accuse him, to scream and shout. But Jared had taken a chance for me tonight. He'd been kind and protective instead of angry and callous. So I looked up, took a deep breath, and asked, "Why did you lie?"

He stood and rubbed his mouth. "I lied because I know that once I tell you what I know, it's going to make you want to look for answers more. Not less. And I don't want you to get hurt. Neither would Danny."

He stooped down to look me in the eyes once again. "Lydia, I need you to promise me that if I tell you this, it's you and me from now on. I promise I will do whatever it takes to get these answers for you if you stop doing reckless things on your own." Jared held out a hand. "Deal?"

"Okay," I said. My voice shook as I took his hand in mine. "What do you know?"

"Danny was my roommate. He got here about a year after I did. He told me," Jared hesitated, "he told me that you were dead." Jared's last words hit me like a punch to the gut.

"What?" I whispered.

"You were all he could talk about. His little sister, who loved movies and coffee and," Jared chuckled softly, "who had a massive crush on his best friend."

I sputtered as Chris's face appeared in my mind's eye. "I did not!"

Jared raised an eyebrow but continued like I hadn't spoken. "He hated it, you know. What he said to you that last day on the beach."

My voice broke. "He told you about that?"

"He told me about everything, Lydia. We were best friends."

My shoulders shook but I said nothing, waiting on tenterhooks for his next words.

"Like I said, Danny was smart. He figured out pretty quickly that he hadn't really been shot. That this place isn't anything like it seems. And the disappearances are just the tip of the iceberg."

I remembered the girl on the gurney. My mouth went dry. "Disappearances?"

"It was a lot worse a few years ago. Now, Reed and the others only take a few per year, and mostly the older ones. But they still go."

"Where?" I whispered.

"I don't know. We weren't able to learn a lot. But it seemed to have to something to do with blood."

I shuddered. I didn't ask how they knew that.

"The longer Danny stayed here, the more convinced he became that he was next. He obsessed over it, spent every moment figuring out ways to protect himself. He wanted out of this place. Danny knew that leaving was the only way we'd ever be safe. Finally, after weeks of searching and sneaking around to places like this, he found something.

"Danny said there was a brick somewhere in this basement that retracted and lead to a passageway out of the mountain. I told him to wait for me, I told him not to go back." Jared swallowed, hard. "But he went without me. The next day, his bed was cleared off. All of his things were gone and so was he." Jared shook his head, staring at the ground. "It's my fault."

I mouthed soundlessly at Jared as his words rolled over me. "He…" I swallowed. "He might have gotten out of here." I didn't say my next thought. *Or he might have ended up on a gurney, pushed down the hallway in the dead of night.*

Jared shook his head sadly. "I'm sorry, Lydia. I don't see any way he could have without getting caught."

I suppressed a sob with my hand. After all these weeks of searching, standing in front of me was irrefutable proof that I wasn't crazy with grief or anything else. Danny *had* been here.

He had also died here.

"I know you're going to want to figure out what happened—who took him and why—but you have to trust me, Lydia. You've stuck out a lot lately. If you try and fight them, they'll just hurt you faster. That's why I've been trying to protect you. I don't want you disappearing the way your brother did."

"I don't care if I disappear," I murmured.

"That was Danny's problem. He didn't care about getting hurt. Once he started to suspect that you were alive, all he could think about was getting back to you and your dad. Don't make the same mistake he did. He's already gone."

"You don't *know* that."

"I do. And I can't watch you get yourself killed for him."

"You don't understand," I gasped, clutching at my stomach. Panicked guilt fluttered through my stomach. "He gave me his gun. He gave it to me, and it's my fault he was captured. It's always been my fault…"

"Lydia!" Jared dropped to his knees beside me, even though I didn't remember falling to the ground. The world spun in a hurricane of tears and guilt and heartache; I was drowning in memory.

"Lydia, I need you to calm down. Class is in just a few hours. Go back to your room, take a shower, and get though the day. Keep your head up, no matter how hard it seems."

Jared squeezed my hand tightly, and I gasped. The world zoomed into sharp focus. "You can't tell anyone what I just told you, okay? Not even those two you hang around with—Aaron and Kat. I don't know if they've been helping you so far, and I don't care. From now on, this is just you and me."

"Are you saying I can't trust my own friends?"

"I'm saying that Danny wouldn't have been caught unless someone close to him leaked his plans to Reed."

"Someone like you?"

"If I was leaking your movements to Reed, you'd be dead by now," Jared said flatly. "All I'm saying is that you've only known them for a few weeks. Ask yourself how well you really know them, and keep your cards a little closer to your chest."

"Closer to you, you mean." I raised an eyebrow.

Jared got to his feet and offered me a hand. "Danny thought it was funny, the way you used to watch so many movies. He said one of his best memories was when he was younger, playing with you and Chris in a lighthouse that faced the south side of the island. Danny trusted me, Lydia. He would have wanted you to trust me."

"I almost want to."

Jared's eyes softened. He moved closer to me and slipped his hands up my forearms to my elbows. "Look, I know I haven't been kind to you. But I care about you, Lydia. I do."

"Yeah, I can really tell by the way you yell at me at your every opportunity," I tried to joke, but my voice wavered.

"About that," Jared sighed. "No one can know about that we know each other as anything more than classmates."

I drew back. "Why?"

"Because I'm not sure Reed ever really stopped suspecting that I was involved in Dan's little escape plan. If he sees us together, he might think I'm at it again."

# CHAPTER THIRTEEN

By the time that I made it back to my room, I had less than an hour to get myself cleaned up and no time at all to sleep. I took a freezing cold shower and braided my hair back, hoping that the deep shadows under my eyes were just a trick of the light. Kat was still asleep when I left to grab breakfast, trying to ignore the steady burn behind my eyes.

I poured myself a cup of coffee and sank into a chair, leaning my chin on my fist. Most of the guilt that had crashed into me last night was gone now, fizzled away by fatigue. But the full weight of what had happened rested just behind the headache that forced my eyes closed, threatening to break free at any second.

"Lyd, is that you?" I jumped and opened my eyes, blinking rapidly. Aaron grinned and set his tray down next to me. It was stacked with pancakes. "Since when do you eat breakfast?"

"I don't. But today isn't happening without coffee." I held up my mug in a toast. Memories as bittersweet as the coffee danced in front of my eyes as I yawned.

"You don't look so good. Are you feeling okay?" Aaron asked. He scooted closer to me and pressed a hand to my forehead. "You're burning up."

"Am I?" I asked woozily. I didn't understand what was wrong with me—I'd pulled plenty of all-nighters on the island, but this felt different. Maybe it was the fresh air in my head after so long underground, or maybe I'd just gone soft from being stuck in this place for so long.

"I think you should see the nurse," Aaron said gently. He put his hands on my waist to steady me. "Can you stand?"

"Yeah." I got to my feet. My knees gave way underneath me. I flailed towards the table to steady myself and knocked the coffee mug to the ground.

It shattered at the exact moment my head hit the floor. Woozy, I stared at the lights that covered the cafeteria ceiling. The last thing that I saw before the world faded away were Aaron's dark, twinkling eyes.

\*\*\*

*"How you feeling, Champ?"*

*I rubbed my red nose, groggy. "Chris?"*

*"Nope. Danny." My brother sat in the chair next to my bed and mock-glared at me. "Hey. Why did you think I was Chris?"*

*I spluttered. "No reason."*

*"Oh, Lydia." Danny sighed. "But I guess I'm not allowed to be mean to you when you're sick, am I?"*

*I sniffled, and my head pounded like an alarm bell. "Nope."*

*"Fair enough. Dad sent me to check on you. You've been asleep a long time."*

*"How long?"*

*"About a day."*

*"Oh, no." I pushed at the sheets with weak arms. "I'm going to be so far behind!"*

*"Lydia, you're eleven years old. Believe me when I say that there are going to be plenty of opportunities to get the drillers when you're older."*

*"I'm plenty old now."*

*"You also have the flu. So, take it easy, okay?" Danny ruffled my tangled hair.*

*I jerked away. "I don't want to take it easy. I want to help!"*

*"If you try and help right now, you'll only get worse. I'll tell you what." Danny lowered his voice. "If you stay here in bed until you're well, I'll show you someplace really special, okay? Somewhere I've never shown anyone."*

*My gut tingled with curiosity. Danny was always out exploring the island while I was stuck inside doing my work—what had he found?*

*"Deal?" Danny asked. "I'd shake on it, but I don't want the flu. No offense."*

*"Deal." I smiled despite the wave of nausea that rolled over me.*

*"Get well, okay?" Danny stood and gave me a salute. "You're the smartest one here and you know it. We can't do this without you."*

*"I know," I mumbled sleepily. Danny's laugh was the last thing I heard before the world faded away.*

\*\*\*

"Melrose? Melrose, can you hear me?" Someone held a cold cloth to my forehead.

"Danny?" I mumbled, eyes closed.

"Donna," the voice answered.

My eyes flew open. The world spun around me, but Donna's face was in sharp focus. "No," I mumbled. "I'm okay…"

"Okay? You've been unconscious for almost three hours. Forgive me, Ms. Melrose, but you are *far* from okay." Donna frowned and moved away. I could see the office she'd used for my checkup all those weeks ago through the open door behind her.

I gritted my teeth and leaned back into the hospital bed I lay on. An IV poked into my left arm, pumping fluid into my veins. Colorful spots danced behind my eyes like TV static. "What's wrong with me?"

Donna clicked her tongue. "Bad case of fatigue, best I can tell. Have you been sleeping?"

"Um, yes?" my voice croaked.

Donna didn't look convinced. "Been feeling under the weather before today?"

"No."

"Ms. Melrose, if you intend to answer every one of my questions with *yes* or *no*, my job is going to be a lot harder."

"I felt fine yesterday," I grumbled. "I didn't sleep well last night, though," I couldn't help but admit. A bad night's sleep didn't necessarily mean plans to escape.

Suddenly, pain stabbed through the crook of my right arm, the one without an IV. A small scab stood against it, and bruises webbed down my forearm. My heartbeat spiked. "What's that?"

"Oh. I know your arms are a little sensitive, so I went ahead and drew some blood when you were out." Donna said the words like taking blood from people while they were passed out was the most normal thing in the world.

"What are you planning on…" I swallowed. "Doing with my blood, exactly?"

"I think I've told you before, dear. Routine tests." Donna snatched the wet cloth from my forehead. "And after today, I'd say I think you need quite a few more."

"No," I mumbled. "No more…testing." Danny's file had mentioned testing, and now he was gone.

"You'll have as much testing as I deem necessary," Donna growled. "We can't have you feeling unwell or fainting every time you have a restless night."

"No, I guess not," I said uneasily. It was incredible how scary a sweet-looking old lady could be. "When can I leave here, exactly?"

"As soon as you can stand without vomiting."

I just glared at her.

"Now, I want you to try and get some rest. I'll be back to check on you." Donna pursed her lips and left me alone in the office. Silence drifted around me except for the sickening drip of the IV from the bag into the tube connected to my arm. With the bright lights in the room and no clock, it was impossible to tell what time it was. Donna said it had only been a few hours—but could I believe her?

I jumped as the door in front of me opened. Was Donna back already? Then, Aaron stepped into the room, and my whole body relaxed. "Aaron," I murmured, lips spreading into a faint smile.

"Hey." Aaron snapped the door shut and leaned against it. "You feeling any better?"

"Not really," I sighed. "What time is it?"

"Dinnertime."

"Donna said it'd only been a few hours," I murmured.

"She probably didn't want to upset you. It's been a full day." Aaron sat on the edge of my bed and took my hand. "I came here earlier, but you weren't here."

My eyes widened. "What?"

"I brought you here after you passed out this morning, but when I came back you were gone." Aaron shook his head. "I figured they took you to a back room, so you could rest."

"Aaron, I've been unconscious since this morning. I don't know where I've been, I don't know what she did to me—"

"Hey, hey, hey." Aaron skimmed a thumb over my cheek. "You're just fine. You're going to be fine."

"I'm not," I stuttered, panicking. "I'm stuck here. My family is dead, and I'm no closer to finding out what happened to them. Donna keeps taking my blood like I'm some kind of feedbag..." My voice tapered off.

"You're going to be okay," Aaron repeated. "You're sick. You're not thinking straight. I'll stay right here until Nurse Donna gets back. No one will take you anywhere." He wrapped his hand around mine, a soft smile on his face.

"Thanks, Aaron," I murmured as I watched clear liquid travel through the IV tube and into my arm. "You're a good friend."

"I know. I'm kind of the best," he said with a wink.

"Ha, ha," I said dryly. I closed my eyes and leaned back into the pillows. "Tell me something," I said suddenly.

"Tell you something?"

"Something to take my mind off all this," I said. "I realized the other night, I don't really know much about you. Where are you from?"

"California," he answered. "Near the ocean. My family owned an old orange grove."

"An orange grove? I didn't think there were any of those left in the world."

"There are a few, and it went surprisingly okay, for a while," Aaron said. The slight smile on his face told me he had fond memories of the place, just like I did about life on the island. "Like you always say, most of the world still works. Like an old car on its last few miles. You know disaster's coming, but for now, you're still chugging along. We farmed the land. The sun shined. The rain fell. The oranges grew... until they didn't."

I nodded, knowing exactly what he meant. "What's your family like?"

"It's just my dad and my brother," Aaron said. "My mom died when I was little."

"I'm sorry," I said softly. "Mine, too."

"It's okay," Aaron said, shrugging. "It was a long time ago."

"Tell me about your brother." I smiled.

Aaron hesitated. "His name's Theo. We don't really get along very well these days."

"You talk to him?" I asked.

"Not often," Aaron said vaguely. "We just see the world differently. But I still remember what he was like when I was little. He taught me how to fly the small plane we had—an old crop duster."

I laughed. "Is there a high demand for crop dusters in the outside world?"

"Not exactly. But flying is a handy skill. There are still planes out there." Aaron paused. "What about you? I know you're from an island. Which one?"

"Somewhere near what used to be Hawaii," I said. "It was gorgeous. Always sunny." A bitter smile settled on my lips. "What I wouldn't give to be back on the island right now, toes in the sand, water rushing over my ankles."

"Sounds perfect."

"Yeah," I said. The world suddenly felt soft and warm and fuzzy. My eyelids were as heavy as lead. My lips fell into a sleepy smile.

Aaron said something in reply, but his voice was muffled like we were swimming underwater. He kept his hand in mine until his face faded out and the darkness swallowed me once again.

\*\*\*

I was discharged from the nurse's office after classes were over the next day, Donna having declared that my bout of fatigue had cleared. The missing time was driving me crazy, but there wasn't any way for me to find out what had happened. Not after my close call in the server room.

My stomach rumbled as I passed the cafeteria. I'd been sleeping for nearly two days, and I hadn't eaten anything since well before I'd been admitted to the hospital. Nothing sounded better than a plate of fries. I was almost to the cafeteria when someone caught my arm and pulled me down a deserted hallway.

"Jared," I gasped. "What are you doing?"

"What am I doing? What are you doing? Where the hell have you been for the past two days?" Jared's eyes searched mine, eyes wide and frantic. "I thought…"

His words died away. Before I knew what was happening, Jared wrapped his arms around me and pulled me against him. I relaxed into his touch, taking my first deep breath in days.

"I'm okay," I mumbled into his shoulder. I pulled back. "I thought that we couldn't…"

"We can't. But I had to make sure you're okay." Jared scanned my face. "Seriously, where have you been?"

"With Nurse Donna."

"You've been in the nurse's office for two days?"

"I… I don't know," I stammered, thinking of the time I'd lost. "I passed out at breakfast a few days ago. Aaron took me to the nurse's office, and I woke up there later that night. But when he came to see me at lunch, I wasn't there."

I rubbed a hand over my mouth, fighting to keep calm. "I don't know where they took me, but when I woke up…" I held out my arm, showing Jared the deep, blue bruises, painful to the touch.

"What did she do to you?" Jared murmured.

"I don't know. But I can't remember a thing from yesterday. You were right, Jared. I'm scared."

Jared put a hand on my good arm. "We'll figure this out. I promise. For now, just keep your head down, and you'll be okay."

"Jared, I didn't do a thing, and they did this to me anyway!" I felt hysteria creep into my voice. "What if they decide to do it again?"

"If they want to hurt you, they will. I can't stop them, much as I may want to. But believe me—the last thing you want to do is give them reason to take you again."

"Why are they doing this to us?" I whispered. "This is a school. Shouldn't it be a safe place?"

Jared let go of my arm and looked away. "You're right. None of us should have to feel afraid here. I don't know what they're planning. But, if sneaking out after hours was bad enough for them to keep you knocked out for two days..." he trailed off. "We have to be careful. We won't do anything else to attract attention until we figure this out, okay?"

"Okay," I whispered.

"Trust me." His face hovered inches from mine. The concern that pooled in his eyes was warm. Undeniable.

"Jared, I..."

"Trust me," he said again.

I closed my eyes for a moment, and when I opened them again, he was gone. I didn't move for a long time after he left, thinking of all of the terrible things that could have happened to me while I was asleep, and wondering what we could do to escape.

\*\*\*

"I thought I'd see you at dinner," Kat exclaimed as she shut the door behind her. She dropped her bag to the ground and rushed over to my bed.

"I wasn't hungry," I lied as my stomach gave a huge rumble.

Kat didn't look convinced. "The cafeteria's still open if you want me to bring you something."

"I'm okay, Kat, really. I'll be back in class tomorrow." I offered a smile.

"What happened to you? Aaron didn't say much."

I pushed myself into a sitting position and dangled my legs off of the bed. "I passed out. I'm not sure why."

"You're okay now?"

"Sort of," I mumbled. "I'm sure I'll feel better after I sleep in my own bed." My own words surprised me—was I finally starting to think of this place as home?

"I hope so." Kat bit her lip. "Do you think that maybe," she hesitated.

"Maybe what?"

"Maybe this has something to do with what happened in the lab," Kat said in a rush.

"The lab?" I couldn't think what she might be talking about.

"The thing with your *blood*," Kat whispered the last word. "Lydia, I have spent the last day and a half in the library researching everything I could about blood and coal dust. Even if the sample was tainted, that wouldn't happen. Ever."

"You think my mystery blood has something to do with why I was passed out for eight hours straight?" *Did the same thing happen to Danny?* I wondered, but I couldn't bring myself to explain my run-ins with Jared and the secrets he'd confided to me.

"Yeah. I do." Kat's words broke through my thoughts.

"That's crazy, Kat." I stood, pushing my hands back through my hair.

"It's not! Your blood is not *normal*."

"You don't know that."

"Isn't it at least worth it to make sure?" Kat asked. She reached for my arm. "I'm worried about you."

"What, you want to draw some more of my blood and run tests on it?" I yanked up my sleeve to my elbow, revealing the web of blue and purple bruising on my arm. "I think my veins are a little out of commission at the moment."

"Oh my God." Kat snatched my arm. Prickles of pain shot through it and I winced, not for the first time that day. "Who did this to you?"

"Nurse Donna." I tugged my arm from her grip, wincing. "I woke up with eight hours just *gone*. I need to figure out what she did to me, because I doubt I just slept in the nurse's office all day."

Kat sighed. "I'm willing to help, but I have to say I think whatever happened to you yesterday starts right there." She pointed at my arm.

"I told you. I don't think it'd be safe to take any more out of here." I shuddered at the very thought of any more needles.

"I didn't say anything about that." Kat's eyes glinted. "Listen. The nurse's office has medical files for every student here. Birth date, allergies, things like that."

Revulsion shuddered through my stomach. "Vials of blood?"

"It might be a long shot, but I think so. If any of your samples are there, we'll get our hands on them," Kat declared as if breaking into Donna's office would be as easy as grabbing a sandwich from the cafeteria.

"I thought you couldn't take any risks," I said. "Aren't you worried about getting kicked out?"

"I'm more worried that my best friend might die on my watch."

"Best friend?" My lips curved into a smile around the words. Something warm and fuzzy gathered in my chest.

"Of course, you're my best friend, silly." Kat wrapped her arms around me, standing on tiptoe to reach around my neck. I held her close, smiling into her hair. She pulled away after a moment, a small smile on her face. "We're in this together, okay?"

"Yeah," I said. "Together."

# CHAPTER FOURTEEN

"How many stealth missions are you planning on doing here, Lyd?" Aaron asked in disbelief.

"Just enough to make sure that Donna doesn't murder her," Kat said brightly. The three of us were wedged into our corner of the library, books stacked high around us and voices hushed. "There has to be a way."

"To break into the nurse's office? I don't think so," Aaron said flatly. "Did you forget that almost every single door in this sector except for the dorms are alarmed after curfew? Donna never leaves her office, not even to sleep. You'd need the glasses to get through every single door in that place."

"Don't you think I've considered all of that?" Kat snapped. "The three of us can do it."

"How the holy hell are you planning on pulling this off?" Aaron asked.

"We're going to do it together," I cut in. "You'll help us, right?"

"That depends on your definition of *help*." Aaron drew air quotes around the words. "If it involves gravely injuring myself in order to get into the nurse's office for example," he drew a finger across his throat. "I'm out."

"Hilarious." Kat rolled her eyes. "Listen, Aaron, we have it all worked out. Later this week, I'll pretend to get sick at lunch. You'll go and get Donna from her office. When she's fussing over me, you and Lydia will leave, sneak back into her office, and search for the vial. Lydia can be the lookout this time," she laughed.

"I'm supposed to just know where it will be?" Aaron furrowed his brow.

"You'll figure it out. You're a smart guy."

"Look at you, Romero. Taking charge for once." Aaron shrugged. "It's kinda sexy."

"First of all, you're not my type." Kat rolled her eyes. "Not that I really have a type, but still. Second, I wasn't there for you guys when I should have been—when you went into Reed's office. But I'm here now, okay?"

I wrapped an arm around Kat's shoulders. I felt a little guilty, letting the two of them take on my investigation, and I felt even worse when I thought of what Jared would say if he knew I was plotting something without him.

"Faking an illness and stealing from the nurse kind of sounds harder than sneaking through one door," Aaron said.

Kat ignored him and opened her Rosett. "Lydia and I were up all night. Donna's office might have an alarm, but I think we've developed a program that'll shut it down for a few minutes."

Aaron didn't smile. "And the glasses? I'll need those to get through the doors."

"I have a pair," I cut in loudly. "There were some down in the janitor's closet."

"Oh, really?" Aaron raised his eyebrows, surprised. "Where are they?"

"Our room." I crossed my fingers behind my back. "I've been keeping them hidden."

"Why didn't you mention them before?"

"I forgot." I offered a tight smile. "Aaron, please. I need you with me on this."

"And if we get caught?" Aaron asked skeptically.

"Since when has that mattered to you?" I asked, hurt.

"It doesn't. It's just, you're hurt, Lydia. We still don't know why you got sick. Do you really think it's a good idea to risk it this soon? What if you pass out again when you're inside?"

"That's a risk I have to take," I said quietly.

"I mean, wow. Okay." Aaron nodded slowly. "Yeah. Yeah, of course I'll help."

"Good." Kat pulled away from me and looked back at her computer. "Let's plan a heist."

Jared's voice whispered in the back of my head, warning me to lay low, but I ignored it. Danny had disappeared from within these walls without a trace, and it felt like it was just a matter of time before I disappeared, too.

\*\*\*

Kat, Aaron, and I decided to stage Kat's illness on Friday, so I'd have a few more days to rest. I spent the next few days in a jumpy panic, looking over my shoulder at every turn. Jared's words were a constant whisper in the back of my mind, warning me that if I did this, if I did anything *like* this, I'd be next to vanish. But I couldn't get something he'd said out of my mind—the brick in the basement. Was it possible that the brick Jared had told me about was the same one I'd been thinking about for weeks? Was it possible that my being able to see the paint that no one else could wasn't a coincidence?

Had Danny been able to see it too?

Aaron had been bugging me to see the glasses, but I'd brushed him off one time after another. As much as I trusted him and Kat, something in my gut told me that my strange ability was something I needed to keep buried. At least until we got ahold of that vial.

"Lydia, wake up." Someone shook my shoulder. I groaned as the last of some already forgotten dream trickled away.

"Kat?" I asked sleepily, throwing an instinctive hand over my face to protect it from flying Cheerios. "Are we late?"

"Not Kat. Aaron."

I opened my eyes blearily as I realized that Aaron was the one standing over me. "What are you doing in here? Where's Kat?"

"She let me in before she left for breakfast," Aaron explained. He smiled, revealing his dimples. Today, he was dressed in a black polo and khakis. It made him look older, somehow.

"Back to question one, then," I laughed and sat up, kicking the blankets off of my legs. "What are you doing in here?"

"What else?" Aaron pulled a cupcake from behind his back. "Ooh. Hold on." He shoved it into my hands and pulled a candle and lighter out of his pocket. He stuck the bright red candle into the cupcake and lit it. He stepped back with a smile. "Happy birthday, Lyd."

I mouthed soundlessly. My eyes filled with tears that I rapidly tried to blink away. I swallowed, watching the flame dance over the candle. Red wax dripped down the candle like droplets of blood. "How did you know?"

"Wish now, questions later."

I smiled down at my cupcake. The fact that Aaron knew about my birthday when I'd barely remembered it myself was better than any wish I could possibly think up. I remembered my last few birthdays—the ones spent alone in my room, my latest pop culture obsession shining from my laptop, wishing more than anything that I could spend them in the lighthouse with Danny and Chris, like the old days. And that's what I wished for now.

*I wish you were still alive, Danny.*

I blew out the candle and opened my eyes.

"So?" Aaron sat next to me and stole a bit of frosting from the top. "What'd you wish for?"

"A pony."

"Funny." Aaron grinned. "I hope this whole sneaking into your room thing before you were awake wasn't too much. I just figured that since you didn't tell anyone it was your birthday, you wanted to keep it on the down low."

"Something like that. How'd you know about it?"

Aaron shrugged. "I have my methods."

"Mysterious." I raised an eyebrow. "What about the cupcake?"

"What can I say? I'm friendly with the cafeteria ladies." Aaron winked. "Well?"

I laughed and took a huge bite out of the cupcake. The taste of rich chocolate filled my mouth and frosting smudged across my nose. I rubbed it away, almost choking.

"You've got something there," Aaron said cheerfully, pointing at the tip of my nose.

I swallowed the massive amount of cake in my mouth and rubbed my nose more vigorously. "Is it gone?"

"No," Aaron laughed. "Here, let me." Aaron pressed one hand against my cheek and used the other to wipe the frosting from my nose. "There. All better."

"Thanks," I said softly.

"Anytime." Aaron skimmed his thumb over my cheek. A nervous shudder ran through my stomach. Aaron's eyes were locked to mine and I stiffened, suddenly aware of how close he was sitting. Was it my imagination, or was he moving even closer? "Happy birthday," he said softly.

The door banged open and Aaron jumped to his feet, clearing his throat.

"Morning!" Kat burst into the room, smiling from ear to ear. She held two paper cups in her hands. "Coffee?"

"Thanks." I got to my feet and took one of the cups. "You guys are spoiling me today."

"You're only eighteen once," Kat pointed out.

"Yeah, I guess," I muttered.

Kat frowned. "Hey, what's wrong?"

"Nothing, nothing." I put the cupcake on my desk and wiped my hands on my sweatpants. "I guess I was just hoping that maybe since I'm eighteen now..."

"That someone from your island would come back and whisk you away?" Aaron asked.

"Something like that."

"Okay, this just got depressing." Kat clapped her hands. "Let's talk about something fun. Who's ready to steal a vial of blood?"

"I'm in," I said as I stifled a yawn behind my hand. "But maybe we should get through a day of classes before then."

"Couldn't agree more." Kat took a swig of her coffee. "I need the time to brush up on my acting anyw—"

Kat pressed a hand to her forehead. She swayed on the spot, blinking rapidly. "I don't feel so well." The coffee cup fell from her hand and smashed to the ground.

"Kat?" I rushed to her side and took her shoulders. "Aaron, help!" Kat slipped from my hands; her knees crumpled. Aaron caught her head before it hit the ground, his eyes wide and frantic.

"Kat? Kat, can you hear me?" Aaron slapped at her face, but Kat's eyes had slid shut.

"Is she breathing?" I asked desperately, groping for her wrist. Her heartbeat fluttered just beneath her skin, faint but steady "Go get Donna."

"Donna? But I thought you were worried about—"

"Get her!" I shouted. Aaron scrambled to his feet and raced through the door, leaving it wide open behind him. The last thing I wanted was to put my best friend in Donna's hands. But what choice did we have?

"Come on, Kat. Wake up." I shook Kat's shoulders, but she was still. I jumped to my feet, pushing my hair back and barely holding back tears. What the hell was wrong with her? Was she going to be okay? If she *was* okay, would she stay that way after a day in Donna's office?

I dropped back to my knees and brushed Kat's hair away from her face. "You have to get better," I said sternly, though my voice shook. "You're my best friend, remember? My *first* best friend. I can't do this without you."

"Move away!" Donna raced through the door, closely followed by a very worried-looking Aaron. Donna dropped to her knees, pulling a stethoscope from her scrub-clad shoulders. "What happened?"

"She had a sip of this." I picked up the coffee cup from the floor. "Then she just collapsed."

"Her airways are swelling—I need to get her into my office immediately. You, Taylor—Taylor!" Donna shouted when Aaron didn't respond. "What are you, deaf? Carry her!"

"Right, of course." Aaron jumped. "I've got her." Aaron picked Kat up, one arm under her legs and the other cradling her small neck.

"You coming?" Aaron asked.

"Of course." I grabbed a hoodie from my desk chair.

"I don't think so, Ms. Melrose," Donna paused in my doorway. "You've barely recovered from your little fainting spell. Besides, there's nothing you can do for her, and I need time to work."

"No, you can't." I withered under Donna's harsh gaze. What was I going to say? That I was worried she'd take Kat to some underground lab like she could have me? "*I* can't leave her," I corrected.

"You can, and you will. She's in good hands," Donna said gruffly. She turned to Aaron. "Well? Go!"

My shout caught in my throat; I was frozen to the spot. Coffee dripped from the cup in my hand down my arm and onto my shirt. I held the cup up to the light. Why hadn't Donna taken this with her?

*What if she was the one that did that to Kat in the first place?* I wondered. Drops of coffee dripped onto the carpet, one after the other.

I'd thought that my worst birthday ever was the one after Danny died. When I'd locked myself in my room and refused to eat, refused to talk, refused to come out. My dad tried everything—a cake, the promise of presents, even bringing Chris to the door. I couldn't even bring myself to get out from under the covers to answer the words he called through the door.

I just lied there all day, corners of my vision tinged with black, like the sadness was a void intent on swallowing me whole. The next years were better. I'd thought that my worst birthday was behind me.

I was wrong.

\*\*\*

The first few hours of the day were torture. Neither Kat nor Aaron showed up to first period, and the anxiety tingling through my gut grew with every second I sat in there without them. Even if Kat was awake by now, I knew Donna wouldn't let her out of her sight anytime soon. But what I couldn't puzzle together was Aaron. The Donna I knew wouldn't let Aaron stay in her precious office a second longer than necessary.

So, where the hell had he been all day?

I all but sprinted to chem lab, eager to get the first half of the day over as soon as possible. I yanked on my scrubs and pushed through the door, barely paying attention to where I was going until I crashed straight into someone.

"Hey, watch—Melrose?" Jared put steadying hands on my arms, eyes searching mine. "What's wrong?"

I shook my head. "It's Kat. She's in the hospital."

"Kat? Kat Romero?"

"She just collapsed," I whispered, "and Donna won't let me see her."

"I'm so sorry, Lydia. Can you try to calm down? It might be difficult to talk about this here," Jared hissed into my ear. I followed his gaze to Ms. Khan, who was frowning at us from across the room. He dropped his hands from my arms. A chill ran over my skin, cold from the absence of his touch.

"You seem awfully cozy with Ms. Melrose for someone who was protesting being her lab partner a few weeks ago," Ms. Khan said, crossing her arms as she stood next to us.

"What can I say? She's grown on me." Jared offered a tight smile. "We'll be going to our station now."

"I don't think so. Taylor, Desai!" Khan called. Two girls, including Lacey from the other night looked up, confused. "We're switching things up today. Taylor, you go with Melrose. Desai, with Carter."

The girls' faces fell into identical looks of annoyance. Lacey's friend, a tall, pretty girl with dark skin and hair whispered something into her ear.

"Whatever, Nikki," Lacey said. "Lydia! Over here."

Nikki mumbled something I didn't catch as I swapped spots with her. I cast a desperate glance back at Jared. If there was anyone, other than Aaron, who could help me figure out what had happened to Kat this morning, it was him. But I turned away from him and forced a smile as Lacey grinned at me.

"I've been wanting to talk to you again," Lacey said. "But it seems like you're busy whenever I see you."

"Oh, yeah. I'm busy a lot. With schoolwork and stuff." I resisted the urge to step away from Lacey. Her pearl-white smile was almost aggressive. Was it even possible for skin to be that clear?

"Schoolwork and stuff," Lacey repeated, drawing out the word. Though the rest of the class had started with the day's work, Lacey couldn't seem less concerned with the experiment in front of her. "Stuff that takes so much time you couldn't stay at my party for more than five minutes?"

"Oh. That."

"That," Lacey repeated, her voice all bubbles and venom. "I thought you were having a good time. What happened?"

"Oh, I felt sick. Lightweight, I guess," I joked uneasily. "We should really get going on this experiment."

"Okay," Lacey agreed. "Just remember that people talk, okay? And it would suck if someone would happen to talk about what they saw at that party."

I dropped my voice, every trace of fake enthusiasm gone from my face. "About what?"

"About nothing. Just that you were out of bed after hours and getting pretty cozy with Jared Carver."

"Are you threatening me?" I asked, shocked. What the hell was going on?

"Maybe." Lacey shrugged. "I guess that's up to you."

"What do you want?" I asked through grit teeth.

"Oh, Lydia, I want a lot of things." Lacey clicked her tongue. "But you can start by staying away from Aaron."

"Aaron?" I repeated, so shocked that the glare slid off of my face.

"Need me to repeat it?" Lacey's voice skipped, but she recovered quickly.

"Aaron and I are just friends," I said quickly. "If you like him, I'm not in your way."

"That's not what this is about. Just stay away from him, okay? It's important," Lacey said sharply.

"Why?"

"Stay away," she repeated. "Please."

I just stared at her.

Lacey took a deep breath. She fixed me with a calm look. "If I see you two together again, you and Jared might find yourselves explaining your little nighttime visit to the basement to Reed."

"Lacey, what are you talking about?" I asked, trying to puzzle together everything I'd just seen cross her face.

"Just stay away, okay?" she hissed. Just like in the hallway, her eyes seemed to be sparkling with more than just the light. With tears.

"Lacey."

Lacey's features snapped into a wide smile as Khan walked by us. "You ready to get working?"

"Yeah," I said slowly. "Born ready." I watched her carefully. My mind was racing. What on earth did she want with Aaron? I'd never even seen them have a conversation. Why was she so determined to keep me away from him? Would she really tell someone that I'd been out of bed after hours if I refused?

I wasn't worried about getting busted for the party. There were hundreds of people there. But I was worried about them checking the cameras and figuring out all of the other times I'd wandered around after curfew.

It took everything I had to keep my hands steady as we completed the experiment. But after a while, my worry about Kat overtook even my confusion about Lacey.

I went straight to the nurse's office after class; lunch was the furthest thing from my mind. I pounded the door. One, two, three minutes passed.

The door opened a sliver. "Can I help you?" Donna snapped. The one eye that I could see narrowed.

"I want to see Kat. Katerina."

"Katerina is still in critical condition. No visitors." Donna made to close the door, but I pushed back against it.

"Wait, wait, wait." Fear raced through my gut. It'd been hours—Kat wasn't awake yet? "What's wrong with her?"

"That's what I'm trying to figure out. Goodbye, Ms. Melrose." Donna gave the door a strong push and I stumbled backwards. I rattled the doorknob, but Donna had locked the door.

"Damn it," I muttered, pressing my hands to my forehead. I needed to find Aaron—he was the only one who would know what to do. Lacey's threats whispered in the back of my mind, but I swallowed my fear down. If I had to deal with Reed, so be it. Kat was more important.

I all but sprinted to the cafeteria, but when I reached it, Aaron was nowhere to be found. Out of breath, I turned away. Where would Aaron be if not the cafeteria? I still had no idea where his room was. Suddenly, the soft chatter from the cafeteria seemed a million times louder. Even though my legs and lungs were burning, I broke into a run, barely paying attention to where I was going until yells filled the hallway.

"And what you did last week, that was part of our agreement?"

"I'm done talking about this. Go back to class."

I froze, pressing my back against the wall so I'd be out of sight. One of those voices belonged to Reed, and the other was familiar but burning with so much rage that it was unrecognizable.

"We're not done here."

I peeked around the corner as the door crashed against the wall.

My blood froze in my veins. It was Aaron.

# CHAPTER FIFTEEN

I didn't go back to class. I couldn't. Numb, I returned to my room, where I huddled on my bed, staring straight ahead. There was a deep brown stain on the carpeting where Kat's coffee cup had fallen. The cupcake Aaron had brought me earlier sat uneaten on my desk. I'd almost forgotten that it was my birthday at all.

The seconds ticked by, bleeding into minutes and eventually hours spent staring across the room at Kat's things. The picture of her and Ivan was still tacked above her desk, shiny and sleek. Sometimes, late at night, I thought I saw Kat looking at it. But I could never be sure.

I thought that someone would come looking for me—Reed, or maybe one of my other teachers—to see why I wasn't in class, but no one came. The clock on my desk read nine thirty, a half hour before curfew, when someone knocked on my door. I jolted upright, staring at it.

Something white and thin slid under the door. I jumped to my feet and snatched it up, heart pounding.

There were only four words written on it.

*Tonight. Midnight. Our place.*

There was no signature, not even an initial. The words were messy, like they'd been scrawled in a hurry. I flipped it over. Still nothing. My gut told me that the letter was from Jared—instructions to meet him in the alcove under the stars tonight at midnight. But then something nagged in my brain— what if it was from Aaron?

*Don't be stupid. If it was Aaron, he would have come inside.*

All the same, it was odd that Aaron *hadn't* come to find me. Lacey was threatening me, not him. As far as I knew, there was no reason why he'd be avoiding me. Unless my nighttime escapades had something to do with the screaming match I'd overheard earlier today.

I shook my head and crumpled the note in my hand. If Reed knew about what I'd been doing, I'd be in the principal's office in the blink of an eye. There had to be a logical reason for Aaron's fight with Reed. Maybe a failed test or a minor curfew infraction. Something normal, completely unrelated to my illness last week. Unrelated to Kat's.

No, the letter had to be from Jared. I watched the minutes tick by on the clock, wondering where Kat was. If she was okay yet. If something had happened to her…I felt sick to my stomach at the very thought.

At twenty to midnight, I stole out of my room, wearing a black hoodie pulled low over my face. I couldn't help but wonder why it was safer for Jared and me to meet in the dead of night in an out-of-bounds area than in one of our rooms, but I was in no position to question it. Jared knew more about this place than just about anyone else, and if he knew something about Kat, I was going to take that risk.

Somehow, I managed to retrace my steps through the basement to the silver ladder. I took the rungs at double speed. By the time I reached the top, all of the breath was gone from my lungs.

"Who's there?" I recognized Jared's voice as I pulled myself off of the ladder. "Lydia! What are you doing here?" Jared jumped to his feet, his face twisted into confusion under the silvery moonlight.

"You told me to meet you," I gasped in between gulps of fresh night air. "You sent a note."

"What note?"

Puzzled, I pulled the message from my pocket and held it out to him. Jared snatched it from my hand, deep lines etched around his mouth. I watched him warily. "You sent this, right?"

"No," Jared said. "Where did you get it?"

"Someone put it under my door," I said slowly. My cheeks were suddenly burning. I'd read *our place* and just assumed that this little alcove was ours. The thought sent a little fluttering feeling through my stomach.

"It wasn't me. Did anyone see you leave your room?" Jared's eyes looked sharp and focused.

"I don't think so. Why?"

"Did it not occur to you that this might be a setup? That someone could have given you this note just to see what you'd do?" My heart pounded; shivers ran up my spine. I slowly turned to face the top of the ladder. *Was Reed at the bottom, just waiting for us to come down?*

"No. I didn't think of that." My mouth was suddenly incredibly dry.

"Damn it, Lydia," Jared breathed, one hand caught in his hair. "Are you sure no one saw you leave?"

"No. Jared, what is it? You're scaring me." I stepped towards him.

"If someone knows that we're here right now, we're dead. I told you last week that Reed suspects that I'm trying to break out of this place. What do you think he'll do if he realizes I discovered the only path to fresh air in this entire school?"

"I don't know," I whispered.

"Lydia, do you even think before you do anything? Your roommate is in the hospital having God knows what done to her and you're still putting yourself at risk by sneaking out after curfew? Who's going to help Kat if they take you away?"

"I thought the note was from *you*." My eyes stung with tears; the back of my neck was on fire. "You said we were in this together, Jared. What was I supposed to do?" Tears streamed down my face; tears of worry for Kat, anger at Jared, and fear that he could be right. "Last week, you risked everything to go to that party with me, and this week you're back to being worried that I'm just some clumsy little girl who'll ruin everything for you. Which is it, Jared?"

"I never said you were clumsy."

"You said I was an idiot," I recited. "You're always so quick to shame me for trying to get answers, but you're running around these tunnels every night looking for that stupid brick!" I shouted.

The anger slipped off of Jared's face. "What did you just say?"

"The brick," I repeated through gritted teeth. "I know where it is. I don't know if it actually leads out of here, like Danny said, but it's there. It's real."

"How do you know?" Jared asked urgently. Moonlight flashed from his eyes, but so did something else. Curiosity. Wonder. Desperation.

"It doesn't matter." I sighed. "I'm going to assume—correctly this time, I hope, that this note is from Aaron and pray that I'm not too late to meet him." *The note had to be from Aaron. Right?*

"Wait." Jared caught my arm. "The brick. Where is it?"

"Why do you want to know so badly?" I stiffened against his touch.

"Lydia, that brick could be the answer to everything."

I yanked my arm away. "You mean the answer you were looking for when you kicked me out of Reed's office that day? The one that got Danny killed?"

"What answer?"

"How to get out of here." I stepped away from Jared, watching his eyes carefully. "That's all you care about—all you've ever cared about is getting out of here, isn't it? Saving yourself before they can hurt you like they hurt Danny?"

Jared didn't answer right away. I could see gears working in his head like the ones in the back of a clock. "It's more complicated than you realize."

"More complicated than my brother's murder?"

"It's not that simple. Look, I'm sorry I yelled at you. I'm sorry for everything. But you need to tell me where that brick is."

"Why, so you can figure it all out and then go back to ignoring me after you get what you need?" I growled. "Apparently, I have someone else I should be talking to right now. I'm leaving."

"There are *reasons* I can't be seen with you!" Jared shouted. "I've already explained that to you."

"Yeah, you have. So, we don't have anything else to talk about." I tried to edge around Jared, but he jumped in front of the ladder before I could.

"Wait. You need to tell me where it is. It's a matter of life and death."

"Kat's life is the only one I care about right now."

"Fine. Go." Jared glared at me.

"Great. Then we're done here." I knocked into Jared as I passed him.

"Lydia," Jared said as I put my hands on the first rung.

I glared up at him. "What?"

"I hope Kat is okay."

I almost laughed. "Sure, you do. See you around, Jared." With those words, I descended the ladder. I didn't look back.

I ran all the way back to the basement stairs. My mind was reeling, and I barely felt the steady, agonizing burn in my lungs. I had no idea how much time had passed. All I could do was hope that Aaron was still in the library. No matter what had happened earlier today, including his shouting match with Reed, I had to see him. He was the one person who cared about Kat as much as I did.

When I reached the ground floor, I kept pace, slowing only to check around corners. At last, I reached the library and skidded to a stop in front of the door, panting. I peered into the dark windows, pressing my hands against the glass. There didn't seem to be anyone inside.

I pulled back and stared at the door handles. Would an alarm go off if I grabbed one of them? I backed away. I couldn't take that chance, especially when I was almost sure that Aaron was already gone. My eyes drifted to the number lock right next to the door. I blinked, and four of the numbers glowed neon green and brighter than ever. I frowned. Was I getting better at this?

*Would the alarm turn off if I punched in the code?*

It seemed unlikely.

I looked down the hall, towards the nurse's office. Fatigue burned my eyes like acid. Now that the adrenaline rush from my sprint was gone, my knees felt like they were about to give way. As worried as I was about Kat, the last thing I needed was a repeat of what had happened last week. I stumbled back to my room. It took me three tries to punch in the right passcode, but eventually, the door swung open.

"Lyd."

"Aaron," I gasped as I flicked on the light. Aaron sat on Kat's bed, his hands clasped in his lap. "Have you just been sitting here in the dark?"

"I thought it would draw less attention," Aaron explained. "Where have you been? Why didn't you meet me in the library?"

"I meant to. I'm really sorry," I pressed a hand to my forehead, reeling for an excuse. "I fell asleep for a few minutes. Still fatigued, I guess." I frowned. "How did you get in here?"

"Kat gave me the password. Are you okay? You look shaken." Aaron moved closer to me and brushed a piece of tangled hair away from my face.

I pulled away and sat on my own bed. "I am shaken. I'm worried about Kat—Donna wouldn't let me see her." I sighed. "I just really need some sleep. Then I can go break down that door tomorrow morning."

"I saw Kat today," Aaron cut in.

My mouth dropped open. "What? When?"

"Right after dinner. She's awake and doing fine. We can go see her together tomorrow morning."

I sighed, trying not to cry. Relief, sweet as honey, spread through my body until all of my limbs were jelly. "She's okay," I whispered.

"Yeah, she is." Aaron grinned. "But that's not even the best part."

"Best part?" I asked weakly. I sank onto my bed.

Aaron opened his fist, revealing a tiny vial of blood. "I managed to snag this when Donna wasn't looking."

I just stared at him, mouth hanging open. While I'd been moping on my bed all night, Aaron had not only gone to see Kat, but had gotten the thing we'd needed in the first place.

"Say something," Aaron suggested. His lips spread into a wide half-grin.

"Wow," I managed. "That's awesome, Aaron. Thank you so much."

"It was easy." Aaron sat next to me and held out the vial. "Happy birthday. Here's a vial of your own blood."

"Morbid," I giggled.

Aaron put a hand on my knee, a smirk on his lips. "Well, at least it's a day to remember." I stared at his hand. Something like fear, but softer, bubbled in my gut. I was alone in my room, for the second time, with Aaron. Suddenly all I could think about were his deep brown eyes, the freckles that ran just over his nose. And his lips, the shapes they made when they curled around a whisper.

*Or a shout.*

I leaned away from Aaron. "I need to ask you something," I said loudly.

Aaron gave his head a small shake. "What?"

"I saw you earlier," I blurted before I could stop myself. "Coming out of Reed's office."

The smirk slid off of Aaron's face. "Oh."

"I just...what was that all about?" I asked timidly.

Aaron didn't answer right away. He rubbed a hand over his chin. "How much did you hear?"

"Something about last week. And an agreement."

"Right. That." Aaron said. "It's complicated."

"Can you un-complicate it?"

"Reed and I have an agreement. Once every few weeks, I get to call out of here. I get to talk to my brother, Theo."

My mouth dropped open. Aaron was allowed to call out of here, regularly? It was *possible* to call out of here?

"He didn't give me my call last week. I missed the time we'd agreed on when I took you to the nurse's office. Not that I blame you, of course—" Aaron raked a hand through his hair, stumbling over his words. "I get why the conversation might have sounded weird. People don't usually argue with Reed."

"I'm sorry." I stood and put a tentative hand on Aaron's arm. "It was none of my business."

"Mm," Aaron replied with a shrug. He seemed to be avoiding my eye. My stomach sank. How could I have jumped to such bad conclusions about what I'd overheard?

"I know what it's like to miss a brother," I offered softly, leaning closer to him. "Tell me more about Theo."

"I don't want to talk about Theo," Aaron replied. He laced his hand with mine and moved even closer to me.

"Okay," I whispered. "What do you want to talk about?"

"I want to talk about us." Aaron put his other hand under my chin, gently guiding my gaze to his. My heart jumped to my throat, beating a million miles a minute.

"W—what about us?"

"Us. This." Aaron slid his hand down to my waist and my whole body tingled with warmth and something like anticipation.

"This," I repeated.

"Am I wrong?" Aaron whispered.

"Wrong about what?"

"That you want me to kiss you right now."

I stuttered. "What makes you think I want to kiss you?"

"Well, you're bright red. And you're not exactly moving away."

He was right. I wasn't moving away. Was it because I wanted this? Wanted him? Or did I just want something? Anything? Wanted to finally be kissed, after eighteen years of watching it happen on a screen?

I tried to swallow, but there was suddenly a knot the size of a baseball in my throat. "I just. I don't…" I trailed off.

My words fell away as Aaron closed the little space that remained between us and pressed his lips against mine. I froze. Movie scenes flashed behind my eyes as they slipped shut, of girls in sleek dresses, boys with dark hair with their arms around them. I wasn't one of those girls—the girls with jewels laced through their hair and gloss on their lips.

I kissed him back, hard. It was electric, intoxicating. Like I'd always thought it would be. But somewhere, beneath the sparks, it felt wrong.

I pulled away, feeling awkward.

"You're incredible," Aaron whispered. "You know that, right?"

I gave an uncomfortable laugh. "I almost believe you."

"Well, you should." Aaron peered at me, trying to catch my eye again.

"Maybe someday I will," I whispered.

He tried to kiss me again, but I pulled back, my lips twisted into a silent apology.

"It's okay," Aaron murmured. "I should get going."

I cleared my throat and stood, stepping away. "Goodnight."

"Come here." Aaron grabbed my hand and pulled me back. I linked my hands around his neck as he pulled me into a hug. "Tomorrow, we can talk more. Then, we'll go to see Kat."

"Right," I whispered, head fuzzy. "Kat."

But Kat didn't seem to matter much right now. As Aaron snapped the door shut behind him, leaving me alone, I found myself thinking about a different set of lips, of hands pressed into my skin in the darkness and a pair of brilliant green eyes.

# CHAPTER SIXTEEN

"Lydia? Lydia, why are you crying?" Danny stepped onto the balcony. The smile slid off of his face.

"Oh, hey, Danny." I jumped to my feet and smeared the tears over my face. The sea breeze felt icy against my wet skin. "What are you doing here?"

"What do you mean, what am I doing here? This was my spot before I showed it to you, remember?" Danny leaned against the rusty railing that ran the length of the lighthouse. His hair was long now; it reached to his shoulders. It made him look older, somehow. Or maybe that was just the stubble on his chin.

"Can it be my spot? Just for tonight?" I asked. I leaned my chin on my hands, sniffling. The night air was calm against my raw throat; the way that the stars and moonlight were reflected in the water below was breathtaking. Standing at the top of the lighthouse was like being in another world, somewhere suspended between the seas of stars above and below. Somewhere that I could slip away from everything and just be.

No war. No problems.

So why couldn't I stop crying?

"Which one was it this time? Ten Things I Hate About You? La La Land? Heathers? That's old school, even for you."

"Shut up."

"I'm serious. Tell me what's wrong."

"Nothing. Nothing is wrong," I insisted. "But please, just for tonight, let me cry over the fact that I'll never fall in love in peace." Silence followed my words, broken only by the creak of the old lighthouse and the summer breeze on the water.

"Lydia, you're so young," Danny said finally.

*"That's the point, Danny. I'm young. I'm fourteen. I'm supposed to be…drinking milkshakes, falling in love. I just feel like I'm missing out, you know? Sure, I might save the world someday. Turn things back to normal for everyone else. But what does that matter if I never get any of it?"*

*Danny stepped away from the railing and looked at me. Something was in his gaze, something more than the reflection of the moonlight. "I don't mean to kick you while you're down, but that's pretty selfish."*

*I turned to face him, my voice low. "Selfish? Having a crush on someone I'll never have is selfish?"*

*"I really hope you're talking about one of your actors, and not about Chris," Danny said.*

*I didn't answer. Of course, I was talking about Chris. The half-smiles he gave me when no one was looking, his brilliance. In a lot of ways, he was just as mythical as the guys I watched onscreen.*

*"We have it good here," Danny said. "There are people off of this island who don't even have food. But instead of focusing on making life better for people who have nothing, you want to mope about not having a boyfriend. Did you ever consider that I'm in the same boat as you? Don't you think I'd love to be captain of a football team with a beautiful girlfriend? But I can't have that. I'm never going to have that. I've accepted it. If I can help end this war so that someday people have that again…" Danny crossed his arms and turned away.*

*"Danny, I'm sorry," I muttered. "I never realized."*

*"It's okay. I know you didn't." Danny's long hair blew away from his face in the wind. "I'm sorry too."*

*"You don't have anything to be sorry about," I sniffled. "You're right. I'm never going to fall in love. But maybe I'm just not meant to."*

*"You don't know that. You have a long life ahead of you." Danny clapped me on the shoulder. "Anything can happen."*

*"Yeah," I muttered, turning back to face the dark, endless sea. "Anything."*

\*\*\*

When I woke up the next morning, all I could think about was Aaron. His dark hair, curly at the ends. His smooth skin pressed against mine. I'd spent the first seventeen years of my life dreaming about something like this—

having a boyfriend to hold hands with in the halls and steal kisses with between classes. But now that someone seemed interested, I had no idea what to do.

How was I supposed to react the next time I saw Aaron? Kiss him? Ignore him? Hug him? Shake his hand? Then there was Lacey, her threats warning me to stay away from Aaron, and my tentative promise I would... a promise I'd now clearly broken.

I rubbed my eyes with the back of my hand and sat up. I looked over at Kat's empty bed and a pang rippled through my gut. It had been almost a full day since I'd seen her, and I'd been so focused on my own problems, I'd barely thought about going to the nurse's office to make sure that she was still alright. I raced through my morning routine and threw my bag over my shoulder, barely bothering to see if I had all of my supplies for the day.

"Donna?" I pounded on the door to the nurse's office the second I reached it, rattling the doorknob with my other hand. "I want to see Kat!"

No answer.

"Donna?" Worry trickled into my gut. What if, even though Kat had been fine last night, she wasn't fine this morning? "Donna!" A few more minutes trickled by. Was Donna simply not there, or was she ignoring me? My eyes went to the keypad beside the door. The code was there, clear as day. I could open it.

But what would happen if Donna was inside? Something told me that advertising my ability to break into any door in the school wouldn't be a great plan. But even as the warning bell clanged overhead, I knew I couldn't leave without knowing that Kat was okay.

I punched in the code and the door clicked open. "Kat?"

"Mm?" A soft voice replied. I raced inside and slammed the door behind me. Kat lay on a hospital bed in the next room, an IV in her arm. "Lydia."

"Kat." Relief flooded my voice as I rushed to her side. "How are you feeling?"

"I've been better," Kat mumbled, rubbing her eyes. Her skin seemed unusually pale; was it my imagination, or were the webbed veins standing out in her face and arms more prominent that usual?

"Has Donna been treating you okay? I tried to come see you yesterday, but she wouldn't let—"

"Hey, everything's fine," Kat said, offering a faint smile. "I'm okay now."

"Now?"

"Yeah, yesterday was rough." Kat looked down, sadness fluttering across her face.

"Rough? How?"

"Everything kind of hurts a lot, to begin with," Kat said with a grimace. "And the dreams didn't help."

"Dreams?"

Kat didn't answer right away. "It's not important. What did I miss?"

I thought about everything that'd happened in the past twenty-four hours: Lacey's threats, my meeting with Jared, the kiss with Aaron...

"Not much," I lied. "Did Donna say what happened to you?"

"Dehydration and stress," Kat replied. "Apparently, that can cause severe pain and fainting. Seems plausible, right?"

"Sure." I nodded but worry tugged in my gut. "I'm really glad you're okay."

"Me too. Hey, how'd you get in here? Donna said she'd be out for a while."

"Magic," I said vaguely. "Did she say when she'd be back here?"

"Hopefully, not anytime soon because if you used the glasses to get in here, you're going to be in a lot of trouble."

"It's okay. I can just tell her that the door was open a crack or something."

"Was it?"

"Nope."

Kat peered at me curiously but seemed to decide against asking me about it.

"I heard you saw Aaron yesterday," I said, and then immediately regretted it. I wasn't sure if I wanted to tell Kat about the kiss or not. I wasn't even sure where I wanted things with Aaron to go. So why had I brought it up?

"Aaron?" Kat asked. "No, he wasn't here. Not that I remember."

"Oh."

Kat sat up straighter. "Did he say he came by?"

"Yeah, he said he talked to you," I said, puzzled.

"Well, I must have been sleep talking. I was out pretty much all day yesterday." Something lingered in Kat's gaze—anger? Disappointment?

"But he said..." I bit my lip. Though last night was a blur, I was certain that Aaron had told me he'd talked to Kat. Was it possible she'd forgotten? "He had a vial—*the* vial of my blood."

Kat didn't smile. "How is that possible?"

"He said he got it when he was in here last night," I said slowly.

"I mean; I guess it's *possible*." Kat's words dropped away, leaving a sterile silence between us. My mind raced. If Aaron hadn't really been here last night, why had he said he was? I fixed my eyes to the door I knew lead to more exam rooms and Donna's office. Could I slip in and out before she got back?

"Don't," Kat warned.

"Don't what?"

"Look, I know that I was planning to fake sick yesterday, but actually *getting* sick was really scary. Let's not try anything until I'm better, okay?"

I took her hand. "Of course. I'll lay low. Promise." I winced as the bell rang overhead. "Guess I'm late for Jamison's class."

"Skip it," Kat yawned. "See if you can snag me something from the cafeteria."

"Are you supposed to be eating solid food?"

"What's your point?"

"I'll see what I can do. Need anything else while I'm skipping class?"

Kat thought for a moment. "Can you bring me my photo?" She asked finally. "You know, the one of Ivan and me?"

"Sure." I nodded. "Have you been thinking a lot about him?"

"About all of them," Kat mumbled. "My mom, my dad, Ivan, Rosa..."

"Who's Rosa?"

"My little sister. She was only about a year old when I left."

I hesitated. "Kat, how exactly did you get here?"

"What do you mean?" Kat asked, frowning.

"Who brought you here? You said you grew up in Detroit, and I'm pretty sure that's halfway across the country."

"I took the test," Kat said, looking at me like that should have been the most obvious thing in the world.

"What test?"

"The placement test," Kat said slowly. "Didn't you take one?"

Wordlessly, I shook my head.

"Sorry," she yawned again. "I assumed you took it sometime before the… the incident with your dad."

She paused again, as if considering where to begin. "I'm sure it was different on your island, Lydia, but back home, things got pretty bad. A few years ago, they decided to implement this 'save the children' program, to keep them hidden away and out of the crossfire. One part of the plan involved setting up advanced schools like this one. Instead of staying on the street or ending up in some group home, I took the test, and was placed here. It's one of the best schools, which is why I'm not crazy about taking risks. I can't afford to get kicked out."

"They gave you a test and then just took you away from your family?" I repeated.

"For someone who knows the exact date of the Battle of Incitement, you're pretty clueless about the world," Kat laughed. "No, they didn't just drag me away. I got a letter and made the choice to leave. I couldn't stay there."

"Is it really that bad?"

"There was fighting nearly every night. We lived in a two-room apartment. I shared a room with Ivan, and Rosa slept in my parents' room. My mom went to medical school before she had us, so people came to us for help a lot. They paid what they could. That's kind of how it is, now. The people who can still afford it go to stores and buy things, but mostly we trade. The only jobs that even pay anymore are government ones."

"Like what?"

"My dad worked for the water treatment plant. It paid, but not a lot. Not enough to support three kids."

I thought of my easy life, back on the island. No matter how isolated I'd felt, I'd had everything. Food. Family. All the books and movies I could ever want. I knew what was happening on the outside world, but somehow, it hadn't seemed real.

It seemed real now,

"Did I ever tell you what happened to Ivan?" she asked suddenly.

"You don't have to tell me," I said quickly.

"I want to." Kat bit her lip. Her words slowed. "When we were about twelve, he got really sick. He was passing out, could barely hold down food…it was like the flu, but worse. Much worse. My mom couldn't help him, so we used the last of the gas in our car to get him to what was left of the hospital. There was nothing they could do."

"Kat," I said quietly.

"He was in a lot of pain for a long time. But he was smiling, until the end. We played wall ball against the wall of his hospital room. I even let him win once or twice. He knew it, but he didn't stop me. We even played the day he died."

"I'm so sorry."

"It was a long time ago," she said in a small voice. "It's just, the doctor said that the disease had something to do with his DNA—with his genes. And we're twins. It was a miracle I didn't get sick when he did. So, when I got the chance to come here, I took it. My life depended on it." Kat's eyes shone; she looked close to tears.

"I'm sorry," I said again. I didn't know what else to say. "I'll get that stuff for you. It's not like I can walk into Jamison's class now anyways."

"Not without getting detention, that is. Though I wouldn't put it past him to punish me for being out sick. We could be detention buddies."

"As appealing as that sounds, I think I'll get going," I laughed. "You gonna be okay?"

"Yeah," Kat said, though she winced. "But Lydia, don't tell Aaron you saw me."

"Why?"

"Because he's lying. I definitely was not awake last night." Kat dropped her voice. "He might be lying about the blood too."

I shook my head as icy cold prickles of dread ran up my spine. "He wouldn't lie. It must be a misunderstanding or something."

"And maybe it is. But until we know for sure, just be careful, okay? Promise me." Kat watched me intently, lip caught between her teeth.

"Okay, I promise." Worry pooled in my heart like tar as I stepped back into the hallway and snapped the door shut behind me.

*He had an explanation for the argument with Reed,* I reminded myself. *There's an explanation for this too.*

"There just has to be," I muttered to the empty hallway, even though I didn't believe it.

# CHAPTER SEVENTEEN

When I knocked on the door to the nurse's office a half hour later, Donna answered the door. "Can I help you?"

I held out the photograph, stuttering. "I thought Kat might like this. Can you give it to her?"

"You should be in class."

"Well, I'm not," I said with a weak attempt at a smile.

"That much is clear."

"Please just give it to her," I said tiredly.

Donna considered me for a moment, dark brows pulled low over her eyes. "Fine," she said finally. She snatched the photo from my hand. "Now *get to class*."

"Right away," I mumbled, turning away. As much as I hated the idea of sitting through more classes while Kat lay alone in the office, I knew I couldn't do anything else for her. In Chemistry, I worked my way through the lab alone. Jared barely looked at me, let alone spoke to me. A tangled knot settled in my chest and stayed there through all of my other classes. When I finally made it to the cafeteria for dinner, I was completely burnt out, both physically and mentally.

I grabbed a hamburger and fries from the cafeteria, but neither of them seemed very appetizing. I just stared at them, occasionally stabbing a fry at a puddle of ketchup until Aaron set down a tray across from me.

"Where were you this morning? I was worried." Aaron frowned. "I thought we were going to see Kat."

I glanced up at Aaron and quickly away again. "I tried. Couldn't get in."

"Was Donna there?"

"If she was, she didn't answer. But you saw her last night, right? I think she's okay." I bit my cheek, waiting for Aaron to latch onto the bait.

"Yeah, I talked to her. She misses you," Aaron said gently. He reached for my hand, skimming his fingers over mine. I bristled under his touch but forced a smile. Something just didn't feel quite right about holding hands with him. My stomach flipped, but not in a good way.

"I miss her too," I said, probably too loudly. A few people at other tables looked over at me and I quickly lowered my voice. "You think we'd be able to get in tonight?"

"I don't think so," Aaron said, frowning down at his food. "If Donna wasn't there earlier, she's probably back now. And besides, we got what we needed, right? As soon as Kat gets out of there, we can take it to the lab sometime and run tests."

"Run tests," I echoed. "Aaron, my blood made coal dust dissolve into thin air. How the hell are we going to figure out what's wrong with me?"

"First of all, there's nothing *wrong* with you, or your blood. And I thought you wanted to do this." Aaron squeezed my hand. "What happened to Kat is scary, but you can't stop looking for answers just because something might happen."

"Something like what?"

"You know, just…something," Aaron said dismissively.

I nodded, looking away from him. A million different thoughts banged against each other in my head like pots and pans. There had to be a good explanation as to why he was lying about Kat. Maybe he was trying to protect me. Or her. But then I remembered the red-hot anger that had colored his voice as he shouted at Reed. The easy way that he seemed to lie about what had happened last night. Who was the boy sitting in front of me right now?

It would be so easy to fall into being with him. We were friends. We got along. He liked me as more than a friend, and I could learn to like him back. Right?

A shock of blonde hair caught my eye from across the cafeteria and I started, pulled out of my reverie. Lacey glared at me. Her eyes flickered between Aaron and me. Slowly, she tilted her head towards Jared, who was sitting alone at a nearby table.

I jumped to my feet. "I have to go."

"What? Why?" Aaron stood, deep worry lines around his eyes. "I'll come with you."

"No, I just have to go," I insisted, swinging my bag over my shoulder.

"You didn't eat anything."

"Not hungry. I'll see you later. I'm sorry, but I have to go."

"I guess." Aaron's frown stuck to his face as long as he was in eyeshot. My heart pounded. Would sitting with Aaron just now be enough for Lacey to make good on her threat? If Reed found out that I was sneaking around the basement...

"Melrose, wait." I whirled around, heart pounding. Jared jogged to catch up to me. "What's going on?"

"What do you mean what's going on?" I snapped, not bothering to slow down.

"You just jumped up in the middle of dinner and left. People noticed. I noticed." Jared waited for a reply, but I gave none.

"Is something going on with you and Aaron?" He pressed.

"One, that's none of your business. Two, why do you care?" I asked tiredly. "I thought you were done talking to me after what happened last night."

"Lydia, you were the one who walked away from me," Jared said quietly.

I hated how he could still make my stomach zing just by using my name. I whirled around. "What is your problem?"

"Keep your voice down," Jared hissed. He pulled me down an empty hallway. "Did you tell Aaron about the brick?"

"I should have known that the stupid brick is all you care about," I spat.

"That's not true. I haven't been using you just to get out of here."

"I know," I admitted, "but I don't think you're just looking out for me, Jared. I think you have it in your head that you owe Danny or something."

The anger faded from Jared's face. "That's not..."

"I think it is," I said softly. This time, when I tried to pull my arm away, he let me. "But I agree with you. Yucca Mountain is not safe. I want out of here as much as you. But where do we go from here?"

"There are places we can go. If you come with me, you'll be safe."

"I can't go without Kat and Aaron."

"Fine—bring them. If you think you can trust them absolutely, bring them." The word *absolutely* bounced around my head. I trusted Kat, but did I really trust Aaron absolutely? *Could* I trust him absolutely?

"That's not all I have to do," I said quietly. "I need to find out what the Latium project is."

Jared's eyes went wide. "Where did you hear that name?" he demanded. "Did someone tell you that name?"

I stepped back, alarmed by the intensity in his eyes. "No one *told* me."

"Then *how?*"

"I hacked the server." I shrugged as if it had been an easy feat.

"That's not possible."

"Trust me, it is. And I need to do it again, unless you want to tell me what the project is."

"I don't know what it is," Jared said slowly. Gears whirred behind his eyes.

"You're unbelievable," I hissed. I shoved his chest with both hands. "Even after everything, you're still lying to me!"

"It's not safe."

"News flash? It's never going to *be* safe," I said. "I don't care about getting hurt, Jared. I care about getting answers. I'm sorry, but nothing you do or say is going to change that." I took one last look at him before turning away.

I ran before he could see the tears gathering in my eyes.

\*\*\*

That night, I stared at the ceiling for hours, exhausted but unable to sleep. Voices—Jared's, Aaron's, Danny's, my own—hissed relentlessly in the back of my mind, no matter how many times I told them to be quiet. When I finally fell into a doze, well after midnight, it was only to be woken what felt like seconds later by something tapping against my face.

I opened my eyes blearily. Kat grinned and threw another cheerio at me. It bounced off of my forehead, but I barely noticed. I jumped to my feet and threw my arms around her, all trace of sleep gone from my mind.

"I have never been so happy to be assaulted with breakfast cereal," I shouted. "They let you go? Are you feeling better?"

"I'm fine," Kat laughed, wriggling out of my grasp. "According to Donna, it was just a nasty bout of 24-hour flu. Hell if I know how the flu virus got down here, but it's gone now."

"Thank goodness," I said weakly. "Are you going back to class today?"

"Guess I have to," Kat sighed, throwing her hair over her shoulder. I frowned. Was it my imagination, or were her collarbones sticking out further than usual?

"We should get some breakfast," I said quickly. "You must be starving."

"Good idea." Kat threw another handful of cheerios at me from the bowl on her desk and I shrieked, shielding myself. Even though my head was pounding with fatigue, I couldn't wipe the smile off of my face for anything. Kat was okay. And she was going to stay that way.

\*\*\*

To my surprise, Jamison barely acknowledged Kat's return to his classroom. Although I didn't *want* her in detention, something about it seemed off. The Jamison who had given me detention on the first day of school would have made a snide remark at least. But he just rambled on about the various renewable energy failures back when the war was just beginning.

I leaned my chin on my hand, actually mildly interested about how the pollution in the atmosphere rendered solar power useless and screwed up the tides.

It was only when the bell rang at the end of the class that I realized that Aaron wasn't sitting beside me. I stared at his empty chair. Fear rippled through my chest. How could I have gone the entire class without noticing that he was gone? What if something had happened to him?

"Kat, hey." I caught her arm as we started towards Chem lab. "Have you seen Aaron today?"

"I was with you all morning, remember?" Kat asked, frowning. "Are you feeling okay?"

"Yeah. I'm fine." I tried to shake away the dread prickling down my neck, but it only pooled in my gut, making me feel sick to my stomach. "Let's get to class."

When we got to the labs, we were greeted by a very irritated Ms. Khan.

"Melrose, Romero? Desai will be joining your lab group today."

I followed her gaze to Nikki, who was already at a station. "Why?"

"Ms. Taylor will be out for a while," Khan said dismissively. "Get to work."

I just stared at her—Lacey, gone? What had happened to her? Did it have anything to do with her threats?

*Don't be insane. No one knew about that.*

"Lydia, come on." Kat tugged on my arm. "People are staring." She pulled me over to the lab station, where Nikki was waiting with a sour look on her face.

"Took you long enough." Nikki raised a thin, shaped eyebrow at Kat. "Go get the acid."

Kat opened her mouth but seemed to decide against arguing. She ducked her head and wandered off to get the chemicals.

I rounded on Nikki the second Kat was gone. "Where's Lacey?"

"Gone," Nikki said shortly.

"For how long?"

"Seeing as I got a new roommate this morning, I'd say quite a while." Nikki pursed her lips. "Now shut up and let's get this done."

I fell silent, mind racing. Lacey couldn't just be...*gone*. I clutched the table as Jared's words from all those weeks ago raced back to me. *It was a lot worse a few years ago. Now, they only take a few per year, and mostly the older ones. But they still go.* Was it possible that Lacey was the latest victim of these disappearances? Was she strapped to a lab table in the basement, or hidden down there beneath a white sheet?

Did it have anything to do with the Latium Project?

I tried to shake the thoughts away, but worry still prickled up my spine as Kat returned with the chemicals and we got to work. Our beaker fizzled, sending pure white vapor into the air. I made notes without really paying attention. All of my thoughts were about Lacey Taylor.

*Taylor.*

I stopped writing and looked straight ahead. I'd heard that name somewhere else—Donna, who called everyone by their last names, had called Aaron "Taylor" when Kat had been passed out on the ground. Was that a coincidence, or were the two related? They didn't look a thing alike, but it was always possible.

Although I had the distinct impression that Jared was trying to catch my eye during the last few minutes of lab, I ignored him. I needed to find Aaron to ask him about Lacey. Now that she was gone, I could talk to him without worrying about what she might tell Reed. Jared and I were off the hook—for now.

I was jumpy until lunch, all shaky hands and darting glances. Every turned page, every cough set my nerves alight. When I finally reached the cafeteria, it was like I couldn't breathe until I spotted Aaron across the room.

"Hey," I said breathlessly as I slid into the seat across from him. "I need to talk to you."

"You didn't seem interested in talking last night," Aaron said. He stabbed a French fry at the splash of ketchup on his plate.

"About that," I sighed. "I'm sorry."

Aaron sighed and pinched the bridge of his nose. "Whatever. What's up?"

"It's about…It's about Lacey."

"What about Lacey?"

"She's missing."

"Missing?" Aaron asked. "What do you mean, missing?"

"I mean she's gone. She's just gone. No one knows what happened to her." I looked across the room, where Nikki was sitting, alone.

"So? What do you care?"

"What do I care?" I repeated. "I care because one second she was here, and now she's not. Her best friend doesn't have a clue where she is. And I can't help but think that it could happen to any one of us."

"Like it happened to your brother?"

"Yeah. Like that." I pushed air out of my mouth. "And I thought that maybe you would care."

Aaron looked up, frowning. "Why would I care about Lacey?"

"I couldn't help but notice that you two have the same last name, and…" I hesitated, "she told me to stay away from you."

Aaron raised his eyes to mine, and a knot grew in the pit of my stomach. There was something in his gaze—anger or fear. I couldn't tell which.

"We're cousins," he said shortly. "We weren't ever really on the best terms." He didn't elaborate.

"Oh." I didn't know what else to say. Thankfully, Kat appeared at Aaron's shoulder a second later.

"Long time no see," she said as she dropped into the seat next to him. "Where were you this morning?"

"Places." Aaron shot Kat a signature smile. "I overslept. It's not like I got sent to the hospital or anything."

"Too soon." Kat pushed his shoulder.

Aaron smiled and draped a hand over Kat's shoulders. Something bubbled in my chest, burning, and stinging as it rose to my throat. "I'm going to get some lunch," I said loudly, hoping they wouldn't notice that the back of my neck was burning bright red.

What the hell was going on? One day, Aaron was kissing me, telling me that I was incredible. Now, because I'd walked away from him once, he was flirting with Kat. It felt like the air was made of maple syrup; each breath was a struggle.

I stared at my faint reflection in a panel of glass. The light hit it just enough that I could see my dark eyes staring back at me. My eyes had always been my favorite part of my appearance—something about their rich brown made me feel older—more powerful than a small, weak girl who couldn't hit the side of a building with a shotgun. They were my father's eyes. They were Danny's eyes.

I imagined what Danny would say if he could see me now, almost in tears over an arm draped over a shoulder. *Are you kidding, Lydia? You're really going to get worked up over* that *guy? You don't even like him that much!* I could almost hear the disappointment in his voice—and the exasperation. In the reflection, my eyes narrowed. Whatever was happening with Aaron, it wasn't worth feeling sick over.

When I returned to the table, I flashed a smile and set down my tray. Aaron still had his arm around Kat.

"We were just talking about you," Aaron said as I sat down. "Now that Kat's better, do we want to revisit the issue of the..." He took his arm from Kat's shoulders and rubbed a hand over the crook of his arm.

Kat's smile slid off of her face as our eyes locked. I bit my lip. After everything that had happened to her, I was just glad she was alive. Jared had been warning me about flying under the radar for months—it was getting caught that got Danny into trouble. Was it really likely that something in my blood had dissolved coal dust?

"I'm not sure we," I paused, choosing my words carefully, "I don't think it's worth the risk. We'd have to, what, sneak into the labs late at night to do that? I can't ask you guys to risk that."

"I think we should wait a while before we go doing anything crazy," Kat agreed. "I'm worried."

"That what?" Aaron asked. "We'll get caught? We can just tell them that it's some extra study time or something."

"It's not that. Listen, I'm not so sure that what happened to me was an accident." Kat said the words in a rush, staring down at her food.

"What do you mean?" I asked.

"I mean I think that there was something in that coffee I drank—I've read up on different kinds of toxins, and my symptoms are completely consistent with an overdose of Anagrelide."

"Anagra-what?" Aaron raised a skeptical eyebrow.

"Anagrelide. It's a blood thinner."

"And you think that someone spiked your coffee with it?

"I think that I need to be careful for a little while." Kat frowned at Aaron. "Is it really so hard to believe that I might have been poisoned?"

"Of course not," I said. "After what we've seen at this school, I'd say it's more than likely."

"I think I thought hearing you say that would make me feel better, but it didn't," Kat said, forcing a chuckle. "I'll see you later, okay? I think I should lie down."

I offered a small wave, and then it was me and Aaron alone at the table. An awkward silence filled the air. I stared down at my hands, wondering what I wanted. I still had no idea. But I knew I wanted to figure it out.

"So," I said finally. "Are we ever going to talk about the other night?"

"What night?" Aaron raised an eyebrow.

"My birthday," I said quietly.

"Oh. That. I think…I think we should just forget about that," Aaron said.

I just stared at him. A sick feeling that had nothing to do with the questionable cafeteria food on my plate rippled through my gut. "Forget about it?"

"Yeah. No big deal, right?" Aaron flashed a smile.

"Yeah," I echoed. I had my answer. "No big deal."

# CHAPTER EIGHTEEN

It felt as though my friendship with Aaron had dissolved. It had been weeks since Kat's accident, and we'd barely spoken since that time. We worked side by side in first period, but never together. The days trickled by like sand in an hourglass. Like blood being drawn through a tube. I spent my time in my room, trying to scheme up ways to get back into the server room, but after a while, I had to face the truth—I couldn't do it. Not without help. And not without Aaron.

But Aaron didn't want me anymore. I was pretty sure I didn't want him, either, but somehow, his rejection hurt.

I kept replaying his words over and over in my head, both the ones from that night, and the ones he'd used to dismiss me faster than one of Jamison's homework assignments.

Maybe it was for the best.

I spent my days in near solitude, hanging out only with Kat, and leaving my room only when necessary. I thought that someone might come to contact me now that I was eighteen. Technically, I was eligible to rejoin the armed forces, and my father had already trained me as a recruit for the Cyber sector. It would be only too easy for me to rejoin. But as the days passed, no one came for me. I aced all of my work quietly, trying to get Aaron and Jared out of my head.

I hadn't talked to Jared in weeks. His ultimatum crossed my mind every now and then, but I doubted it still stood. If he got out of here...he'd get out of here alone.

"So, I've been thinking," Kat said one night, well after curfew, "Maybe we should look back into the blood."

"No," I said quickly. "Remember what happened to you? Remember what happened to Lacey?"

"We don't know for sure what happened to Lacey," Kat pointed out. "You said she's Aaron's cousin, right? If something had happened to her, don't you think he'd be more worried?"

I bristled at Aaron's name. "I'm not sure he has a clue what happened to her. Do you have any idea what's going on with your parents? With Rosa?"

"That's different."

"It doesn't change the fact that we're completely cut off from everything that happens outside these walls."

"I hear, you, I do. It's just, shouldn't we find out as much as we can about where we are?"

"Where we are doesn't have anything to do with my blood," I said shortly. "I'm eighteen now. They have to let us out of here eventually, right?"

"What happened to you?" Kat burst out. "What happened to the crazy girl who'd do anything to figure out what happened to her brother— break into Reed's office, run through the basement after curfew...Where did all of that fire go?"

"Maybe it's gone," I snapped, jumping to my feet. "Maybe I realized that I could have had everything I'd ever wanted here, and I blew it because I couldn't trust that something could finally be *normal* for once."

"Do you even hear yourself right now?" Kat stood and crossed her arms, her small face twisted in anger. "I was poisoned, Lydia, I'm sure of it. And you think that's a reason to keep laying low?"

"Kat, you're the one who wanted to lay low!"

"Yeah, the day after it happened, but I don't really feel like sitting around and waiting for it to happen again!"

"So, you, what, want to go to Aaron for help?" My insides burned at the thought.

"Why wouldn't we go to Aaron for help?"

"Maybe because he lied—to both of us?"

"We *think* he lied to you."

"Kat, he said he talked to you. He didn't."

"Maybe I was, I don't know. Talking in my sleep or something. What?" She added as I raised my eyebrows. "It's possible."

"Yeah, maybe it is, but I still don't want to talk to him."

"Why not?" Kat yelled.

"Because he kissed me!" I shouted back.

Kat's mouth dropped open. "He *what?*"

"We…kissed. That night you were in the hospital," I mumbled. Unable to look at Kat, I ran through everything that had happened—Lacey's threats, Aaron's anger, the confusion I felt after finally having my first real kiss.

The more I told Kat, the less sense everything made. I still had no idea why Lacey wanted to keep me away from Aaron, but I'd put the thought out of my mind for weeks. I didn't want to think about the fact that Aaron had kissed me and then shut me out like it'd never happened.

Danny was right. Real life was nothing like the movies.

"That's…that's awful, Lydia. I'm sorry." All of the anger had drained from Kat's voice. "You should have told me."

"Yeah, I should have," I said quietly. "Part of me thought that maybe there was something between you two."

"God, no," Kat said. "He's not my type, remember? Actually, I'm not really sure that anyone's my type. Is that weird?"

"What do you mean?" I asked.

Kat sighed and flopped onto her back. "I don't know. My parents were so in love," she said. "It was like they couldn't stand the thought of living a single day without each other. They were always holding hands, kissing, doing little things for each other. I always figured that when I grew up, I'd find someone that I wanted to be with as much as they wanted to be with each other. My friends were always talking about how they liked this boy, or that girl, or whoever, but I never felt any of it. No crushes. No dreams about kissing... or anything else. Nothing like that."

"Maybe you just hadn't found the right person?" I asked.

"That's what I thought, too," Kat said. "But it's been two years since I started school here. I'm surrounded by some very attractive people my age. I think if I was going to feel something, I'd have felt it by now. For someone. Anyone."

"Maybe you're just not wired that way," I said. "And there's nothing wrong with that. It's not like you need to fall in love to be happy."

"I wish I could believe that." Kat stared at the ceiling. "I wish I wanted to like, kiss someone or something. You know? But honestly, it just sounds gross."

"Huh," I said quietly. "I can't imagine that, honestly."

"It's weird. I know." Kat sighed. "I can't tell you how often I've wished I wasn't like this."

"Oh, Kat," I said, taking her hand. "If you don't need romance to be happy, you don't need it. Don't let anyone or anything make you think you do. You're amazing with or without it—smart, pretty, kind, funny…You're my best friend. I love you. Isn't that enough?" I teased.

"Well, you are practically famous," Kat reasoned. "So, I guess your love counts extra. Thanks, Lydia."

"Of course," I said softly. For a moment, we sat in silence.

"Honestly, I can't imagine not wanting to kiss anyone. Even back on the island, there was this boy," I said, my voice soft.

"Ooh, a boy," Kat said, wiggling her eyebrows at me.

"Yeah," I said quietly. "Chris. He was older than me."

"What was he like?"

"Practically perfect," I sighed. "Smart. Strong. Kind. He was all I had after Danny disappeared."

"You loved him?" Kat asked quietly.

I didn't answer right away. "I think. Maybe. I felt something. But sometimes, I wonder if I fell for him because he was my only option."

"That might be how it started, but that doesn't mean your feelings weren't real," Kat said. "I'm sorry you lost him."

My chest tightened. "Yeah. Me too." I shook my head. "Listen, I'm sorry. I should have told you about Aaron. I thought I could trust him. I guess I was wrong."

"Yeah, maybe." Kat shook her head as she sat up. "But I still think we should run some tests on your blood, just to see."

"Which would require getting the vial from Aaron." I frowned. "Wait. If Aaron got the vial of my blood that they had on file, wouldn't Donna want more of it?"

"More of your blood? Why would she want more of your blood?"

"Same reason she wanted it in the first place. If we give Donna the maximum benefit of the doubt, and she needs samples from all of us for medical reasons, she still needs a sample on file. So why hasn't she tracked me down to get a new one?"

"Maybe she hasn't noticed that it's missing," Kat said. "She does have other people to look after, you know."

I bit my lip. "I don't think so. She's got eyes like a hawk. She'd know right away if something was missing from her office."

"What are you saying? That Aaron bled into a vial and pretended it was your blood?" Kat looked at me. "Speaking of getting over things, how would you feel about getting knifed?"

I barked out a laugh. "Are you kidding?"

"Not really, no. We can go to the lab, and you can slice into your palm with a scalpel or something. Nothing too deep. The cut will heal within the week."

"It still sounds painful."

"More painful than talking to Aaron?"

"Good point." I pushed my hands back through my hair. "When do you propose we do this?"

"I don't know. The sooner the better, probably." Kat shrugged. "We'll need to reconfigure our program to shut down the lab alarms instead of the nurse's office one. Sneaking out is second nature to you now, right?"

"Kind of." I bit the corner of my mouth. Sneaking out wasn't just second nature for *me*—it was second nature for Jared, too. What if we ran into him while we were sneaking around after curfew? I hadn't told Kat anything about Jared, not even his original warnings about Danny. Not even about the night we'd spent together in detention. God, that felt like a million years ago.

"Lydia, I think we need to do this. Are you in or out?"

I looked at my best friend and smiled. "I'm in."

\*\*\*

Kat and I spent the next few days in our corner of the library, whispering back and forth and trying to make a plan. Breaking into the labs was shaping up to be substantially more challenging than the basement; there were more cameras, more alarms, and more risks. I considered just "injuring" myself in class one day, but we wanted privacy, and I couldn't risk our teacher calling Donna in to help a hurt student. I didn't want her to pay any more attention to me than she already had.

"But what if they *do* happen to look at the cameras?" I asked.

"If you were worried about that, I don't think you'd have gone down to the basement all those times," Kat pointed out. "This is for Danny, remember?"

"Kat, how in the hell is this for Danny?"

"In case you forgot, Danny's your brother."

"So?"

Kat rolled her eyes. "*So*, you two have similar DNA. Don't you think that if something in your blood is messed up, his might have been too?"

I frowned. "I guess. But without a way to access his file again, we'll never know for sure."

"One thing at a time."

"Right. So, tonight it is." I tapped a few keys on my laptop. "I'll be in our room, and you'll be here. You'll go in first and get things ready. Then when I get there..." I winced. I could already feel the scalpel slicing into my flesh.

"Hey, don't worry. We don't need much blood for this to work." Kat tapped her fingers on the table. "Come to think of it, you should probably give me the glasses so that I can get into the supply cabinet before you get there."

I bit my lip. I'd almost forgotten that I'd told Kat and Aaron that I had a pair. "About that."

"You still have them, right? You didn't lose them?"

I considered Kat, my heart and mind pounding together as I tried to buy myself time. Kat had just offered me the perfect explanation for not having the glasses—all I had to do was say the word, and she'd think I'd lost them. My secret would be safe. But what would we do once we were inside the lab?

"I don't have a pair of glasses," I mumbled to my shoes.

Kat leaned closer. "Speak up."

"I don't have a pair of glasses," I repeated, louder. "I never did."

"Then how did you..." Kat gestured around us, trying to find words. "All the doors!"

"I can see it. I can see the paint."

"You can what?" Kat asked weakly.

"The keypad has a glow. The first number's the faintest. They get brighter."

Kat sank into a chair. "I need a minute to process this. Your eyes can see the magical glowing numbers on the keypads around the school and you just thought to mention this *now*?"

"I'm sorry, I just—" I said.

"Didn't think you could trust me." Kat crossed her arms.

"Kat, that's not it," I snapped. "You think it's been easy being here, knowing it's where my brother was murdered? Figuring out that my blood is *toxic* or something, that I can somehow see paint that no one is supposed to be able to? This isn't about you, Kat. It's about me."

Kat's deep scowl softened. "I get that this is scary, but I'm here for you. I guess I just thought you knew that."

"Hey, I do. I do. I'm sorry. I'm here for you too, okay?"

"Well, duh. I know that." Kat stood and hiked her backpack over her shoulder. "But we do need a slight change of plans. We're going to the labs right now, and you're going to tell me the code. Then, tonight, you'll get there first. I'll come later."

"If I'm getting there first, can't you just knock?"

"And attract the entire school? Great plan." Kat pushed my shoulder. "Let's get out of here. We have a big night ahead."

\*\*\*

I left well before curfew that night, planning to wander the halls and attempt to make time go as slowly as possible—I definitely wasn't looking forward to having my skin sliced open. So, I wandered around this way and that, never going down the same hallway twice. I stared at my feet, barely paying attention to where I was going until I smashed headfirst into someone.

"Hey wa—Oh." Aaron took his hand from my shoulder and stepped away. "Sorry."

"My fault," I said coolly. I stepped around him.

"Hey, Lyd—Lydia, wait," Aaron called after me.

I didn't turn around. "What do you want?"

"Can we talk?"

I whirled around. "What about? How you decided that I was perfect for you, and then I meant nothing to you all in the span of about a day?"

"It was never like that," Aaron implored. "You don't understand."

"Explain it to me, then!"

"I…"

"I trusted you, Aaron! You were my first kiss, and that meant something to me. I'm going through a lot right now, but I felt like maybe we could try to be more than friends. But, as soon as I was ready to open up a little, you threw everything away because I didn't want to eat dinner with you for one night." I wasn't sure where my rage was coming from, but now that it was pouring out of me, I couldn't seem to stop it. I felt like I was talking to Jared again—not my friend, Aaron.

"I'm telling you, that's not why!" Aaron shouted. "Can we please just go somewhere and talk about this?"

"Somewhere like where?"

"My room's right around the corner. Just come with me." Aaron sighed. "Please. I want things to get back to the way they were."

"So do I, Aaron, but do you really think that's possible?"

Aaron held out a hand. "We won't know until we try."

I bit my lip. There wasn't much time before I had to meet Kat. Could I really justify going with Aaron when we had so much to do? Aside from Kat, Aaron was the best friend I'd ever had. I wanted it back—the fun, the laughter, all of it.

"Fine," I said stiffly. "You get five minutes. Then I have to go."

Aaron raised an eyebrow. "You got somewhere to be?"

"It's almost curfew."

"Never mattered to you before. Come on. Five minutes is fine."

"Fine," I echoed. Silently, we walked to Aaron's room. I looked down as he punched the code and held the door for me.

I whirled around when he snapped it shut. "Why'd you shut the door?"

"That's kind of the point of a private conversation, Lyd. Why are you acting like you hate me?"

"I don't know," I said in a small voice. "You said you wanted to explain, so...explain."

"Theo's dead," Aaron blurted.

My veins turned to ice. "What?" I whispered. "Theo, your brother?"

"Yeah." Aaron's eyes sparkled. "I've been in a really bad place lately, and I just don't know what to d—"

I threw my arms around Aaron and buried my face in his shoulder. My heart ached. "Oh, Aaron," I whispered. "Why didn't you tell me?"

"I don't know," Aaron murmured into my hair. "I just really miss him, you know? Things weren't perfect, but he was still my brother. You know, sometimes, we used to go climb in the orange trees. The best ones were always at the top. He'd lift me up, and I was so small that I could get to the very top. It's those things that I remember now, you know? Not our fights later on. The things I'd say or he'd scream that seem meaningless now."

"I know. Trust me, I know. I'm so sorry, Aaron."

"It's not your fault." Aaron pulled back and offered a faint version of his signature smile. "But the way I've been acting is definitely my fault. I never meant to...I like you, Lyd." Aaron took my hand. "I'm sorry that I made you feel otherwise."

"You *told* me otherwise," I pointed out.

"I know. I messed up, and I'm sorry. But I miss you," Aaron murmured, drawing closer. "And I know you miss me too."

My heart spiked as he pressed a hand to the small of my back. "Y— you sure about that?" I breathed. I wasn't sure. Not even close.

"Yeah. I am." For a heartbeat's second of time, he just stared at me.

And then he kissed me again. I expected something to feel different this time. Like being apart had only made what little fire there was between us grow hotter, more intense. But even though there was a warmth in my stomach, fluttering and tingly, it wasn't enough. It just felt like something was missing.

I pulled back, eyes wide open. "I have to go."

"Wait, what? Lydia!" Aaron caught my arm. "I thought we were…"

"There's just something I have to do."

"What?"

"I need to go, okay?" Gently, I pulled away. "I'll see you at breakfast tomorrow."

"Sure," Aaron said slowly. He hooked a hand around the back of his neck. "Be careful."

"What did you say?" I demanded, heart pounding.

"Getting back to your room," Aaron said slowly. "It's almost curfew."

"Oh. Yeah." I offered a weak smile. "I'll see you tomorrow."

"So you've said." Aaron kissed my forehead. "Go."

I offered one last smile and left. I shut the door behind me, and the click sounded like a gunshot that echoed through the empty hallway. Kat was almost certainly at the labs by now, probably worried that something had happened to me. I sprinted there. By the time I skidded to the door, I was completely out of breath, and my hands were shaking so badly that it took me several tries to key in the right code.

Hands grabbed me the second I was inside. "Where the *hell* have you been?" Kat hissed as she snapped the door shut behind me. "I've been waiting here for twenty minutes, and *you* were supposed to get here first!"

"I know, I'm sorry. I…I got held up." '

"By?"

"Aaron."

Kat blew air out of her cheeks, completely exasperated. "I don't even want to know. Tell me later. Or don't. Just get over here, I've set up everything I can."

Kat dragged me over to a lab station at the back of the room, where she'd set up a row of beakers. Different colored substances, both liquid and solid, sparkled inside them. "I got everything I could out of the student cabinets, but we're going to need more supplies. Can you get those open for me?" Kat gestured behind us to the locked cabinets that (hypothetically) only Khan had access to.

The tips of my fingers tingled as I unlocked the cabinet. Now that Kat knew my secret, using my ability felt different. Real.

"What do you need?"

"I need you to take *this*." Kat handed me one of the silver knives from the experiment all those weeks ago. "Oh, don't look at me like that. I sterilized it," she added when I paled. "Just slice into your palm and bleed into this beaker a little. No big deal."

"You're not the one stabbing yourself with a knife half the size of your arm," I muttered.

"No, you're right. I'm just here after hours risking detention. So, bleed, or I'll make you bleed."

"Geez, pushy." I laughed nervously and ran the knife over my palm, just hard enough to tickle. I took a deep breath and sliced my skin apart. I gasped at the white-hot pain, and the knife clattered to the floor. Just like when Donna had pierced my arm with the needle, the edges of the cut I'd made seemed to tingle with electric nerves.

"Here, here." Kat put a beaker next to the river of blood dripping off of my hand and caught it.

"I didn't mean to cut that deep," I said faintly, unwillingly fascinated by the way my blood was pooling in my hand, running through the lines in my skin like ruby-red rivers.

"Well, we'll definitely have a lot to work with," Kat said mildly. She handed me a white handkerchief that I wrapped around my hand while I watched her measure out the blood in the beaker.

"What's the plan?"

"You remember the murder mystery lab?" Kat asked.

My heart pulsed in time with the pain throbbing through my hand. I'd done that lab with Jared. I cleared my throat. "Yeah, of course."

"That was all about the different chemical compositions of the substances. The liquid changed colors based on how it reacted with the samples."

"So, we're just going to mix my blood with a bunch of random stuff to see what happens?" I picked up the beaker, watching the blood splash on the sides of the glass. "How are you going to tell anything from that?"

"There's more to being smart than solving calc problems and hacking into the FBI, you know." Kat rolled her eyes. I sighed. She was right— chemistry wasn't my strong suit. All those different substances and reactions…they were like a puzzle I couldn't solve. Just like this school.

"You're right." I settled back against a counter. "Just let me know if I can help." As I watched Kat pour tiny amounts of blood into the various beakers she'd set up, my mind wandered back to that day with Jared— watching bright colors burst through the ordinary while our hands skimmed within a veil's space of each other. And then suddenly I wasn't thinking about class anymore, I was thinking about that night in the basement—our night of dancing and darkness and his hands against my skin for real this time. We'd almost kissed that night.

I pressed the handkerchief harder against the slit in my palm. The jab of pain jolted me back to reality. What was I doing, thinking about one night with Jared when Aaron was probably thinking of me right now? Aaron. Other than Kat, Aaron was the one person that I knew cared about me—really cared about me. So why couldn't I learn to love him back?

"Woah…" Kat pointed at one of the beakers. White smoke poured from it. "That shouldn't be happening."

"What is it?"

"It's…dirt," Kat replied.

"You're kidding." I reached forward. When I touched the beaker, it was burning hot. I jumped back as pain rippled through my hand. "Jesus!"

"What?"

"It's *hot*!"

"That's odd."

"You don't say," I scoffed. Now, pain shot though both of my hands instead of just one. "What does that mean?"

"I don't know." Kat leaned both of her palms on the counter. "Listen, maybe you should just go. I'm going to have to stay here all night to figure this out."

"I'm not leaving you," I said immediately, hopping up onto a counter. "We'll make a night of it."

*Maybe I'll tell you about Aaron, and you can help me work out how I even feel.*

"No, seriously. I think you should go. I work better on my own."

"Kat..."

"Seriously. I'll be fine here."

"It might not be safe." I looked behind me even though I knew the labs were deserted. "Remember the girl on the gurney? Remember what happened to Lacey?"

"I'm not Lacey. I can actually take care of myself beyond fixing my hair." Kat rolled her eyes. "I mean it—get to bed. No offense, but you look like you could use the sleep."

"I'm not even tired," I lied.

Kat glared at me.

"Fine." I threw up my hands. "I'll go. But you're coming back the second you're done, okay? And you're going to wake me up when you get back, so I know you're safe." I hopped down from the counter and pulled her into a hug. "Thank you for doing this."

"What are friends for?"

"You are the *best* best friend," I muttered into her shoulder. "I love you."

"Love you, too." Kat pushed my shoulder towards the door. "Everything's going to be fine."

"I hope you're right," I murmured as I closed the door to the labs behind me.

# CHAPTER NINETEEN

As I walked away from Kat, the reality of what I'd just seen started to set in. My blood had lit dirt on fire. *Dirt.* I didn't even know that dirt was flammable—but, then again, I wasn't the best with chemistry. I walked the silent halls as slowly and quietly as I could, trying to think of some kind of explanation for why my blood would have dissolved it. All I could conjure was the distant echo of Danny's voice from that awful, awful day.

*Someone will make a breakthrough soon. Discover that you can actually make electricity from dirt or something.*

I stopped in place, my mind racing to remember everything I'd ever learned about generating electricity and how it was done before so much of the fuel ran out. I didn't know much, but in everything I'd learned, there was a common denominator.

Heat.

For some inexplicable reason, my blood heated up that dirt until it burned to the touch. What the hell was wrong with me? And more importantly, how was I alive right now? If my blood was that potent, that toxic, why weren't my guts jelly? Had I always been this way? No. I'd had plenty of cuts and scrapes as a kid, playing on the beach with Danny and Chris. Those injuries never hurt like the cuts I'd gotten since coming to Yucca Mountain. This was something *they* had done to me.

Or something they'd woken inside of me.

I blinked. I'd been staring down the hallway ahead of me for the past minute and a half without really seeing. But now I noticed a flash of blond hair disappearing around a corner. I tilted my head. *Jared?*

"Jared," I shout-whispered down the hallway, but he was already gone. I stole after him. Was he still going down to the basement to look for the brick? I knew he'd never find it. Not without my help. So, what was he doing down there?

I caught up to him as soon as we entered the basement. I wasn't sure why I'd followed him. Maybe I wanted to tell someone other than Kat what I'd seen tonight. Or maybe I was thinking about the night of the party again. About how I felt.

"Jared," I called.

Jared turned. "I thought you'd given up these little fieldtrips."

"I have. Kind of." I walked to him and leaned back against the wall. "Any luck with that brick?" My eyes fell onto the backpack slung over his shoulders. "What's in there?"

"So first you follow me, then you think I'll answer your questions? Cute, Melrose." He turned away.

"Jared, wait. You didn't…you're not…" I sputtered.

"I did, and I am. I'm getting out of here. Tonight."

"Tonight?" I repeated incredulously.

"Yeah, tonight. Since you've made it clear you're not interested in coming with me, you should probably just go back to your room." He grinned at the dumbstruck look on my face. "Smile, Melrose. You never have to see me again."

My heart swooped to my shoes. Jared was just…leaving? The last person who knew my brother, who admitted that he'd ever existed, was about to be gone. I was never going to see him again.

"Where are you going to go?" I asked quietly.

"I'm not sure. That's what this is for." Jared hiked his backpack higher onto his shoulder as we turned a corner. "Anyways, what do you care? You have Aaron, now… and Kat. You haven't even looked at me in days."

"Only because you're always lying."

"Well, maybe I lie for good reasons."

"I'm sure you do, but…"

"But nothing. I told you to stay away from all of this. I asked you to stay away altogether or team up with me. You chose them instead of me… or yourself. You couldn't trust me, Lydia, so I couldn't trust you."

"Jared, *please.* If you leave, I might never—"

"Find out what happened to Danny? You'll never figure that out, anyways! You need to let it go. Maybe then, you'll survive this place."

"So, you're just leaving me to die, is that it?"

"I *asked* you to come with me," Jared said. His voice softened. "You still can."

I swallowed, hard. "What about them?"

"I can't help them. Just you." Jared shrugged. "I'm sorry."

"I won't leave them," I said quietly.

"I know you won't." Jared sighed and continued his walk down the hallway.

"If you're leaving, why can't you just tell me?" I asked tiredly. "I know that you know what the Latium project is."

"I can't tell you because it'd destroy you," Jared burst out. "Once you know what it is, you'll never look at yourself in the mirror the same way again. *Everything* will change."

"Can it really be that horrible?" I whispered thinking of the white smoke that'd curled out of the beaker tonight.

"It can."

"More horrible than never knowing why my brother was murdered?"

Jared didn't hesitate. "Yes."

"I don't understand."

"I don't expect you to. Just trust me. I'm trying to protect you."

"So you've said." As we came to a fork, I turned automatically to the left. The brick wasn't far now.

"Where are you going?" I frowned as Jared turned right.

"The exit." Jared drew out the word. "Are you feeling okay, Melrose?"

"I'm *feeling* fine," I snapped. "But that's not the way to the exit."

"What are you talking about?"

"I found it weeks ago. It's this way." I jerked a thumb to the left.

"You must be remembering wrong." Jared shrugged.

"Hey, wait," I said, catching up to him. "Something's wrong. I know the place I found was back that way."

"Well, the place I found is up here. Straight ahead, actually." Jared pointed ahead, at the dead end I hadn't even seen until we came to a stop in front of it. I frowned at the wall. At first, it was blank. None of the bricks glowed; it was just a wall. After a moment, a faint red glow appeared on the edges of the brick in the middle. It grew until the entire thing was bathed in soft red light.

"Right here," Jared said, reaching for it.

"Wait!" I caught his arm and pulled it back. "Something's wrong," I repeated. "The light here is red, not green."

Jared turned to face me, deep lines between his eyebrows. "What are you talking about?"

"The brick is glowing red," I repeated, knowing that I'd just betrayed my secret to the second person today. "I don't think you should touch it."

"Of course, I have to touch it," Jared scoffed. He looked down at the place where my hand wrapped around his arm. "Mind letting go?"

"Actually, yes." I stepped closer and tightened my grip. "You can't do this, Jared. It's not safe."

"You're one to talk about not safe," Jared breathed.

"I know I haven't made the smartest choices." I swallowed. "But you said you've been looking out for me. I'm trying to look out for you now."

"Why do you care?" Jared asked, leaning closer. My breath hitched in my throat.

"I don't want you to get hurt, either. And I don't want you to leave."

We stood for a second, staring at each other. For a heartbeat's space of time, there was nothing but us; nothing but his deep, green eyes locked to mine.

When Jared finally kissed me, the very last traces of the world beyond *him*, beyond his gentle hands on my waist and the smell of cinnamon, melted into nothing.

This wasn't like daydreaming about Chris. This wasn't even like kissing Aaron. Kissing Jared was everything the movies promised and more— the perfect night, the perfect clothes, the perfect boy. Nothing about this moment was perfect. In fact, almost everything was wrong. But somehow, nothing besides the two of us seemed to matter at all.

When we pulled apart, my hands were linked around his neck. I only had a faint idea of how they'd gotten there. "Jared," I whispered. "Please don't go."

"Come with me," Jared said gently, skimming his thumb over my cheek. "We'll keep each other safe. Look out for each other."

My lips parted as I looked at Jared. I wanted to. I wanted to go with him more than I'd ever wanted anything. More, even, than I wanted answers. My lips started to move, to tell him that of course I'd go with him, that I thought I was in love with him. But then I remembered that Kat, my best friend, was holed up in the lab right now, risking her safety for me. If I disappeared, she'd never understand why. She'd think I was dead, or worse. I couldn't do that to her.

"I'm sorry," I whispered. "Kat..."

Jared pulled away "I know."

"But Jared," my voice caught in my throat like it was made of flypaper. "I'm serious about the brick. I don't think this is the right place."

"Nothing you say is going to get me to stay." Jared's hard expression was back, the warmth in his eyes replaced by a glare.

"I'm not trying to do keep you here," I protested as Jared yanked his hand out of mine. "Jared!"

"I'm sorry, but I'm leaving." Jared pressed his palm flat against the brick. It pulsed red, like a warning. For a moment, nothing happened.

And then, out of nowhere, the world was alight with flashes of red. "Jared, freeze!" I shouted.

"What? Why?" Jared asked. His voice pulsed with alarm. "What's happening?"

I mouthed soundlessly. Jared and I were trapped in what seemed to be a maze of bright red lasers that filled the entire hallway.

"Lasers," I breathed. "You just set off an alarm!"

"I don't *see* anything!"

"They're like the paint on the bricks and the locks. You can't see them."

"Oh, and you can?"

"Yes, I can," I snapped. "I don't know why. Kat is in the lab right now trying to figure it out. If you want to get out of here without Reed storming down here, you'd better do exactly what I tell you."

"I don't see anything, Lydia."

"Do you see that brick doing anything? It's a decoy."

"A decoy for what?"

"I don't know yet," I muttered, holding a trembling hand steady over one of the lasers. "But I know we can't get caught here." I studied Jared as he craned his neck to look at me. Five lasers were dangerously close to him; two zapped low near his shoulders, one under his arm, over his head and directly behind him. I took a deep breath. "Okay. Lift up your right hand until I tell you to stop. Stop! Now step backwards. Lift your foot higher."

To my surprise and relief, Jared followed my instructions without question as I guided him through the maze. Though my heart pounded against my ribs, my voice was strangely calm. Jared followed my instructions with careful, deft movements. Soon, he was almost at the edge of the maze.

"Good job." I nodded approvingly as he stepped over another laser. "You're almost there."

"This is the most bizarre thing I've ever done," Jared grumbled. I rolled my eyes and gave him the last few instructions. Finally, he ducked under the last laser.

"You're out," I breathed. I gazed at the web of lasers around me. At least I could see what I was up against. My limbs felt tight after standing still for so long, and my whole body shook as I ducked under the bright red lights, careful to keep each line intact. I didn't know what would happen if I broke one, but I knew it wouldn't be good.

My footing on the floor slipped. I fell towards one of the lasers. My hand slammed into the hard ground. I caught myself just in time. My nose hovered centimeters above the sharp red line.

"You're scaring me," Jared called.

"I'm scaring myself too," I snapped. "Shut up so I can concentrate." Slowly, I pushed myself to my feet. I wasn't far from the end now—only six lasers stood in my way. I ducked under the first, twisting my arms at odd angles to avoid the other two. My heart pounded as I jumped over the final laser between Jared and me. I fell to the ground, completely exhausted as relief flooded my body.

"Woah, you okay?" Jared asked.

"Yeah, I'm fine." I raised a hand and Jared grabbed it. He pulled me to my feet. "That was a close call," I breathed. I didn't take my hand from his. He didn't move his either.

Jared looked back at the maze of lights. "I still don't see anything."

"I know. Thanks for believing me," I said softly. "I don't know what would have happened if we'd set that alarm off."

"Well, I guess I'm stuck here for one more day," Jared said, turning his eyes back to me.

I swallowed. "I guess you are."

His hand left mine and trailed to the small of my back. "I'm glad you were here. And not just because you just saved my ass."

"I'm glad, too," I whispered. I stepped closer to him. Slowly, tentatively, I reached a hand to skim his cheek. Sparks, warm and tingly, raced through my body as he pulled me even closer. "We should probably get out of here," I whispered.

Jared's lips spread into a soft half-smile. His eyes flickered to my lips and back up again. "Maybe not just yet."

"Yeah, maybe not." I grinned and tangled my hands in his hair, drinking in everything about this moment. The dust, the darkness, his hands on my waist and the magic in the air.

"Adorable." A voice sounded from further down the hall. My stomach dropped to the floor, into an icy, frozen lake. I jumped back from Jared, and his hand latched onto my wrist like a vice.

All of the blood left my face as Reed stepped into the light. His thin face was twisted into a rage that was somehow both calm and terrifying.

"Either of you want to explain this to me?"

I stepped back. Fear flooded through me. I opened my mouth, but no words came out.

"Going somewhere, Carver?" Jamison appeared behind Reed and pointed at the backpack slung over his shoulders.

"Nowhere. We were just headed back upstairs," Jared said. His hand was tight around mine.

"I would certainly hope you were. It's almost midnight," Reed said. "In fact, I think we should all head upstairs together."

"We're good," I said loudly.

"I don't think so," Reed said. "You're coming with me. Jamison will deal with Carver."

"No," I said immediately.

"Excuse me?"

"You're the principal, right? Why would a teacher take Jared and you take me? It just seems counterproductive, Sir." I babbled as my legs went to jelly. I felt like I was going to faint all over again.

"As principal, it's up to me to decide what is or is not counterproductive," Reed said. "Let go of each other. Now."

"Don't you touch her," Jared said, stepping in front of me. "Lydia," he whispered.

"Now," Reed said again. He pulled a small weapon that looked like a taser from his pocket. "This doesn't have to get ugly, but it will if you keep this up."

"Jared?" I breathed.

He let go.

I met his eyes, shocked.

"Just go with him." Jared stepped towards Jamison and nodded. Fear raced through me as I watched them go, along with a knot in my gut that told me I would be lucky to ever see him again.

# CHAPTER TWENTY

"I think I've made it clear that you're not leaving this office until I get a satisfactory explanation, Ms. Melrose." Reed drummed his fingers on his desk. Frustration lined every inch of his face.

"I told you. Jared and I sneak down to the basement sometimes to… you know…" My face burned bright red. "Spend time together."

"I see. And can you tell me why Mr. Carver had a backpack full of survival supplies on him when you two set off the alarm?"

"You'll have to ask him that."

"Oh, I will, if Jamison can't get it out of him." Reed leaned forwards. Rage burned behind his dark eyes. "And I suppose neither of you knew that you'd stumbled upon the entrance to a classified research facility either, is that right?"

I stuttered. "R—research for what?"

"Ms. Melrose, do you have trouble understanding the phrase *classified*?"

"Why is there a research facility inside a high school?"

"You're not in any position to ask questions here, least of all when you've refused to answer mine. You'll be staying here until you decide to give me a real explanation. I don't care how long it takes."

Fear rippled down my spine. "What about class?"

Reed didn't answer. He left the room, leaving me alone in his office. I raced for the door the second he left. When I tugged on it, it was locked up tight. I swore under my breath and slammed my fist against the door. My heart pounded with fear for Jared. What was Reed going to do to him? With *me*?

I hit the door again, and pain stabbed through my cut hand. "Damn it," I whined as I slid to the floor. What were Kat and Aaron going to think when I didn't show up this morning? What if Kat had found some incredible answers last night?

Answers.

I turned around slowly. My eyes locked onto the file cabinet in the corner of the room. My skin tingled as I remembered the day I'd broken in here. Jared had ruined my chance to see the files when I could. But who was going to stop me now? I was already in deep, deep trouble. What was a bit more?

I raced to Reed's desk and tugged the drawer open. The neat arrangement scattered, and the keys clinked to the front of the jumble. I held them up to the light, but none of them seemed to be marked as the key to the server room had been. Luckily, there were only six keys on the ring, but every second I stayed here was another second that Reed had to return. One, two, three wrong tries. My heart pounded as I tried the fourth. What was Jared telling him?

Finally, on the fifth key, the cabinet clicked open. I pulled the handle, revealing dozens of manila folders. I yanked on the first one—it was a profile on *Warren, Michael.* I shoved it back into the mess and picked up another. And another. And another. The files weren't in alphabetical order—they didn't seem to be in any order at all.

*How was I supposed to find Danny's file in this mess?*

Charlotte, Anne. Bucan, Holly. Collins, Wende.

Melrose, Lydia.

I pulled my own file from the cabinet, heart pounding. At least ten pages filled the folder, each one covered with inky black text. I chose a page at random and scanned it.

*Melrose, Lydia. Eyes: Brown. Hair: Brown.*

*Latium Status: Positive*

Latium. I touched the word as if information would soak through the ink and into my skin. The same word that had been in that file about Danny. Jared's words bounced around my head: *It'll destroy you.* What could possibly be so bad?

I skimmed the rest of my file, but nothing out of the ord… there, just my personal and academic records. I jabbed it back into cabinet and kept going. Five, ten, fifteen minutes passed. Nothing, n nothing.

I slammed the cabinet shut and replaced the keys, breathing heavily. . needed to get out of this room and find Jared. If Reed figured out that he was trying to leave the school, I didn't know what he'd do to him. The locked door loomed over me, reminding me that I had no way to get out of here. I rattled the doorknob again.

Nothing.

But then I spotted the keypad next to the door. I knelt so that it was at eye level. *Please, please, please.*

It stayed dark for one, two, three seconds. And then the numbers appeared. I punched them in and waited for the door to click open.

Nothing happened.

"What?" I breathed desperately. I slammed my palm against the wall. It was hopeless—I was trapped in here until Reed decided what to do with me.

I grabbed the doorknob again. It didn't budge. But then I stopped and looked at it. While before it had been solid, there was now a keyhole in the center of the shiny silver orb.

Keys! Of course! I stumbled back to the desk and yanked the keys from their spot. The six of them glinted in the bright light, mocking me. But this time, I got the right key on the first try.

I stumbled into the hallway and slammed the door behind me. The crowd milling through here didn't even flinch; the chatter filled the space so completely. Frantically, I grabbed onto the nearest arm I could. A small girl with long red hair stopped, looking startled.

"What time is it?" I demanded.

"What?"

"What class period is it?" I shouted.

"Second!" The girl yanked her arm away and hurried away from me. I raked a hand back through my hair. Second. That meant Kat was going to be in lab. Finding her, making sure that she was safe, was my first priority.

Then I could tear this place apart looking for Jared.

I pushed past body after body, looking frantically around for Kat, for Reed, for anyone else who would drag me back to the office. That word—*Latium*—bounced around my head. According to Jared, knowing would destroy me. But what about not knowing? Not knowing what happened to Danny. Not knowing where I stood with Aaron, with Jared, with anyone. What was wrong with my blood.

The slit on my hand throbbed as I rocketed around the last corner. The bell clanged overhead—if I'd wanted to go to class, I'd be late.

I burst into the lab, breathing heavily. I scanned the room. No Kat. No Jared.

"Melrose—why aren't you in your scrubs?" Khan demanded.

"Where's Kat?"

"I was hoping you could tell me that." Khan crossed her arms. "You are her roommate."

"Right," I said slowly. I backed away. "I don't feel very well."

"Melrose, put your scrubs on and start the lab. You're already behind."

I didn't answer. I just turned and ran. My heart and mind pounded as I skidded over the floor. It was entirely possible that Kat was asleep in our room after her long night of research.

I dodged the last few stragglers on their way to class on the way back to my room. Guys in khakis and black polos. Girls in bright red dresses. They passed in blurs of color. Something in my gut told me that if Kat wasn't in our room, something was very, very wrong.

Finally, I stumbled through our door. "Kat?"

My eyes raked over the room. Unmade bed, messy desk. Nothing out the ordinary.

But no Kat. I turned around on the spot, both hands caught in my hair. Where the hell could she be? The nurse's office? Worse? I needed to get out of here, to find Jared and Aaron.

Aaron. Oh God. Aaron. Jared. What a mess.

But I couldn't think about that now. I grabbed my backpack and raced from the room, running over all the places that Kat could be. Nurse's office, Reed's office, class, basement. Basement? I couldn't string two thoughts together, let alone form a theory about where she might be.

Lungs completely out of air, I skidded to a stop. Sweat dripped from my forehead as I leaned back against the wall. Somehow, I'd managed to circle back to the hallway I'd seen on my first night here—the hallway with the class photos. I stumbled towards one of them, towards the one I knew I'd seen Danny in, and skimmed my fingers over the glass.

"Where did you go?" I murmured as my finger came to a rest on a much-younger Jared, who stood in the top row. For some stupid reason, the sight of his floppy blond hair made me smile in spite of everything that was happening.

Out of nowhere, someone grabbed my arm and spun me around. I tried to scream, but the noise caught in my throat like a fish in a net.

"Hey, hey, hey. It's okay. It's me."

I relaxed immediately and wrapped my arms around his neck. He pulled me close and rested his chin on my head. Warm relief, like sweet as sugary syrup, flowed through my body and leaked into my voice. "Aaron."

"Yeah, what's going on?" Aaron asked, eyes searching mine. His hands settled on my forearms. "Are you okay?"

"No, I'm not." Out of nowhere, I was crying. Crying out of exhaustion. Out of worry for Kat and Jared. But mostly for the boy missing from the photograph on the wall. For the brother who'd wanted the same things as me but had never let it control him.

I wondered if he'd found what he was looking for here at Yucca. I hope he was happy before he died.

"Hey, slow down." Aaron pushed my hair away from my eyes, worry tattooed all over his face. "Just tell me what happened."

"I think Reed," I stuttered, stumbling over my words as the tears trailed down my face. "I think Reed's going to kill me like he killed Danny."

"Hold on—*kill* you?"

"Maybe."

"Lydia, that's crazy, okay? Reed may have hidden some stuff about your brother, but he'd never kill anyone."

"How do you know?" I whispered. "How do you know that he hasn't been killing them all along?"

"Them—them who?"

"Them like Lacey. Like the girl we saw on the gurney. Like Kat! She's missing, too, and it's all my fault," I sobbed. "Jared told me about the missing kids. I think they took Kat, and I think we're next." Aaron pulled me closer to him and I buried my head in his shoulder. *Kat. Gone behind the red brick in the wall, locked in stone forever.*

"Lyd, Kat's fine." Aaron pulled back and brushed the tears from my face. "I just saw her. She told me she was worried about *you*."

"W—what?"

"Kat is *fine*," Aaron repeated. The dimples in his cheeks stood out as he smiled reassuringly. "I went to your chemistry class. She's pissed that she has to work with Nikki again."

"You went to my class?"

"Of course. I was worried when you didn't show up to history this morning."

"Kat was in history?"

"Lydia, yeah," Aaron said slowly. Something like lightening flashed in his eyes. "Come with me, and we'll find her." He locked me in an embrace.

I tried to back away from Aaron, but he had me pressed against the wall. My heart pounded. There was a chance Aaron had gone to the labs after I'd left, but a very, very slight one.

"I actually need to…" I trailed off as his hands tightened around my hips. "I need to go…"

"Go where, Lydia?" Aaron asked, tilting his head. "I thought you said you wanted to find Kat."

"I mean, you said she's safe," I said with my best attempt at nonchalance.

"Then, who do you have to go look for?"

*Jared.* "No one." I tried to edge away from him again, but Aaron just held me in place. "Aaron, let me go."

"I can't. I can't let you *go*." The mild expression twisted off of Aaron's face, giving way to something dark—a kind of frantic anger that matched the pace and intensity of his next words. "I can't let you leave here. That's what you were trying to do, right? All those times down in the basement…you can see it, can't you?"

I shook my head frantically. "I'm not trying to leave, Aaron. I just want to get back to—"

"You can see it, can't you?" Aaron repeated.

"See what?"

"The paint. The numbers. You can see the way out."

All of the breath jerked out of my lungs like someone had punched me in the chest. How did Aaron know that I could see the lights that no one was supposed to see? Had he puzzled it out on his own? Had Kat told him?

Aaron shoved one of my shoulders and my head cracked back against the photo. It fell from the wall. The glass shattered at my feet.

"Tell me you can see it!" Aaron yelled. "Just tell me you can see it, and everything'll be okay, Lydia. Trust me." Aaron's voice shook, but not with fear like mine.

The tears were drying on my face now, leaving icy trails across my cheeks and nose. "I can see it," I whispered.

Aaron's whole body relaxed at my words, except for his hands that still held my hip and shoulder in place. "I knew it."

"I'm sorry I didn't tell you," I said slowly. "What's this about?"

Aaron released me, nodding to himself. "It's all going to be okay."

"Yeah, it is," I agreed, inching away from him. I didn't know what was wrong with Aaron, but something told me that I needed to get away from him. Fast.

"Where are you going?"

"I'm, I'm…" I stuttered.

"You're not going anywhere," Reed said smoothly. He stepped around the corner, leering at me.

I whirled around and found Aaron's face an inch from my own. "It's all going to be okay," he assured me. Then, he grabbed me.

"Aaron—" My shout melded into a scream as something sharp jabbed into the side of my neck. Immediately, all of the feeling left my arms and legs. I crumpled to the floor, and I barely felt it when my head cracked against the cement. The world was spinning; their voices distorted like we were floating, floating underwater.

The last thing that I saw before the world faded to black was a pair of shiny black shoes stepping into my frame of vision.

# CHAPTER TWENTY-ONE

The world came into focus slowly, like a film fading in. Each time I blinked, the world sharpened, but my mind was filled with disorienting clouds of fog. Where was I, and why did my head feel like it had been smashed in by a brick?

"Melrose." A blurry face appeared in front of me, but I only had the faintest idea of how it'd gotten there. I tried to lift my arms, but my wrists were bolted down, face-up. A thrill of revulsion rattled through me as I realized that there were needles embedded into the crooks of both of my arms.

A pair of fingers snapped in front of my eyes and I gasped sharply when I realized who was standing in front of me. Reed. And he wasn't alone "Aaron?" I murmured. My words were slow and bogged, like the air had turned to molasses. "What...what are you doing?"

"My son and I will be asking the questions today, Melrose. Not you."

My jaw dropped to the floor as his words crashed over me. *Son?*

"Don't look so surprised," Aaron pouted, moving closer until he and Reed were shoulder to shoulder.

"I don't understand," I whispered. "Aaron, we're friends, we're more than friends." *We weren't. Not after I admitted my feelings for Jared, but Aaron thought we were.*

"More than friends? Adorable." Aaron laughed. The cold sound echoed off of high, wide ceilings and I realized where I was—the amphitheater. He put a hand on my shoulder and leaned close. "Didn't anyone ever tell you not to trust a pretty face?"

I jerked away. "Where's Kat?"

"Oh. About that."

"You didn't see her this morning. You were lying," I growled. I strained my wrists against the bonds and sharp, electric pain raced through my veins.

"Of course, I was lying," Aaron chuckled. "I've gotten pretty good at lying lately."

"Enough," Reed snapped. "I didn't bring you down here to gloat."

Aaron's face soured. "You're just mad that I did something right. It's more than you can say for *her*."

"We're not here to discuss Lacey either," Reed snapped.

"Lacey?" I repeated. "What did you do to her?"

Reed raised an eyebrow. "Do to her? We didn't do anything to her. She's been sent home."

"Home where?"

"The base, of course. Something had to be done after she tried to warn you about Aaron."

"Warn me?"

"She's gone soft. Her father will get her back in order soon, I'm sure," Reed said.

My mind raced. Lacey was alive. All that stuff about staying away from Aaron was her way of trying to protect me. But why hadn't she just said? Unless she couldn't. Unless it was too dangerous.

"The base," I whispered. A horrible picture started to form in my mind, clearer and worse with each passing second. What I was thinking couldn't be true. I looked away, thinking. My eyes wandered from the walls to the floor and settled onto Reed's shoes—black and shiny as midnight, with a flash of silver on the toes. I'd seen those before, when the world was fading to black. As Chris took his last breath. "It was you. It was all you! You killed him." My voice broke. *I loved him, and you killed him.*

"Killed Jared Carver? Unfortunately, I haven't had that pleasure yet," Reed said idly.

"Not Jared. Chris. You're the ones who attacked the island." Fury pulsed through me. "You killed my *father*." My voice shook. "Why? Why are you doing all of this?"

"It's nothing personal, really. More of a...*national* issue." Reed's eyes glinted.

And my stomach dropped to the floor. "You're Drillers."

"Very good." Reed grinned, his lips spread tight over his shiny white teeth. "I must say, I'm surprised it took you this long to figure it out, what with all of your excursions throughout the school."

"You knew about that?" I whispered. "You knew all along?"

"Of course, he knew," Aaron laughed. "There are cameras everywhere watching everything. Did you really think it was an accident that you saw that picture of your brother? We wanted to see what you would do once you saw him. We needed to know if you had the same abilities that he did."

"Don't talk about Danny," I growled. "You killed him too." My voice choked, like I was trying to squeeze it through a funnel. "You're going to kill me."

"No one said anything about killing you." Reed waved a hand dismissively, like I was crazy to suggest it. Like I wasn't tied to a chair with needles in my veins.

"Then what do you want from me?" I shouted. My voice bounced around the room, again and again and again.

"I want the *truth*," Reed growled. He leaned down until there were less than six inches between our eyes. I could feel his breath on my face, count every one of the faint lines in his pale skin. "I want to know what went wrong with you."

I leaned as far away as I could, but it was no use. "W—what are you talking about?"

"The Latium Project. I want to know what makes you different. What makes you special."

"I don't know anything about the Latium project," I stuttered. "I don't even know what it is."

Reed looked at Aaron. "Is that true?"

"She never told me anything about it." Aaron shrugged. "Not beyond the name."

"How could you?" I whispered. "How could you tell me those things and…" I couldn't finish. There was a huge knot in the back of my throat. My eyes burned.

"We're in a war here, sweetheart," Aaron said. "I turned on the charm a little."

"Why? Why am I so important to you?" I asked. "What do I possibly have to offer?"

"More than you know," Reed murmured. "Do you know how much some people would pay for the blood running through your pretty little veins?"

"What about my blood?" I demanded. "What did you do to me?"

"Do to you? We didn't do anything to you. No, your father is to thank for that," Reed said. "He's the one who signed you up."

"I have no idea what you're talking about," I said weakly.

"Then why you can see paint that's supposed to be invisible?" his mouth quirked as if he found our entire conversation amusing.

I sighed. "I have no idea why I can see all of those things. I have no idea why my blood sets dirt on fire—"

To my surprise, Reed began to laugh. "It set dirt on fire? Oh, very good. We weren't able to get *that* little piece of information out of Romero, were we, Aaron?"

"Kat?" I demanded sharply. "Where is she?"

"Dead," Reed said. One syllable. One monotone, four-letter word that shattered my world into a million tiny shards of glass that embedded themselves into my heart until shocked tears gathered in my eyes.

"No," I whispered. Kat couldn't be dead. Because if she was dead, it was my fault. She died because of what she discovered about this place. I should have never left her alone that night. I should have never thought that she'd be safe! No, Kat was alive. They were lying. Aaron had been lying all along. So why would he tell the truth now?"

"I'm afraid so," Reed said, his voice completely flat and neutral.

"You're a liar!"

"If you'd like, I could arrange for her body to be brought in here. She's looking a little pale at the moment, however, seeing as we already drained all of her blood."

Bile gathered in the back of my throat. "You're lying. I know you're l—lying."

"He's not," Aaron cut in, and even through the tears that trailed down my face, I could see the tiniest of frowns around his lips.

"Did you kill her?" I demanded. I kicked against the ankle restraints, yanked my wrists until I felt my skin bruising. White hot rage filled my body, obscuring everything—even the grief. All I could think about was getting out of here and wrapping my arms around Aaron's neck. Not to kiss him. To kill him.

"It wasn't my decision," Aaron said uncomfortably.

"But you did it anyways? You killed my friend—*your* friend, just because he told you to?"

"I did what I had to," Aaron snapped. "Do you really think you'd be alive right now if it weren't for me?"

"What are you talking about?"

"We're here to offer you a deal," Reed cut in. "Very soon, Yucca Mountain School will be gone." A twisted grin spread over his lips.

"I'd rather die than make a deal with you," I spat.

Reed chuckled. "That offer's certainly on the table, but don't you want to hear the full story first?"

I didn't answer.

Reed nodded at his son. "Aaron, do it."

"Sir…"

"I won't ask again. Four will do."

Panicked, I looked between them. Four? Four what?

Aaron moved closer to me and I instinctively leaned away. If he ever touched me again, I felt sure that I'd throw up.

But he didn't try to. Instead, he moved behind me. I tried to see what he was looking at, but I couldn't crane my neck far enough to see. "What are you doing?" I asked, panicked.

"Nothing too bad. Yet."

The sound of a switch flicking came from behind me, followed by a mechanical whir. Tingles shot through the crooks of my elbows like millions of tiny arrows. And then the clear tubes attached to them turned red.

I screamed.

"Don't be dramatic," Reed snapped. "We're not taking enough to do any permanent damage. Do you know how much blood a human can lose before they die?"

The faintest touch of dizziness ran through my head. Someone had told me, once. But I couldn't string two thoughts together, let alone remember something like that. "No…"

"Forty percent. I've just had Aaron remove about four percent from you. Every time I ask a question and I don't like the answer, I'll take a little more out. This time it was four, next time it'll be six. Eight, ten and so on. I'm sure you realize that this game can't go on forever."

I nearly vomited but fought to keep calm. I was going to die tonight. I knew that. But if I wanted to die with the truth, I was going to have to stay sane.

"You were going to tell me about the Latium Project," I said slowly. "About your deal."

"Yes. I was." Reed paced in front of me and Aaron rejoined him. Was it my imagination, or did Aaron look the tiniest bit troubled by what he'd just done to me? "I'm sure you're familiar with the energy crisis? You also know I would be more than happy to drill for oil and let things be. But your side went after some more innovative solutions.

"The Latium Project is the future. It's a way for everyone to have an unlimited, totally renewable source of clean energy. Can you guess what that source is?" Reed asked, his eyes glinting.

My voice was hollow. "No."

"It's you."

I shook my head. "I don't understand."

"The blood flowing through your veins is liquid gold. When combined with the right substances—even something as simple and common as dirt—it produces an incredible amount of heat."

Panicked waves rocked through me. If Reed was telling the truth, then the war I'd been fighting for years was absolutely pointless. We'd had a solution all along. I *was* the solution. But being the solution…was this what that looked like? Strapped to a chair and drained of just enough blood to keep me alive for the rest of my life?

*It'll destroy you*, Jared had said. He'd been right.

"Is this it, then?" I asked weakly. "You're going to keep me down here for the rest of my life and use my blood for fuel?"

"Have you been listening to a word I've said? The Drillers aren't interested in solutions. We're interested in *drilling*," Reed emphasized. "We're interested in power."

"What do you need me for, then?" I spat.

"There's something different about you. Your DNA doesn't just make energy, like that of everyone else here. It lets you see things no one should be able to see. And that could just be the beginning of your abilities. *That's* what we're interested in, Melrose. We came so close to discovering the truth with your brother."

"What did you do to him?" I strained against the bonds. I didn't care that pain burned through both of my arms. Or that blood was leaking from around the needles like tiny beads of ruby.

"We're not here to discuss that. We're here to discuss *you*," Reed snapped.

"Lydia, calm down. You're only hurting yourself," Aaron said hesitantly.

I rounded on him. "Oh, like you even care."

"I…I care…"

"You don't. You *murdered* Kat and helped him hook me up to that thing. You made me believe you cared about me and then stabbed me in the back."

"Hey, the only reason you're *alive* right now is because of me."

"Oh, so I'm supposed to thank you for killing my best friend?"

"Yeah, maybe you should!"

Rage rose in my gut, burning hotter than ever. Every fiber of my being yearned to be free, so I could rush to Aaron and smash his face against one of these stone walls.

"Enough," Reed cut in sharply. "If you speak again without being spoken to, we'll take another six percent. Understood?"

Fuming, I clamped my jaw shut and nodded.

"Good. Like I said, we're here to offer you a deal."

"I don't want any de—"

"Aaron, do it." Reed waved a hand.

I shook my head frantically. "Wait. N—"

Spots danced in front of my eyes as Aaron powered the machine back up; the tips of my fingers and toes went numb. Even though my eyes were closed, I was seeing bright red.

Someone snapped their fingers in front of my face. "Are you ready to listen?"

I didn't answer. I just stared at him.

"We've determined that it would be beneficial to our cause if you would agree to be studied. You can come with us to the base, where you'll be treated well—much better than all of our other prisoners. All you have to do is agree to be tested, so that we can see what other abilities you may have."

I didn't dare say a word. The effects of the blood loss had dulled, but I knew if they took any more, I wouldn't be able to think straight.

"These tests would primarily be physical, which is why we need your cooperation. It's a good deal, Melrose. You'll be under my protection."

*Like I am now?*

"And if I refuse?" I asked quietly.

"Then, Aaron will simply turn the machine up to one hundred."

I looked at Aaron. "You'd do that? You'd kill me?"

Aaron looked down at his shoes instead of at me. He didn't answer.

"After everything, you'd stand there and flip a switch that would end my life? I don't believe that, Aaron."

"Melrose," Reed warned sharply.

"You have feelings for me." I raised my voice. "You have feelings for me, and you know it. Are you really going to let your father decide if the girl you love lives or dies?"

"I don't love you," Aaron snapped.

"Well, I love you," I lied boldly. "I love how you were friends with me from my first day here. How you were the one that helped me through everything when I was trying to find Danny. That you were thoughtful enough to bring me a cupcake on my birthday. Aaron, you were the first person who ever kissed me. I never thought that someone as handsome and smart as you would even look at me."

"Melrose, stop talking or so help me, I will drain you until you pass out and we can continue this conversation on the bas—"

"I know you don't really want to hurt me," I continued in a voice as sweet as sugar. "Just tell him to let me go and everything will go back to normal, Aaron. We'll go back to school and I can be your girlfriend. Just like it's supposed to be."

"This is getting ridiculous. Aaron, turn it on."

I held my breath. Aaron didn't move. "Can't we just take her with us?"

"Are you seriously falling for her act?" Reed shouted. "Do it or I'll do it myself."

One, two, three seconds passed. Nothing happened.

"Ridiculous." Reed circled around the back of my chair, and a bang like a gunshot sounded.

I whipped my head around, trying to see the source of the noise, but I couldn't see anything. What the hell was going on?

"Lydia, are you down there?" Someone shouted. My heart leaped. It was Jared.

"Jared!" I shouted. "Jared, I'm here!"

Aaron's eyes went wide; he sprinted behind me.

"Aaron, don't," I shouted. "Don't hurt him!"

Grunts and fist falls filled the air. "Jared!" I shouted. "Jared, are you okay?"

Everything went quiet.

Reed and Aaron dragged Jared into my view and threw him at my feet. He looked up at me. Blood poured from his nose, pooling on the ground.

"Jared," I murmured. "Why did you come back?" If he was free, he could have left. He could have saved himself!

"I couldn't leave you," he whispered back.

"Adorable." Reed kicked Jared in the ribs.

"Stop it!" I screamed.

"Why? If you love my son, this boy's life shouldn't be of any consequence to you." Reed shrugged. "But if it does have value, I'd be more than happy to update our deal."

I narrowed my eyes. "To what?"

"Your life isn't the only one on the table anymore. His is too. Agree to the testing, or I'll kill both of you."

# CHAPTER TWENTY-TWO

"Lydia, don't do it," Jared groaned. A bruise was forming on his jaw. "You can't let them take you."

"They already have us, and I'm not letting you die!"

"You have to!"

"No, I don't! I won't!" I shook my head. My words fell over each other like soldiers running from a dragon. "They already killed Kat, I can't lose you too."

"You've already lost," Reed reminded us. "Either agree, or I'll just shoot you both." He pulled a handgun from inside his jacket. "We're running out of time."

"Time for what?" I asked. Jared's head was pressed into the ground, his chest heaving.

"This entire mountain is rigged with explosives," Reed said. "We'd do better to keep you here and let the flames take care of you like the rest of your classmates."

"No," I said quickly. "I'll do it. I'll do whatever you want, just don't hurt Jared." I looked at Aaron. "Aaron, please. Help us."

Aaron's face twisted with anger. "You don't love me," he snarled. "You…you and him…"

"I do love you, Aaron," I said quickly, ignoring the hurt look that crashed over Jared's face at my words. "But Jared is my friend. I don't want him to die either. He doesn't deserve to die."

"What use does a common *Lateral* have to us?" Reed scoffed.

"Lateral?" I couldn't help asking.

Reed ignored me. "The only thing I can promise is that Jared won't suffer when he dies."

"What about you?" I asked. "Won't you suffer at the hands of your supervisors when you return without me?"

"Your life isn't of any consequence to them. Or to me. I'll give you thirty more seconds. Either take the deal, or I leave you both to die."

"Aaron?" I asked weakly. Aaron crossed his arms, his mouth pressed into a thin line. "Aaron, please. Come with Jared and me."

"Come where?" Aaron scoffed. "There's nowhere to go."

"Anywhere but here," I said desperately. I looked down at Jared, heart pounding. Though his head rested against the floor, his palms were flat against the concrete. His eyes were alert—he was looking for a window, I knew it. "Please," I whispered.

"Ten seconds," Reed cut in. "Melrose, this silly, love-struck schoolgirl act is growing tiresome—"

Reed's words grew to a strangled yell as Aaron grabbed him from behind and slammed him against the wall. "Go!" Aaron shouted.

Jared was on his feet and at my side in an instant. "This is going to hurt." Jared yanked the needles out. Blood leaked from deep gashes in my arms. "Are you alright?"

"No, I'm not!" I had one eye on Reed and Aaron's struggle and the other on Jared as he searched for a way to unlock the bonds. The ones around my wrists clicked open, followed by the ones around my ankles. I sprang to my feet, and the word spun.

Jared caught my shoulders to steady me. His eyes, green and familiar and teeming with panic, met mine.

"You came back," I said weakly.

"Of course, I did," Jared murmured.

"Jared!" Aaron shouted, his voice choked. Reed punched him square in the jaw and Aaron crashed to the floor. Jared moved towards Reed, but Reed had the gun pointed between his eyes in an instant.

"Don't test me," he growled. "If you think this changes anyth—"

Aaron lunged for his father's ankles and Reed crashed to the ground. His yell was barely discernable. *"Go!"*

Jared grabbed my hand. My heart was yanked from my chest as we ran. And left Aaron behind.

"Are you okay?" I panted. "What happened?"

"There's no time for that. Do you remember where the exit is?"

"This way." The blood loss began to affect me. But, though the world spun, and the floor warbled under my feet, I managed to pull Jared in the right direction.

A gunshot sounded behind me. "Aaron," I shrieked.

Jared clapped a hand over my mouth and shoved me against the wall. "Do you want to lead him right to us?"

"We shouldn't leave Aaron."

"Why? Because you love him?"

"I only said that to get him to help us," I hissed. "You should know that after… Forget all that for right now, Jared. We need to get out of here."

Jared's eyes searched mine for a split second longer. A million unsaid words sparkled in his gaze. "You're right." We took off again. Yells and heavy footfalls echoed behind us.

*What were we going to do when we reached the exit?*

"Here, here." I skidded around a corner, pulling Jared with me. Blood spattered over my arms and hands. "It's down h—"

Another gunshot banged through the air. The bullet ricocheted off of the wall, inches from my head. Dust and debris burst from the point of impact. I ducked my head away from it.

We'd reached the last, long hallway leading to the brick. "It's right down here." My lungs burned, but I kept pushing. The wall was fifteen feet away. Ten. Five.

One final gunshot, much louder than the last, rang through the air.

At first, I didn't realize what had happened.

But then I felt the blood seeping through my shirt and down my arm. And then I felt the pain. Searing, red hot pain in my shoulder that rocked through me like a knife and knocked me to the ground.

"Lydia!" Jared shouted, falling to his knees. The world flashed bright red.

"Jared," I gasped, gritting my teeth. "Jared, the brick...seven up, thirteen over..."

"What?" Jared whispered frantically. He pushed my hair off of my forehead. "Stay with me. I'm going to get you out of here."

"The brick," I murmured, but the world was fading fast. I'd already lost ten percent of my blood. How much more was draining out of the wound in my shoulder? "You have to..."

The blood pooling underneath me was warm, like a hot bath. I closed my eyes and exhaled, letting the warmth and fog surround me. Someone was calling my name from far, far away.

But I was already gone.


*"I thought I might find you up here."*

*I turned and smiled as Chris emerged from the stairwell. The salty air threw his hair back. When it settled on his forehead again, it was messy in just the right way.*

*"What are you doing here?" I asked as Chris pressed a hand to the small of my back and guided me back to the railing. It was the perfect weather for a day on the sea; the sun sparkled off of the blue waves and white crests and made the entire ocean below us look like an endless field of sapphires. "Aren't you supposed to be working? With Danny?"*

*"I needed a break. And I wanted to see my favorite girl." Chris pressed a kiss to my cheek. The warmth of his skin against mine mingled with the heat that the sunlight trickled over my face.*

*"Favorite, huh? I've gotten an upgrade?"*

*"You've always been my favorite and you know it." Chris put a hand under my chin and tilted my head until our eyes met. I studied the familiar lines of his face—his sharp jaw, dark lashes, green eyes. God, his eyes. I felt sure that every movie ever made had been thinking of Chris when they spoke of love.*

"You only like me because you know I mean less work for you in the labs," I quipped. "How's that going, by the way? You must hate spending so much time in there, knowing I finished days ago."

"I do miss having something nice to look at while I work," Chris winked. "It's going okay. No guarantees, but I think we can do it."

"I almost believe you. But you realize that this is the Driller's central database, right? Not something silly like the CIA. It'll be a miracle if they don't brick our entire server before we can get one hit in."

"They'll be the ones getting bricked," Chris assured me. "We've got a pretty good team, even if our best members are under twenty years old."

"Do you ever do anything except compliment me?"

"What else is there?"

"Fair point." I pressed my hands against Chris's chest and gazed into his eyes. That shade of green was everything—running through the grass in the summertime, the wave of the palm trees down by the shore. But as I looked at him, something changed. His face fizzled like an old television and was momentarily replaced by another face—one framed in messy blond hair.

My heart spiked, and I pushed away from him—who was that guy?

Chris reached for my hand. "What's wrong?"

Something clicked. Memories rushed towards me like summer rain from the sky. I remembered blood. I remembered pain.

"This...this isn't real," I said slowly. "I...I watched you die."

"Watched me die? I'm right here." Chris pressed my hand against his face. "See? Right here. Are you feeling okay?"

"No. I'm not. You're dead. Danny's dead." My heart lurched. "Am I dead?"

"What are you talking about?" Chris asked. "You're scaring me."

I took his hand in mine as a tear rolled down my cheek. "You have no idea how many times I dreamed about a moment like this." Chris and I alone on the lighthouse, looking over the dazzling sea while he whispered into my ear.

*"You don't have to dream. I'm right here. I've always been right here."* Chris's face fizzled again, revealing the hidden features behind it. This time, a name tingled on the tip of my tongue.

*"Jared,"* I whispered.

*"Who?"*

*"Jared. I need to find him. I need to help him!"* I pushed Chris aside and raced down the stairwell. The familiar smell of mildew and rust filled my nose; mist peppered my face. Something was very, very wrong. Sunlight streamed through the door at the bottom of the spiral staircase. I burst through it.

And found myself back at the top of the lighthouse.

I spun around. *"What the hell just happened?"* I demanded.

*"I thought I might find you up here."* Chris smiled and moved towards me.

I backed away. *"What's going on?"*

*"I needed a break. And I wanted to see my favorite girl."*

*"Just shut up."* I curled my hands around the rail, breathing heavily. *"I need to figure out how to get out of here."*

*"You've always been my favorite, and you know it,"* Chris said robotically.

I looked back at the stairwell. Something told me that if I ran down it again, I'd just end up back here.

*"Where are we?"* I asked Chris.

*"I do miss having something nice to look at while I wo—"*

*"Shut up!"*

Chris fell silent but continued to gaze at me like a lost puppy. I couldn't stay here—wherever here was. I needed to find a way out.

*"How do I get out of here?"* I tried again.

*"No guarantees, but I think we can do it."*

*"Damn it,"* I muttered under my breath. When I was younger, I used to lie in bed and imagine a moment like this with Chris. How things would be

*if Danny had never died. And here and now, he was following that made-up script to a T.*

*I looked away from him and out at the sparkling sea. It glittered some thirty feet below me, all shimmering gems, and snow-white waves. Once, when we were younger, Danny had fallen from the top. He'd emerged from the water, soaked and laughing, but the thought of falling that far through the air with nothing to catch me was terrifying.*

*I pressed my hands against the railing and took a deep breath. Rust flaked under my fingers as the soft sea breeze blew my hair over my shoulder. I had no idea what would happen if I jumped from here, but I knew that I couldn't stay.*

*Heart in my throat, I turned back to Chris. "I think I always sort of loved you."*

*Chris smiled. "We're a pretty good team."*

*I closed the space between us and wrapped my arms around his neck. "I miss you," I whispered. But then I turned away. I followed the railing until I found the old gap in the metal. The weathered rock felt unsteady under my feet, even before my toes were teetering off the edge. I took a deep breath.*

*And stepped into open air. The air rushed around me as I fell, pushing my hair back and rushing over my skin. For a moment, all was peaceful. And then icy cool water rushed over every inch of my body and I sank deep underneath the waves. My lungs screamed for air, but I fluttered easily to the surface.*

*I gasped and swiped my sopping hair away from my eyes. Even though I'd sunk deep into the water, my bare toes found the sand as I pushed to my feet.*

*"Water's great, right?" A voice called from the beach.*

*My heart shattered. It was Danny.*

*"Danny," I breathed. I sloshed through the shallows as fast as I could. Gritty sand gathered on my feet and in between my toes, but I didn't care. I couldn't think about anything except for getting to my brother.*

*"Danny!" I threw my arms around him, heart pounding.*

*"Hey, hey. You're all wet." Danny pushed me away and looked down at the wet imprints on the front of his blue polo shirt. "Thanks."*

*I just beamed. "I can't believe you're here."*

*"Lyd, we literally walked down here together. Are you okay?"*

*"I'm more than okay. You're here. You're okay."*

*"Of course, I'm okay. It's tomorrow we've got to worry about."*

*My smile faltered. "Tomorrow?"*

*"What is with you today?" Danny gave me a strange look. "It's like you're a different person."*

*"No. I'm me. I'm Lydia, I'm your little sister, and you're alive..."*

*"Of course, I'm alive." Danny frowned. "Why wouldn't I be?"*

*"I...I don't know." I frowned. Something tugged in my gut, signaling danger. But I brushed it away. What could be wrong? My brother and I were enjoying a day at the beach, just like always. "Hey, let's skip some rocks."*

*"Get ready to lose, then." Danny pushed my shoulder as he ran to the waves. I followed him, laughing. Cool water splashed over my skin. I shrieked as he threw water into my face.*

*"I thought we were skipping rocks!"*

*"You were never any good at it."*

*We paused for breath, soaking wet and knee-deep in the ocean. "I could've learned. Maybe."*

*"What do you mean, 'could've'? You still can." Danny shook water out of his hair and gazed down into the crystal-clear shallows below us. "Here, I'll find you one."*

*"No," I said softly. "I can't."*

*Danny frowned. "Why not?"*

*"Because you're not real," I whispered. As I said the words, Danny's figure faded to a silhouette, soft and bright. But it was back in an instant.*

*"You can learn," Danny insisted. "You just have to do one thing for me. Just one."*

*"What's that?"*

*Danny grabbed my wrist and squeezed, hard. "Wake up."*

*"I don't understand."*

*"Wake up!"*

*The world dissolved into darkness around me; the sea rose and turned black, curling its tendrils over the scene. I closed my eyes against it, heart beating furiously. When I tried to open them again, there was only darkness.*

*And Danny's voice echoing in my head over and over and over, "Wake up! Wake up! Wake up!"*

# CHAPTER TWENTY-THREE

The first thing I noticed when I woke up was the pain. In my jaw. In my head. But mostly in my shoulder, which felt like it had a hole burned through it. I gasped, and my eyes flew open. Someone pressed a hand to my forehead, calming me. A pair of deep brown eyes swam into view.

I mouthed soundlessly. I must be dead.

"Danny?"

"Hey, Lyd." Danny's mouth spread into a wide smile. "How's it going?"

"Am I dead?" I blurted. This place certainly had the right color scheme for heaven; everything I could see was white. The walls. The floors. The sheets that covered my body, the bandages that wrapped around my arms.

"No, you're not dead." Danny took his hand from my forehead. "You certainly tried hard enough, though. Blood drained from both your arms, not to mention getting shot in the shoulder..."

"Danny, you're not *alive*," I shouted. "There's no way for you to be here right now!" It was like someone had put a band around my chest; each breath was rushed and difficult. Danny wasn't alive. Something was wrong— I was locked up somewhere in the basement of some Driller stronghold, drugs in my veins and my mind making me see things that weren't there.

"I am alive. Just calm down. I'll explain everything."

A monitor to my left beeped sharply, signaling that my heart rate had spiked to a dangerous level. I didn't care. I stuttered. "They killed you. They said they killed you."

"Calm down and listen to what I'm saying," Danny said over my babbling. "I know you were at Yucca, and I know you thought I was dead. But I'm not. I escaped. Look at me." Danny took my hand. "I'm your brother. I know that you love movies and coffee. You always wore your hair in two braids when you went to sleep. And you're terrible at skipping rocks."

Something inside me broke. The tears that poured silently down my face had nothing to do with the searing pain in my shoulder. "Danny."

"It's me." Danny sounded close to tears himself. "I missed you so much." I studied my brother's face, the face I hadn't seen in three and a half years. Some of it—the warm brown eyes, the sharp jaw—were the same, but the weathered look of his skin, the stubble that dotted his chin, were new.

"Where are we?" I asked, craning my neck to see around him. A white door that blended almost perfectly with the wall was the only sign that the world existed beyond this room.

"We're safe. We're on a hidden base in on the coast. I think it used to be part of California. It doesn't have a name now, except for the base."

"Military?"

"Yeah. Commander Mathews is here."

My eyebrows shot up. "I thought she was dead!"

"She's not. She's fine. We're all fine." Danny grinned.

My heart dropped. "Chris?"

Danny looked down. The tiny bit of hope in my chest drained away.

"Oh," I said quietly.

"I miss him, too," Danny said. "He was my best friend."

"Mine, too." My voice shook. A tear shuddered down my cheek.

"Everyone's worried about you," Danny said. "Jared especially."

I shot upright. "Jared is here? He's okay?"

"He's fine," Danny assured me. "Thanks to you. He couldn't have found the exit without you."

"Danny, I don't understand. Reed was there with a gun. How the hell did Jared and I get out of there?"

"We were waiting for you guys. On the other side," Danny explained. "I'd been planning to get Jared out of there for a long time. When I heard that you were inside, I knew they'd go after you. So, we sped things up a bit."

My heart lurched. "Danny, Reed said something about the school...explosives..." I swallowed, hard. "Did you get anyone out?"

Danny looked down at his hands.

"There was a girl," I said desperately. "Her name was—"

"No," Danny said abruptly, cutting me off. "Whoever you're thinking of, she's dead. I'm sorry, Lydia. You and Jared were the only two who made it out."

The words carved a hole in my gut like a hunting knife. They hurt more than the bullet in my shoulder, than the tunnels in my arms. Kat, my best friend, was dead. I thought Reed was lying, but even if Kat was alive then, she wasn't any longer. Aaron and his father had tortured Kat before she died. Drained her blood like they would have mine. My stomach heaved, but it was empty.

"She's dead," I repeated over and over, trying not to cry.

"I'm so sorry. Do you want to talk about it?"

"Do I want to talk about it?" I repeated, my voice deadly. "Are you fucking kidding me, Danny? I thought you were dead. I thought you were dead for three and a half years, and you think I want to *talk* about it?"

I kicked the blankets off of my legs, ignoring the pain that raced through my arms and shoulder. "I want to know where I am and what's going on."

"Hey, slow down. You can't move yet, you're very weak."

"I don't care!" I screamed. "What do you know about the Latium project?"

Danny paled. He stood, rubbing a hand over his jaw as he looked down at me. "How much do you know?"

"I know that I can see invisible ink, do other things I shouldn't be able to. I know that my blood can set dirt on *fire*," I growled. "I know that they took me because of it. I just don't know why!"

"It's a long story, and you just woke from a week-long coma. We shouldn't do this now."

"When do you suggest we do it, Danny? When I've had a few more days to process the fact that everyone I've ever known is dead?"

"I'm right here, Lyd." Danny reached for my hand again, but I yanked it away.

"You're not my brother," I breathed. "My brother died three and a half years ago. That brother would have gotten a message to me somehow—let me know he was alive! But you...how long have you been on this base, hanging out while I grew up, wishing you were there with me? I..." I took a deep, shuddering breath. "I don't even know who you *are*."

"I'm your brother."

"I'm not sure I believe that anymore." I shook my head. "Just go."

"But I want to see you."

"You should have thought of that before you let me believe you were dead for three years."

"Lydia."

"I just need some time, Danny." I turned away. "Please leave me alone."

Danny lingered for a moment, but then he left, leaving me alone in the white room. I stared after him, numb. Danny was alive. He'd been gone for years, but here he was, right in front of me like the attack had been yesterday. I buried my head in my hands. All this time, I'd been following breadcrumbs trying to figure out what had happened to him, when he'd been here all along.

I stared at the steady drip of liquid—saline, presumably—through the IV that hung above my head. How they'd found an undamaged vein in my arm to connect it to was beyond me. Every one of them felt bruised and broken, just like the ties between Danny and me were fractured.

I jumped as the door opened again, just moments after Danny left. "I told you to go aw—" I fell silent when I saw it was Jared who'd walked through the door. "Hi."

"You're okay," Jared said weakly. He was dressed modestly, in a light blue t-shirt and jeans—softer colors than I'd ever seen on him. "It's been so long. I thought..."

"That I was dead? Believe me, I did too," I said, remembering the dreams that had flowed through my mind. They'd been so meticulous, so detailed. I could still see every inch of Chris's face. His green eyes, his crooked smile.

But another pair of green eyes met mine as Jared sat on the edge of my bed and pulled my hand into his. "You were in a coma for almost a week."

"How much blood did I lose?"

"Enough that you should be dead."

"Don't look so disappointed that I'm not," I grumbled. My voice softened. "How did you get us out of there?"

"I managed to get you into the tunnel and lock Reed out. Dan's people found us pretty quickly after that. They got you out of there." A pause. "He's still your bother, you know."

"I don't know anything anymore," I muttered. "Where's he been all this time? Why didn't he try to get to me? Write to me or something?"

"He thought *you* were dead, Lydia. I told you that before, remember? Beyond that, you'll have to ask him." Jared looked down at our intertwined hands, a frown pulling at the corners of his lips. His skin was warm against mine. I'd lost so much these past few days, but he was still there. I wasn't sure what he was—a friend? More? But he was here. And that was all that mattered.

"Fine, I'll ask you something else." My voice was barely a whisper. "Why did you come back for me?"

"I could never leave you," Jared whispered.

"You were about to," I pointed out.

"I wouldn't have gone through with it," Jared said, leaning close.

"Really?" I whispered.

Jared didn't answer. Instead, he closed the last of the space between us and pressed his lips against mine. My eyes fluttered shut and warmth spread to the tips of my fingers and toes. For this moment, I couldn't feel anything beyond him, not the pain or the grief or any of my tangled-up emotions. Just this moment. Just us.

"Does that answer your question?" he asked softly, pulling away.

It took me a moment to find my voice again. "Yeah. Yeah, I think it does."

"Besides, I was going to come back for you the next day. With Dan."

I pulled my hand away from his. Shadows dipped over my face. "Wait. You knew? You knew Danny was alive?"

Jared's eyes went wide. "Lydia, listen."

"Are you kidding me right now? You watched me worry about what had happened to him—watched me risk my life for *weeks* and you knew he was alive the entire time?"

"I didn't know at first."

I laughed derisively. "What in the hell does 'at first' mean, Jared?"

"I found out a few days ago," Jared confessed. "I didn't tell you because I thought you'd be upset—"

"That my brother decided to tell you that he was alive before me? Why would that make me upset?"

"That's not my fault, and you know it."

"You could have *told* me."

"He asked me not to."

"Oh, well, that makes it all fine."

"I was wrong, okay?" Jared said loudly. "I should have told you that he was alive. But I was scared that if you knew…"

"That I'd try to escape and find him?"

"That you'd try to escape before they'd be there to help us," Jared said patiently. "And thank God they came when they did, or we'd be dead right now."

Dead like Kat was dead. Burned alive in an explosion set by Reed and Aa—

"Aaron," I whispered. "Jared, what happened to him?"

"I don't know."

I buried my head in my hands. Was Aaron dead, left behind and murdered by his father because he tried to help us? Or had he escaped?

"He saved us," I mumbled. My voice trembled. "We would have died if he hadn't attacked Reed."

"I know."

"Do you think he's alive?"

"I don't think we'll ever know." Deep lines settled around Jared's mouth. "I'm sorry. I know you two were close."

I nodded, not wanting to think or talk about Aaron anymore, at least not for a while. I had to know if Jared really did feel for me what I felt for him, or if it was all some kind of act. I looked into his eyes. "Jared, did you only come back for me because you feel guilty you let your best friend's little sister get hurt?"

"Lydia, you're more than Dan's little sister to me and you know it." Jared's voice was tinged with hurt.

"Could've fooled me."

"Lydia, I just kissed you."

"You can't just kiss me and make everything okay."

Jared looked down. "I know."

"Then tell me the truth for once. Where are we? How did they get us out of there?" I looked at Jared through the tears that sparkled in my eyes.

"It's a long story. You should rest."

I glared at him, angry all over again. "If I'm not just your friend's little sister, then stop treating me like a child."

He sighed. "Dan figured out the truth about the Latium project about three years ago. The code is in our genetics. It's always been there. But the experiments do something to activate our blood so that we can be used for fuel. The government used the school as an excuse to bring all of us whose DNA they messed with to the same place—but then the Drillers infiltrated it, and Reed was put in charge. Dan knew that if we stayed there long enough, they'd take the experiments too far. Or kill us. So, he found a way out."

"The paint," I said slowly. "He could see it too. Why can we see the paint?" I wondered.

"I don't know." Jared looked pained. "I don't have all the answers, much as I'd like them."

"Do you honestly expect me to believe that after everything you kept from me?"

"Believe what you want, but I don't *know* anything else," Jared said. "I didn't tell you the truth before because I was worried about you, Lydia. You know that."

"Just tell me one last thing," I pleaded.

Jared sighed. "If I have the answer, I'll tell you."

"Who did this to me?"

"Lydia..."

"Who did this to me? Who was it that put this..." My fingers shuddered up and down my arms. "Who made me like this?"

Jared didn't answer. Gears turned behind his bright green eyes.

"I know you know."

"I think you do, too."

Denial rippled through my empty stomach like a wave of nausea. "He wouldn't." There was no way that my father would have taken part in something so dangerous—something so cruel! No way he would have subjected Danny and me to it.

"You wanted to know." Jared said. "I'm sorry, Lydia. Our DNA was altered before we were even born. There was no one else who could've done it." Jared sighed. "My parents did it, too." He stood.

"Where are you going?" I demanded. My voice broke. I'd just woken up from the most bizarre, terrible nightmare I'd ever had. And it was real.

"I think I should let you rest." Jared said with his back to me.

"Wait." I shifted so that I sat higher. "What happens now?"

"Now, we hope to God that no one here or anywhere else discovers the truth about us." With those words, Jared left, leaving me alone in the white room once again with nothing to do but consider his words.

Somehow, I'd escaped from Yucca. I was okay.

But something told me that even though I'd survived, even though my brother was alive, and we were together again at last, things were further from okay than they'd ever been in my life.

# EPILOGUE

The flame flickered in front of my eyes, creating a small pool of light that traveled no further than the palm of my hand and did nothing to combat the dense darkness around me. I flicked the top of the lighter back over the flame, and the darkness returned.

I don't know why they let me keep the lighter.

I don't know if I'll ever see the light of day again.

"How did you get that?" A hoarse voice called to me. I tensed, but then I remembered. The speaker couldn't reach me even if he wanted to. And even if he could...what could he do to me that's worse than what's already happened?

I sighed and leaned back against the brick wall. Dampness seeped through my bloodstained shirt. Chills ran up and down my bruised skin.

"It was in here when I got here." My voice caught in my throat. When was the last time they brought me water? That I spoke even a single word? I flicked the flame on again and held it in front of my eyes. Burned its blue-white image to the back of my mind, wishing that memories were a film reel. That I could destroy them.

"Why haven't you said anything before?" I asked abruptly.

The speaker shifted. This time, I could tell where the noise came from—the cell across from mine. "I've been in here so long that I was sure I was imagining it," the voice explained. "After a while, it's hard to know what's real and what's not." The voice was male. Not young, but not old either.

"Don't I know it," I grumbled.

Flame on. Flame off.

"You haven't been here long," the voice observed. "A few weeks, maybe."

"What gives you that idea?"

"I heard them bringing you in. I've always been good at determining the passage of time, even in the dark like this."

"Well la-dee-da," I said blandly. "How's that served you down here?"

"Not too well," the speaker chuckled. "How's your pessimism served you?"

"Pessimism, huh? Harsh judgement from someone trapped in a jail cell."

"It's not harsh at all. You've been here barely two weeks, and you've already given up."

"Who said I've given up?"

"Your voice did."

"Yeah, well, you don't know me. Maybe I deserve to be down here." Guilt rippled through my stomach. God, I wish I could have saved her. Both of them.

"You sound about my daughter's age," the man cut in as if I hadn't said anything. "Seventeen or so? You can't have done anything bad enough to land you here."

"You'd be surprised."

These past few weeks of darkness and silence gave me a lot of time to think. About everything. Like how my best friends are dead because of me.

"I think you may be slightly overestimating the morality of our captors," the voice mused. "They took my son from me three years ago, and then they came back for my daughter. Lydia. That's her name."

The lighter clattered to the floor. My mouth dropped open. The man in the cell across from mine was supposed to be dead. Everyone thought he was dead!

"Y—you're…"

"Sebastian Melrose. Pleasure." A pause. "And you are?"

"Aaron," I whispered. "Aaron Reed."

# COMING SOON
# LATIUM BOOK 2: SPECTRUM

## Chapter 1: Aaron

"Sebastian Melrose. Pleasure." A pause. "And you are?"

"Aaron," I whispered. "Aaron Reed."

"Reed," Sebastian echoed.

"Yeah. Reed as in Dominic Reed," I muttered bitterly.

"I knew your father was cruel, but I never dreamed that..."

"That he'd throw his own son in the dungeon? You thought wrong."
I flicked the flame back on.

"What could you possibly have done to make him so angry?"

I didn't answer. I'd made plenty of people angry over the past few
months. But considering what else I'd done...

"Whatever it was, your father won't keep you down here forever.
Whatever he's done...he loves you."

I almost laughed out loud. "You don't know anything about my
father."

"Maybe not, but I am a father. He won't leave you here to die."

"Like he wouldn't murder my best friends in cold blood?" I asked
dryly. A familiar pang of nausea creeped up my throat.

"I'm sorry," Sebastian said.

"Just shut up," I snapped. The lighter slipped between my fingers as
I raked my hands back through my hair. Pressed my nails into my scalp, like
it would drown out the sound of her screaming—

"Son, are you alright?"

"I'm not your son!" I shouted. My voice bounced through the empty space, echoing over and over and over.

"I didn't say you were," Sebastian said mildly. "But you need to calm down. It's cold down here. We're very weak. You need to get rest, if you can."

"Rest?" I echoed. Every time I closed my eyes, all I could see was the blood running down Kat's arms. The flames licking at the dust that coated the floor as she died. As she begged me to help. As I stood by and watched as my father…

I scrambled to find the lighter and flicked it on again. I inched my fingers closer and closer to the flame. The metal underneath my thumb burned. But I kept it there until the white-hot pain was all I could see, hear and feel. I didn't let go until it seemed like my skin would blister against the metal. I gasped and wrapped the lighter in my hand.

"You're hurting," Sebastian said after a moment.

"What gives you that idea?"

"Don't give up hope. Find something you love and hold onto it. Focus on that instead of hurting yourself."

"Something I love."

"Something. Someone."

"Everyone I loved is dead," I said in a hollow voice. Everyone I loved is dead because of me.

"I'm sorry."

"Just shut up, okay? I never asked for a heart-to-heart with you."

"I know. Maybe you just remind me of my son."

"Well, was your son also a cold-blood murd—"

"Well, this is adorable. Seriously, guys—ten out of ten." A new voice rang out, and suddenly the space flooded with light. The light was like fire against my eyes. I slammed them shut against it.

"Oh, come on—you're not even gonna look at me?"

Nothing but the shock of hearing that voice could have made me force my eyes open. At first, the world was nothing but an endless sea of searing, painful white. But then his face zoomed into focus.

"Theo?" I choked.

"In the flesh, little brother." Theo leered at me through the bars of my cell. It'd been years, but he looked exactly the same—angular face, dark eyes, close-cropped hair. My polar opposite. My father's favorite son.

"How long were you standing there?"

Theo glanced behind him, at the man lying on the floor. This place was a maze of metal cages; endless rows of black bars that reached to the ceiling ten feet above us. It was impossible to see where any given cell began or ended. At least I was afforded the privilege of a single concrete wall.

"Long enough. You should know better than to talk to the enemy."

"And he's the enemy?" I pushed myself up, but my arms shook. Even though it'd only been a few weeks, all of my muscle was gone. "Seems to me that my enemies are the ones who threw me in a box and left me here for three weeks."

"Oh, it hasn't been that bad. We gave you food every three days. Most of them only get it every five. If we remember."

"How fucking generous," I growled. "Is there a reason you're here?"

"Yeah. Dad wants to see you." Theo unlocked the padlock that held my cell shut and swung the door open. "You coming?"

"Yeah, wanna race?" I tried to push myself to my feet, but my arms gave way and I crashed back down. Sharp pain punched through both of my elbows.

"You're not in much of a position for sarcasm."

"I've noticed." I met Theo's eyes. "So, are you gonna help me, or will Dad have to march down here himself?"

"Can't ever do anything for yourself, can you?" Theo grunted as he knelt down and tugged me up by my arm. I fell against him as he marched me from the cell.

"Oh," Theo called over his shoulder as he pulled me along, "I wouldn't waste any more hope on that daughter of yours. She's dead."

Ice flooded my entire body. Lydia's face flashed in front of my face—her eyes, her smile, the way her lips felt on mine… The blood, trickling down her arms as she begged me to help her—

"Come on." Theo yanked my arm so hard that I nearly fell to the floor. "Dad doesn't have much time, and this is important."

"Maybe he should have thought of that before he starved me."

"Maybe you should have thought of that before you went rogue. Seriously, what were you thinking?"

"I was thinking that she didn't deserve to die," I said weakly.

# ACKNOWLEDGMENTS

This book would have never reached the place it is now without the advice and support of so many. First and foremost, I want to thank my mom and dad for always supporting my writing and keeping me supplied with notebooks, pens, coffee and laptops, and for reading a very, very bad first draft of the book you hold now. Also, thanks to my older brother Shane for always being generous and supportive, and to Corey for inspiring my creativity since I was a kid.

Next, a HUGE thank you to anyone and everyone who read all or part of this book before it was actually decent, especially Autumn, who was the VERY first, and Joann, who reads basically everything I shove at her. This book also wouldn't be anywhere without my amazing friend Holly, who read this book three times and not only offered advice, but more importantly opened my eyes to the magical ship that is Kat and Cheerios. Thanks to Liyan, my best friend in the world for not only being incredibly supportive and amazing, but taking all of my official headshots. Thanks for taking my gorgeous author photo that can be found on the back of this book, and of course, for all of your fabulous music recommendations!

Endless thanks to Diana, for being the most amazing friend and listener ever and always being generous with her never-ending supply of watermelon. To Abigail, for being my lechuga niña and always being willing to read the snippets I shove at her! Love to my amazing roommate Amanda, for listening patiently to me as I ramble on about my latest ideas and always sharing her cosmic brownies with me. Thanks to Melinda for not only reading this book last summer, but helping me get through field camp, college and everything in between. You'll always be my loamy clay bae. And of course, much love to my first collaborator and best friend Sandra. I wouldn't be the writer I am today without all of our stories, characters and memories. Wishing you LOTS of mashed potatoes and Spanish Rice. You look good in plaid (and stripes too, I guess…)

I also need to thank all of the incredible internet friends I've made over the years. Whenever I was feeling down, or needed a name for a character, they were right there, always there to listen and make me laugh. You've all changed my life for the better. First, thanks and lots of love to one of my best friends and earliest supporters, Wende. Thanks for all the laughs and support. Love also to Dragana, Kace (Shemory!), Brittany, Ava, Marsyee, Colette, Liviara, Heather, Mica and of course my writing partner in crime, Anna! Your positivity and encouragement has meant the world. Also, to Annie, for being a great listener and helping me with last-minute tweaks! Finally, lots of kisses (and windex) to everyone in that one group chat. You know who you are. I hope to meet all of you IRL very soon.

Lastly, a huge thanks to my superstar publishers, Megan Cassidy-Hall and Steve Hall for believing in this story and helping me take it to the next level. I can't express how much I appreciate Megan's unending patience with my phone calls and killer suggestions and advice. Thank you for everything, from the gorgeous cover to the line edits. I couldn't have asked for better editors and publishers for Latium. Thank you so much for giving me the opportunity to share this book with the world.

# ABOUT THE AUTHOR

Samantha Martin is an actress, filmmaker, and author. Latium is her debut novel. When not writing, she can be found reading or wasting time on Twitter. She can't sing or dance but enjoys covering her favorite songs in sign language. After she finishes her degree at the University of Kentucky, she hopes to work in the film or publishing industry while, of course, writing.

Connect with Samantha on Twitter @am_i_write
Or read more about her work at www.5050press.com

# THANKS!

If you think other readers would enjoy Latium, we would love it if you would leave a review!